Tecate Peak
The Edge

A novel by

Michael Joseph Hudon

Published by MOHOMBRE Media, San Diego, CA.

Printed in the United States of America

Cover Design by Michael Joseph Hudon

in Collaboration with Carol Shamrock and Derek Murphy

ISBN-13: 978-0578127651 (Mohombre Media)

ISBN-10: 0578127652

Table of Contents

"Jake, the Big Handy Home Store over on Chestnut—you know where it is?"

The man named Jake nodded. "See the manager about a shoplifter, and take Dugan with you."

Jake McGinnis was in his later thirties, handsome and easygoing, but not afraid to speak up in any situation and not hesitant to address the boss by his first name.

"But Phil, shoplifting, for God's sake. Isn't that something that could be handled by routine police patrol? Don't you think our skills could be put to better use somewhere else?"

Bradshaw seemed to take no offense at McGinnis's brashness. "Trust me on this, Jake, we need you there."

He opened his mouth as if to say more, then shut it and turned away. Harry followed Jake, who was already out of the conference room and heading toward the self-opening doors at the center front of the building. Like himself, Jake had been a fast-tracker at SCABS, though he had started at a much younger age. That and a couple years in the military. A quick thinker.

Harry wasn't quite sure how he felt about Jake. He hadn't had a regular partner for his first two years on the force, beginning in 2007; but he'd probably been paired with Jake more than any of the others in the last three. They got along okay, not the same kind of rapport he'd had with John Saunders, back in Dover, both on the job and off, but that was a whole other world. Just as they had started out the door Bradshaw spoke again, a bit louder.

"You can find the Big Handy, can't you?" Jake nodded.

As Jake and Harry walked across the parking structure, Harry tossed Jake the keys. "Since you know where we are going."

Harry looked over at Jake and smiled as he hopped into the passenger's side of a black pick-up truck. Jake eased the official truck out and drove two blocks in the general direction of Chestnut Street. The truck looked pretty average, black crew-cab, short-bed. Nothing unique, except for the gray lettering on both front doors that read simply "SCABS." Most of the members of the force referred to their employer as "scabs" or sometimes "security blankets." Some even got philosophical about the metaphorical meaning, seeing themselves as part of an organization that was in some way responsible for healing the wounds of society, or at least some of them.

Harry Dugan could never get into that psychological crap. He just had a job to do—a job very much like that of his father and grandfather, although in a different place. Like them, he believed in doing his job well, and he believed a job well done was its own reward.

On passing a gas station parking lot that had been filled with dozens of matching evergreens, Harry snorted, "Can you believe this shit? It's just the beginning of December and already they're selling trees."

Jake responded in kind.

"Been there since last month. Don't listen to the radio either. There has been nothing but "songs of the season." That and television commercials are enough to drive you bonkers."

Jake looked over at Harry quizzically.

"Hey, buddy, you do know where this place is don't you?" "I thought you said you did," Harry barked back.

"I think I do, but I'm not gonna say that to Bradshaw. It's on Second or Third Street— right near the corner, isn't it?"

Harry reached up scratching his head.

"Sounds right. I been there a few times. Stay on the surface streets.

It's only a few miles down. Big building.

I don't think we can miss it. And don't worry—it's no emergency — just a light-fingered Lizzie."

Jake, never missing a chance to correct someone, perked up in the driver's seat.

"Or 'Light -fingered Louie.' Shoplifters aren't always girls, you know. Should I turn at the light?"

"Yeah, that should get you there. I know it's right next door to Cuzins Cafe. Harry pointed at a row of smaller commercial buildings. "You'll see the home store first. The cafe's set back a little, then there's more little places, almost like a strip mall, but not on the main drag.

"Cuzins—that sounds familiar," Harry said, "but I'm having a hard time figuring out why."

Jake had another come back ready for Harry.

"Now that I can answer" Jake smiling sarcastically, "It's the place where all the old farts hang out. You know, retired cops. Even one or two of our guys on occasion. They meet there every Wednesday for breakfast. The ones that haven't had heart attacks or drunk themselves to death, or have nothing better to do."

Harry nodded. "Today's Wednesday."

Jake and Harry realized something was going down in front of the Big Handy as soon as they pulled into the parking lot and saw an ambulance, red light still revolving. Jake sped to the area and came to a screeching stop as close as possible. The two SCABS detectives encountered a surreal scene involving about a half-dozen old men, one sitting on the curb clutching his shoulder where blood was seeping out just above the breastbone. He looked to be about sixty-five and well-built for his age; he kept muttering that he was all right and why were they wasting time trying to put him in an ambulance.

Another of the old guys, who were all presumably the retired police officers, was standing near him and addressed the detectives as the ambulance driver pressed a large gauze pad to the sitting man's shoulder. Several other men, appearing to be between sixty and seventy, milled around to the right and back a ways, near the door of the little cafe, speaking among themselves and watching the proceedings furtively.

Off to the left, a man in black slacks and a torn white shirt was bending over, picking up coins and bills, as was another in a Santa suit.

A few people near the store and in the parking lot looked on, immobilized by shock. Harry, trying to take in everything at once, noticed blood on the sidewalk in front of the sitting man, who was now being lifted onto a stretcher. A lot of blood. Too much blood to be from the victim going into the ambulance. His collared shirt was still pale blue, except for a little area around the compress, which he now held for himself. He had stopped protesting and was instead giving instructions to the ambulance crew to call his wife. Two of the crew got in the vehicle with him; the driver remained standing near the closed front door.

"What the bloody hell happened here?" Harry asked the man who had greeted him, immediately regretting his choice of words.

"A lunatic shoplifter attacked my friend with a knife," the self-appointed spokesman reported in a firm, steady voice.

He waited a minute for that to sink in, then added, "A couple of my friends and I came to his aid, subdued the attacker and put him in cuffs."

Noticing that the man was wearing civilian clothes and apparently a customer at the coffee shop, Harry asked,

"You had handcuffs with you in the restaurant?"

"Not with me, but always in my car." The man stopped and pointed to an older, mid-size sedan twenty feet or so down from the ambulance, in the first marked parking spot. "That's it right there."

"Where is the perpetrator?" Jake looked around. The man they were speaking to didn't utter a word; he simply stepped several feet to his right. The pool of blood in front of him became a trail leading back into a dark corner shaded from the soft mid-day winter light that shone on the parking lot. This corner was where the man-made stone of the Big Handy Store met the brick of the restaurant, which was set back about fifteen feet. No windows faced it. For a second, Harry thought he saw a body there. When he looked again, he was sure he saw a body.

"He alive?" Harry asked. As if on cue, the prone figure started making loud moaning sounds, interspersed with some demeaning curse words, and some Harry had never heard before. He threw in a few 'mother-fer's', 'damn geezers', 'what-the-hell's' and threats to retaliate through the courts.

"I know lawyers," he said. "I know bikers—you guys are dead meat." His speech was somewhat garbled.

"Is he drunk?" Harry asked.

"I don't think so. I think he might have broken his jaw when he fell." The standing man then offered his outstretched hand. "Jim Patterson

here. Sergeant Patterson, retired. Station thirteen is where I worked last." Both he and Harry knew he didn't have to break out his badge.

McGinnis spoke next as Harry shook Sergeant Patterson's hand.

"So, you guys rough him up a little?"

"We are not like those cowboys out there."

Patterson pointed in the general direction where the U.S. Border Patrol outpost was located, almost intentionally in Jake's face.

Patterson looked just a bit taken back by the question. "Besides, he was okay when we pulled him off Jerry."

He nodded toward the ambulance and said, "We was walking' with him back to the sidewalk, and he tripped right here on the curb." He pointed to where he had been standing. "Hurt himself pretty bad, looks like. Then he starts flailin' around and cussin', hittin' himself against that stone wall." Patterson pointed over at a blood stained portion of the wall. "We had to pull him away and put the cuffs on him. He finally settled down. Reckon he'll be needin' an ambulance."

"Is another ambulance on the way?"

"Damned if I know."

"You didn't ask for two? "

"I didn't ask for any," Patterson responded. "Someone from the store called, I guess. Or there—he nodded toward the coffee shop, where people were watching from the doorway and from inside." The ambulance driver told Harry he was taking off.

"Hold it a minute. You heard what he said, right." The man nodded. "Is that what you saw?"

"Hell if I know what happened," the driver said.

"I saw what you saw. Got here just a minute before you did and started tending the man with the knife wound." The driver started closing the doors to the ambulance.

"You better call for another bus—we can't put that guy in here." Jake was already on the radio, giving the location.

"Yes, I know. We need another one. Yes, second bus, same location. And hurry. This guy's hurt pretty bad."

Harry grabbed the ambulance driver just as he was closing his door.

"Can you at least leave one of your guys here to check out that poor bastard— and some kind of first aid kit?" The driver complied; one of the uniformed paramedics started walking warily to the man lying in the corner, now softly moaning again. The medic rolled the other man onto his side and placed a gauze pad against one nostril,

saying in a soothing tone, "I'm here to help you, stay calm and try not to move much."

By the time Sergeant Patterson finished his explanation, two of the other former cops had joined him. Harry turned to one of them.

"Tell me what happened."

"Just like Pat says; he tripped on the curb."

"And how about you? " Harry said to the third old man who was trying not to get involved.

"Not much I can add—it happened like Pat said. We were just walking with him. He wasn't paying attention to his feet and fell. Hurt himself, had a nosebleed, then he started screaming and pounding the wall." The man pointed to the same spot Pat had.

Harry sighed a deep sigh and got out his clipboard. "I'm going to need brief statements from all of you."

Wrapping it Up

"Well, looks like we're going to be here most of the day," Harry said to Jake as they waited for the second ambulance and made an attempt to run some yellow tape from their car to a building support post.

"And I guess we better call in the real cops."

The crowd from the restaurant was staying back pretty well, but as Harry and Jake worked, a van drove up with so much equipment on it that it looked top-heavy, like it shouldn't be on the road—one of those mobile broadcasting stations.

"Looks like the press has finally made it," Harry studied the van.

"Vultures," muttered Jake.

Harry preferred the term "termites" because they crawl out of the woodwork. He didn't say that out loud. Jake continued, "Don't know who made the first call, but if they didn't pick up on it, they surely heard your call for the second bus. Bastards."

He used his favorite term of non-endearment, although the press corps members they interacted with were as likely as not to be women, just doing their jobs. Unfortunately, it sometimes interfered with police work. The press van parked a discreet distance away and people began scurrying around with cords and electronic boxes. A giant antenna unfolded and rose like the head and neck of a skinny monster emerging out of an asphalt sea.

Over the din of voices, cars, and equipment, they heard the siren of the approaching ambulance. After it slid in next to their unmarked car, the two quasi-police border agents made quick introductions and summarized the situation, leading the crew to the injured shoplifter. As they discussed the next order of business, which was to interview the store manager, Harry moved a step closer to the injured man.

"That guy got any I.D. on him?"

"Just a minute," said the crew leader.

He whispered to the other paramedic, who procured a wallet that was then passed to Harry. The man on the ground said something that may have questioned the parentage of all those present and accused them of stealing his money. There wasn't much money in the wallet, Harry noted, less than a hundred dollars. But a few other items caught his attention: a driver's license, a card that indicated he was, or had been, an iron-worker, a credit card with a name that wasn't the same as the other I.D., and a folded piece of wax paper that had in it something Harry thought might be an illicit drug in the form of a wafer. He collected the items of interest in a baggie, wrote down the man's name, Jeff Van Zandt, and his other information, then tossed the closed wallet back to the paramedic.

"Which hospital? Harry asked. "We'll send the cops there sometime today to book him."

"He ain't goin' nowhere," the ambulance driver answered.

Harry knew the drill. If the cops, who were just arriving as he spoke, arrested the guy now, the city and or police department might be on the hook for the ambulance cost and all the hospital bills incurred, which were likely to be huge in this case. The cops would work that out with the hospital staff, so that someone was present to take care of the arrest just as he was released. Harry had a pang of sympathy for the man as he watched him being lifted onto the stretcher.

Earlier that morning, at about the same time dispatcher Phillip Bradshaw had entered the conference room, and a few miles away at the corner of Chestnut and Third Avenue, the first assistant manager of the Big Handy had ascended a short flight of carpeted stairs. Otto Yates was young, with dark slightly receding hair and large brown eyes, emphasized by the thick contacts he always wore. Though his height and weight were average, he had smooth skin and slightly sloped shoulders that gave him a sort of round look at first glance. At the age of thirty, he felt pretty good about having advanced to the position he held at the largest Big Handy in the San Diego area. Often, as today, he was in full charge of the store, and it wouldn't be too long, he felt, before he would have his name and photo on the store-manager board near the main entrance.

Otto was a conscientious leader and organizer; one of the areas in which he took special pride was that of mitigating the losses that all big-box home stores were sure to suffer from theft. His store was consistently one of those with the lowest reported shoplifting- related losses. The look-out loft was one of his main tools in this endeavor. As in many other stores, the loft was designed to be as inconspicuous as possible, and mirrors were placed strategically throughout the entire huge lower floor. The only places he couldn't see were the hardware aisle where rolls of tapes and small items like tacks and nails were displayed, and the garden center; but not too many thieves were likely to try to make off with bags of mulch, sand, cement, or plants. Nothing ever surprised him, though. People who attempt this crime are often not the brightest bulbs in the box.

Like the guy who expected a different Big Handy to give him change for the counterfeit one million dollar bill he presented. The store was laid out so the expensive and tempting items, be they small or large, could easily be watched from his perch, and anyone trying to lift one of them would have to go a ways to get to an exit; the stairs from the loft were directly on that route. Immediately in his view, and closest, were several aisles filled with tools. Many people not in the business would be surprised by the amazing advances in tool design, and both the compactness and the value of tools, especially things like saws, drills, routers, shapers or kits that combined them and even newer ones that incorporated electronic technology. Those were the most costly. Some kits were smaller than laptop computers, and worth twice as much.

Otto also found it surprising—unbelievable sometimes—how easy the perpetrators made his job. His store, like most others, was at its busiest most weekdays in the early morning between 5:30 am and 7:30 am. Hordes of construction guys (and occasionally a few gals) would show up in their crew cabs with ladders or lumber racks and pick up supplies for the day. They almost always knew exactly what they wanted, grabbed or ordered and picked up with great efficiency and got out on the road before the commuter traffic started to back up.

But there were many customers; and if a low- life decided to slip a flat tool- kit under his shirt and walk out with it in the middle of all that commotion, he might just get away with it. Otto wouldn't have had the luxury of viewing the action from his sky-box, because he was needed then on the floor. Now, at almost 10:00 am, the perp was a sitting duck.

Otto smiled as he watched the man look warily over his shoulder, both directions, then slip the tools in their bright red high-impact plastic container into his unbuttoned shirt, under which he wore a T-shirt. Buttoning up his shirt, the man sauntered toward the exit at a normal pace, as Otto slid down the stairs with the quickness and stealth of a cat locked in on its prey. He reached the floor just in time to intercept the thief. Sometimes thieves would bolt and Otto would have to hope the security guard was on duty, could give chase and bring him down.

He planned to look into installing a different type of automatic door that allowed him to lock it shut with a small remote device, but they were a new and costly option. More often than not, the thief would try to act nonchalant and give some absurd answer like, "Wow—how did that get there?"

Arresting them in the store was not an option. They could always say they planned to pay for it and just chose that unconventional way of carrying it to check-out. But Otto wasn't vindictive towards a thief; he just didn't want his expensive products to leave the store. In addition, any shoplifter he questioned that way was very unlikely to return. Otto's timing was perfect.

"Are you planning to pay for the tools?" he asked. Before he finished the question, he knew something was wrong. He saw the man's right hand slide from the shirt button and pull something out of the belt; something slid in on an angle at the waistband, something shiny. He saw the reflection on metal of fluorescent lights high above. Before he could process the information and even begin to react, Otto was confronted by a knife blade that appeared to be about a foot long, and it was moving toward him at a speed that precluded action, evasive or offensive. Instinct must have kicked in, and without realizing he did it, Otto twisted his shoulder and chest ever so slightly. He heard his shirt tear, he felt the blade touch his skin, but when he looked, there was no blood. The shoplifter, still balancing the computer design kit against his chest with one hand and waving the knife wildly in the other, shuffled toward the door. Otto took another look at himself, unable to believe that he hadn't been sliced open like a watermelon. Almost too late, Otto realized that he wasn't hurt seriously and decided to give chase himself. He knew he was a decent athlete, which might have seemed surprising given his stature, and he knew the stupid man was not letting go of his ill-gotten goods or his weapon. The door might slow him down, if no one was using it.

Sure enough, the thief had to hesitate a second, and Otto was close enough to make it through behind him without getting hit by the closing door.

To his left and down a ways, he was vaguely aware that two or three retired cops were standing around in front of the coffee shop, where they hung out some mornings. To Otto's right, he noticed a man dressed like Santa next to a big kettle, ringing a bell to call attention to his charity. But Otto barely acknowledged them. His full attention was focused on the guy with his property.

Now the action was over for Otto, and he was being questioned by two men he assumed to be plainclothes policemen, and two others in uniform.

"Otto Yates," he told them as they took notes. He went through the whole story with amazing calmness and clarity, but when it came to the moment he was shoved or thrown into the kettle, he was vague.

"I think I hit my head." Otto paused, placed his hand on his head. "But I can't be sure what happened next. I'm pretty sure I made him drop the knife, but then I thought I saw it again."

Patterson reached up to hold the sore spot on his head.

"I just don't know."

"I know." It was the voice of the salvation army volunteer, who had taken off the Santa hat and red jacket and settled himself rather inconspicuously on a bench in front of the home store. "Did you see what happened after the shoplifter—make that alleged shoplifter--after he shoved Mr. Yates?"

"Sure did." replied the half dressed Santa. "Only there is no alleged about it." The man became animated as if in a game of charades. As he spoke, he acted out each action with body movements. It had added a little entertainment to the situation for the moment. The topless Santa continued on. "The man was runnin' out of the store fast as he could holdin' his chest cause he had a big ole' plastic box under his shirt, halfway under, anyhow. This guy," he put his hand on Mr. Yates's forearm, which the manager accepted without noticeable disapproval, "this here guy caught him, don't see how, but he's faster than he looks. Mr.--" he peered at the store badge, still hanging sideways from a thick part of the shirt pocket, the only place on the shirt that wasn't in shreds, "Mr. Yates ."

"OK, go on." Harry encouraged.

"Well, just as soon as Mr. Yates's head bounced off that pillar and he fell into my collection kettle, the crazy guy, he takes the tool thing and slings it under a car. It's still there, over yonder." Harry looked in the direction where the man was pointing, and sure enough, there was a bright red item under the nearest parked car.

"I'll get that," Jake said, putting on a rubber glove and pulling a plastic bag from the inside pocket of his jacket. The media people were closing in on them, now that the ambulance had left. Cameras were everywhere, so Jake McGinnis wanted them to see everything that he did was by the book. The bell-ringer, whom Harry had learned was named Terrance Smith, waited until Jake got back, then went on with his story.

"Mr. Yates here would be dead if it hadn't been for the old man coming over." "Dead?" Harry looked puzzled. "Explain, please."

"Well, see, the guy, he didn't look like he was drunk or drug-crazed, you know, but he was sure, well, he was just as pissed as a horse with a bee under its saddle, pardon my French. Soon as he threw that toolbox, he picked up the knife again. Mr. Yates here was on his belly on the ground, out cold for a minute and I was too far away to stop him, not that I felt exactly like trying to be a hero, but I probably would have."

Mr. Smith leaned back a little and puffed his chest a bit as if to show he was a manly man. Harry was amused, but kept his composure.

"But I wasn't close enough, you know what I mean?"

Santa continued without waiting for an answer. "The guy had that big old knife and he was standing just as tall as he could and bearing down on Mr. Yates's back." Mr. Smith looked over at Otto. "And then Mr. Yates here—"

the forearm touch again, well, sir, he's just not in any state to protect himself, tho' I know he could have otherwise , but it looked like he was a goner."

"And?" Harry prompted once more.

"And I didn't even know he was there. Or anybody was there. But out of nowhere comes this guy—had to be way over sixty but he could move like a--well, he was fast, and strong for an old man. He grabbed that guy and he wrestled that knife out of his hand, and got cut in the process, but I think he did some damage to the guy, too. Looked like the knife guy had a bloody nose and he was holding his chin and screaming bloody murder, like he was in real pain, but you know, the old guy was saving a life. Mr. Yates here he would have been run right through with that big ole knife."

Harry was taking notes as he listened to Mr. Smith speak about the event. "Did you see anyone hitting the shoplifter?"

"Well, maybe the old man that got cut—I didn't see it, but he must have hit him after he got the knife away. There was another old guy here by that time, couple more on their way. The guy was cut, he sat down a little ways away on the curb, still had the knife in his hand. The others...they grabbed Mr. shoplifter and led him around the corner.

I heard some screaming and shuffling, but I didn't see nobody hit nobody. Does that answer your question?"

"You've been very helpful, Mr. Smith, " said one of the uniformed officers. "We may have more questions for you later, but that should do it for now. Thank you very much for your help. We have your number— we'll call you if we need you." "You're free to go now."

He turned to Mr. Yates, and noticed for the first time a big lump on the man's face, just above the eyebrow. The swelling may have just appeared, but it was definitely swollen, and seemed to be getting more so. "Looks like you need some medical attention—shall we call another ambulance?"

"No, I can get myself to a doctor."

"Well. I don't think it's a good idea to ignore that—have it looked at," Harry said.

"Oh, I will. Just as soon as I get someone to look after the store." He then turned to Terrance Smith, who was still hovering in the general area. Yates put out his hand. "I believe you saved my life, young man, or would have," he said, although the volunteer was probably only a few years his junior. "I'd like to stay in touch. Do you have a business card?" The man produced some kind of card, and wrote something on it before he handed it to Yates and they left in opposite directions.

Jake turned to Harry.

"Well, I guess that's that. We might have to run the media gauntlet, but soon as we can, what say we break for some food?"

As Jake and Harry walk towards Cuzins Cafe Jake continued,

"I didn't have any breakfast and it's past lunch time. The real cops can get this evidence turned in and try to contact Van Zandt's loved ones. If anyone loves him, that is."

Harry looked back over his shoulder as they were entering the door of Cuzins, "Hey, who was Patterson calling cowboys anyway?"

"He didn't mean much, accept the recent incidents of misconduct by a few rogue border patrol agents."

Sandcastles

Nine miles due south of downtown San Diego, two men in a black crew-cab pickup truck headed west on Palm Avenue. The vehicle's radio buzzed with guitar riffs and drums thumping, or screeched with loud clanging commercials. It was tuned to a station that called itself an "oldies" venue, although Harry, the one in the passenger seat, grumbled with mild disdain that the songs they played were all too new for him, and all sounded pretty much alike.

"Why don't we turn that damn thing off so we can hear the scanner?" Harry asked the one driving, his partner Jake McGinnis. Jake's response was pleasant, but not without the little barb that often accompanied his conversations with Harry.

"Come on, New Guy, you know I never miss a call, and I got extra good hearing. And, even if I didn't, we get the vibrate mode, too. Remember, we both got the same state-of-the-art equipment on our belts." Jake, at thirty-seven, was about ten years younger than Harry, but he was a six-year veteran of the force when Harry hired on, and never

missed an opportunity to remind Harry of that fact. That's also why he was still technically the senior partner when they worked together, which was a lot. But Harry knew Jake respected him for his intelligence and many years doing police work. The pecking order rankled Harry, but not enough to interfere with the friendship that had developed in the years they'd handled this strange assignment. Harry was confident that someday soon he would be the senior partner.

Jake had a thick crop of light brown hair that always seemed to dip onto his forehead in a way that highlighted his eyes. It made him look like a slightly guilty ten-year-old His smile, those rare times he displayed it, (cliché). But even with a serious expression on his face, he was attractive.

Their truck proceeded west on Palm, also labeled Highway 75—a major route that connected the 5 and the 805 freeways. These two main north-south freeways started together just above the International Border, though each had it's own crossing. The two sets of gates comprised the busiest border crossing in the world. The two freeways eventually merged again twelve miles north of downtown in a nightmare of traffic gridlock that was always being addressed by Caltrans but never quite solved, and called simply "The Merge" by most San Diego County residents.

To the east, at the backs of the two patrolmen, ruler-straight Palm Avenue crossed the 805 and continued as a two-lane road, curving east and south toward Otay Mesa. That was the location of a huge concert amphitheater, an Olympic training sports facility, Brown Field regional airport, and a large, popular water-park. It was also home to tens of thousands of mostly Hispanic suburbanites and the location of the SCABS extensive main compound. The SCABS teams were scattered about this area for good reason. In the recent past few years, organized criminal enterprises from both sides of the international border had targeted law enforcement professionals. These included border patrol agents, immigration, customs agents, and just about anybody they could try to bribe. There were even local gangs that tried to get in on the action, which kept the local cops as well as federal agencies very busy.

They moved away from all that at approximately 70 mph. The border area was just south of the compound campus and the even wilder terrain—harsh, dramatic, untamed and uninhabitable---further east--- that they referred to as "The Edge." It was their main theater of operations. Technically, SCABS jurisdiction extended into Arizona; after all they were a sub-contractor for Homeland Security, but their territory was presumed to be from the border of Arizona and Mexico and westward to the Pacific Ocean. Most of their work took place between the Otay Mesa truck crossing and Tecate. It was there, just a few miles east of the Tijuana International Airport, that the border fence abruptly ended, allowing anyone who was brave or foolish enough to just walk around it into the United States. There were many who tried different and more evasive measures to get themselves and their families to El Norte.

Continuing the west Highway 75 would bend north and follow a narrow strip of land between San Diego Bay and the Pacific Ocean, ending up on Coronado Island--an city of lovely, exclusive homes, owned mostly by retired military--that had once been accessible from San Diego only by ferry, or by the long circuitous route that involved driving ten or twelve miles south to where they were now, and the same distance north. As he looked into the glare of early afternoon sun, Harry wondered if something special was afoot in the department. It was unusual for them to drive west for the six miles between the main border gates and the water's edge, if you could apply that term to a slough. This stretch of land was usually taken care of by the coast guard or the Department of Homeland Security, which had a strong presence there since 2008. But the border patrol, of which they could loosely be considered an adjunct, did operate in that zone.

The northwest part of the Coronado Island, more than half of it, was Naval Air Station North Island. Inland from that was Coronado. The beaches there were some of the best in the country, if not the world, and the small city was famous for a very conservative population of mostly retired military officers and for the grand old Hotel Del Coronado, commonly known by it's nickname, "The Del" is the site of movie filming

and visits by several presidents. The "Del" was well over a hundred and twenty-five years old; in the 1880's, its lighting was converted to electricity by Thomas Edison himself.

But today, they weren't going to Coronado. Harry pulled down his visor to block out the bright early afternoon sun directly ahead, and caught a glimpse of his face in the mirror. He wasn't as handsome, or as young, as the man in the other seat, but that wasn't what bothered him. His dark brown hair hadn't receded much, and there was just the slightest trace of silver, not at the temples where it would be expected, but in a strip over his left forehead. He was still attractive enough, he knew that, but wasn't particularly interested in having a girlfriend--especially one like Jake had.

He took a last look at his reflection, feeling quite comfortable in his weathered skin, then tilted the visor to banish it. He wondered what the community of Imperial Beach was like.

Almost as if reading his mind, Jake asked, "Ever been to IB, dude?"

Harry, who had never thought of himself as a dude and wondered why Jake would use the term, let that one go.

"Nope," he said. "I can't believe I've been here six years and never had occasion to go to Imperial Beach. What is it, some sort of a hippie place?"

"No, not exactly. That's probably Ocean Beach you're thinking of. Hasn't changed in decades. Still got a "head shop" even. The Black."

"Head shop?' Harry wondered out loud.

"It's a ways up north from here, about even with downtown, but out on the edge of the ocean. It's the farthest south beach on the mainland unless you drive out all the way to Point Loma. But that's not a beach really, mostly cliffs with a big military cemetery and a lighthouse that's a popular tourist spot. And tide-pools. And Navy facilities, of course."

Harry listened closely as Jake gave the tour of the area. "You've probably noticed them."

Harry wasn't much of a talker, except when he was talking to Trish, but he was glad Jake was. He appreciated Jake being a sort of tour guide all these years, as well as teaching him the ropes of working on a "police-assistant" unit. They weren't quite para-military, like Blackwater, and that was a good thing, as far as Harry was concerned. He was a cop, not a soldier, and sometimes the line got blurred. Harry knew, even with his police background, that he had a lot to learn when he first signed up. Born and raised on the East Coast, Harry had had a traditional upper-middle class family, and everything about California was new to him-- sometimes an adventure, sometimes a frustrating enigma.

"So what about the other branches of the military? Are there any of them around?" Harry always eager to add to his knowledge of local lore.

"There's the Marine Corps Air Station Miramar—MCAS," Jake explained. "You've probably heard of it. It used to be a Naval Air Station; it's where they filmed "Top Gun. They closed it down—the politicians. Said it was budget constraints, but I think they just wanted to get a major Marine Corps presence here in this corner of the country. If you ask me, they had it all planned, to be ready for major wars in the Arab countries. Desert Storm and Iraq were just practice. They've got plenty of oil and somehow we need it." Jake was getting all worked up.

"Our esteemed leaders are always going to find some excuse to have a war over there. Better than here. But when it comes to training for Afghanistan or Saudi Arabia or any of those places, the California desert is perfect. Almost the same conditions. They already had Camp Pendleton, and then they got Miramar and Yuma, just across the Arizona border. That's not our worry though. We got an International Border to take care of." Harry finally spoke. "Ya know Jake, it's funny how prophetic you are."

"Huh?" Jake was perplexed.

"You said there would be more wars over there after Iraq, and already there's been two. And one's not over yet."

"Maybe no war is ever really over."

"You're sounding pretty philosophical all of a sudden, Jake. Is that part of your growing up?"

"Not to worry. No chance of that—it ain't happening," offered the eternal surfer boy.

Jake paused as he moved into the left lane at the intersection where 75 turned northwards and Palm Avenue continued into Imperial Beach.

A moment later, he spoke again. "See over there?" Harry was trying to see what Jake was pointing to. "I bet you've never seen one of those."

He pointed to a facility about a mile south that looked like a huge circular fence, like you'd find enclosing a trampoline, but a hundred times bigger, with an equally large satellite dish inside it and a few small buildings around it.

"The Outlying Landing Field IB, they call it, though it would be a challenge to land anything bigger than a piper cub there. They do have a few helicopters. Everything between them and the ocean, about a half mile wide and a couple miles long is a wildlife refuge—a slough, really. The southern edge of that's the Tijuana River's mouth, dry this time of year, but a mess when it rains. It becomes a horrible mess; you don't want to be there. Beyond that, another reserve extends inland four or five miles. A state park and a regional park, then the border. Not much there, except the new DHS site on Spooner's Mesa."

"Why is the river delta so bad?" Harry wondered aloud.

"The river starts in Mexico and it carries a lot of raw sewage. Even though they try to treat it, the smell is sometimes unbearable. It gets putrid if they open the dam gates, 'cause the flooding can be extensive. Sometimes a lot of people die. People in Tijuana —that's where the dam is, near a lot of poor people crowded into cardboard shacks in the colonias."

Harry pictured what it must be like to have to live in those conditions.

"And we have no say if they decide to open those floodgates," Jake went on, "even though that nasty water floods over on to our side too. Most people just stay away from that area when rain is in the forecast." "The park's not a very popular place, except for biologists and such, or people up to no good. Once in a while, some poor bastards like us have to go in and rescue horses when it floods; there's one little area with residences, and some ranches. Oh, and we don't call it a delta—its "The Slough" or the "Tijuana Riverbed.""

"But didn't the Department of Homeland Security fix that?" Harry asked.

"They're in the process," answered Jake.

"The governments, all of them, have tried to improve things over the years. They had a great idea. At least I think it was," Jake said.

"They had a plan for a place where people from both countries could get together to visit. Sort of like family day in the pen. Illegals, families that got separated."

"Get out of here." Harry blurted out. "Family day at the pen?"

"It would be clean and safe, a joint project with Mexico. A park on both sides, administered by two countries."

Harry found the plan difficult to imagine. "So, how'd that go, where is this park?"

"Ha! You know how hard it is for one country's government to figure out what the other hand is doing. Multiply that by two, and the fact it's one of the hardest places in the world to maintain, to even get a vehicle into, well, I just don't think it was destined for success. From what I hear, it deteriorated pretty fast. Not that I think it's a bad idea. Don't get me wrong. I just don't think there's a chance of a snowball in Hell that they can pull it off." "They got it going--called it Friendship Park-- but security was sorely lacking. It wasn't fenced well, not even close. Evidently the politicians gave up, or had more important things to worry about, and it wasn't long before the junkies and coyotes took over, and a few homeless and even fewer whores. Brave or stupid ones. The place the DHS is working now, where they built the two-mile-wide mesa and the roads— that canyon, those gullies, it was called Smuggler's Gulch. I guess they're trying' again, though." "That ought to be interesting whenever they finish."

"Now that you mention it," Harry interjected, "I did hear about that pilot project some time ago. I just didn't realize it was so close." Harry noticed that Jake had attention issues whenever girls in bikinis were around. Harry had taken a moment for himself as well to have a look at the surroundings. At the stop sign, Jake spoke.

"I have to focus on driving through this section of town, I don't want to hit any pedestrians."

"So I will tell you what I have learned about that park project, and you can correct me if I am wrong."

Jake nodded his head while focusing on the lime green bathing suit's bikini top.

Harry began his spiel on what he remembered about the joint park project between Mexico and the US. "They started digging in 2008, after five years of environmental impact reports and negotiations about the cost of the land. The tree-huggers put up a big fuss, of course, said it was worth half a million an acre. The state and county settled on just under $20,000 an acre if I recall right. I'm not sure I'd pay a dollar for it. People tried to fight them, but the feds won."

"They always do, don't they." Jake replied.

"Usually. But, hey, maybe they have the right idea. Maybe it could work, if they can keep the undocumented workers who just want to see their families now and then separated from the low-lifes and gang-bangers, keep the access roads open and safe, keep the border patrol agents from getting hurt, or going bad and hurting someone."

Before Harry could finish they had arrived in the heart of the small town, which seemed to be only a few blocks long.

"We're here," Jake said as he maneuvered the truck around a set of barriers and found a space big enough to park at an Italian restaurant where they had arranged to meet.

A few other VIP drivers had squeezed their cars in, but almost every inch of remaining space was taken up by bicycles—dozens of them.

Harry had never seen so many bikes in one place.

"What the hell— is this town off limits to cars?"

"No, they have regular streets and people drive on them, well, just not very many of them. But today is the Sandcastle Festival, remember. That's why they sent us here, 'though it's unlikely we'll see any action. So anyway, today, they have some of the streets closed and the rest will be so crowded with cars in a few hours that it will take longer to get out of here than it does to build the winning entry. Have you ever seen a sandcastle contest?"

Harry had to admit that, being from New Hampshire, he had not. They had beaches, of course, but this sure seemed different—all the women in bikinis and in perfect physical shape. And they weren't even at the water yet.

"Not such a big deal," Jake explained, as they waited for the "walk" sign, then crossed a two lane road running parallel to the ocean and walked west.

"Happens every August if they don't run out of money. Groups sign up ahead of time, and then they're given a square of beach and certain amount of time to make something glorious with just sand and water— tools OK, but no props. While they're doing their thing, fifty thousand or so people watch, or just hang out.

That's the fun part—'cause more than half are women, my friend, and almost all of them wearing bathing suits. We are gonna get to see us some skin today--some gorgeous tanned and toned bodies in strips of cloth. Maybe some thongs."

Both men stopped walking and reached for their thighs simultaneously. The casual observer might not have noticed, or might have wondered about the synchronicity of it, but for Harry and Jake, it was a common occurrence. Like dancers in a tango or birds in flight, they moved almost as one, grabbing their all-purpose phones from their clips, finding a place to sit on a low stucco wall that bordered the sidewalk, and listening intently. The female caller spoke in a relatively calm voice, but one thickly accented with Spanish: "This is police, si? I don't know who should I call but something is--is estrange, you know. Truck is parked, long time, no move. Yesterday was parked, same truck, unload but no go. No es happen like this— you know, just stay."

"Thank you ma'am, but I don't see the nature of the emergency," the operator answered. "Was the truck involved in an accident?"

The call was to 9-1-1 and SCABS personnel were automatically alerted to any such call made within their district.

"No—maybe. I don't know. It just stay all day--today too. People, men, they take boxes off—many boxes. All day. Too many boxes. Truck can no hold but still more boxes."

"Does the truck have writing on it? What is in the boxes?"

The 9-1-1 operator asked the questions by rote without a change of inflection in her voice, but the woman with the accented voice was becoming a bit excited, and both Jake and Harry, listening without the knowledge of either party, had their interest piqued. The truck in question was apparently a one-ton, enclosed, something like a small moving van, according to the information gleaned by the operator, and had been in the same spot for days, half a block from the Mom-and-Pop grocery where the call originated.

It was down a short alley in a parking lot off Hollister, near the corner of Dairy Mart Road, in a little enclave of low- income homes, duplexes and commercial enterprises that was entirely surrounded by the Tijuana River Regional Park. The dispatcher had decided to send a police unit, but neither of the officers she talked to seemed to be familiar with the area.

Jake jumped off the wall with a start. "Let's go."

"What? Why? They already got cops going out there, and it doesn't sound like anything is going on."

"Maybe not, but I got a funny hunch about this—something just doesn't seem right. And those two dildos taking the call will take forever to get here."

"Here? It's not in IB is it?" asked Harry.

"No, but it's close as the crow flies, over toward the San Ysidro crossing, south of Nestor. But you can't get there from IB, or from anywhere else, hardly. There's only one road in and it comes off the I-5, sort of. They'll never find it."

"And we will? News flash—we're not crows. And we're a heck of a way from the 5." "Yeah, but we don't need a road."

They were in the agency pick- up, which had been equipped with the best four-wheel drive available, and Jake took it south in the direction of the giant antenna instead of north toward Palm Avenue. Their speed was well above the 35 limit, and their route was a zig-zag, past homes, a high school, even a small community police station that appeared to be unoccupied. Jake was in full control at the wheel and he knew where he was headed. At the

Naval Outlying Landing Field, he made an abrupt left and followed a road that soon turned into a pair of ruts, or tracks. It snaked its way south and east along the north bank of what was called the Tijuana River, but in reality it was nothing more than a wide mud bog, dry in most places this time of year. A few scattered trees were visible, and occasionally shacks, tents, or other signs of living—sleeping bags, an abandoned grocery cart. The road got rougher by the minute, and even with his seat belt on, Harry had to hold one hand against the overhead to keep from bumping his head on it.

Jake was calm. "Good thing we have driver-operated four-wheel drive," he smiled. "Even at that, we wouldn't be doing this in the rainy season."

Two minutes later they came to a street marked Hollister and took a sharp right. It was a paved road, with only a few potholes, and Harry released his grip on the grab bar over the door, stretching out his fingers to see if the knuckles still operated correctly. In a block-long commercial section, Jake pulled up behind a "Roach Coach," whose operator had apparently closed up for the day or was taking a siesta. Two doors ahead, on the same side of Hollister, was the grocery store, the only one around, whose employee or owner had made the call. Outside the store were tables filled with trays of fruits and vegetables, sort of an open-air market. Both men knew that, from there, a person would be able to look down the short alley that was across Hollister on their left. The cab of their truck also presented a view of the same parking lot, sort of like a narrow-mouthed cul-de-sac. The truck was there all right, a one-ton with a lift-gate— an older model, painted an off- white color-- a haphazard paint job that looked like it was done by amateurs to cover up an old business name. Harry thought he could see orange and the hint of a logo, when he used his standard issue field-glasses—it was probably a truck that had been purchased from a rental company when they upgraded their fleet.

Hollister Avenue

As they sat in the truck with the engine turned off and both their windows cracked open a few inches to allow for the slight breeze, they saw two dark brown Hispanic men, both small, wiry and muscular. They were working methodically, taking boxes about two feet square, boxes that weighed, by Harry's guess, thirty or forty pounds each, from inside the truck and loading them into a van parked conveniently close, sliding them forward and stacking with maximum efficiency. As they watched, unnoticed, Jake's phone rang. Harry scowled. It was a particular ring that Harry recognized as signifying that his girlfriend Trish Hester was calling. Though their windows were down, they were far enough away and the ring-tone did not attract the attention of the subjects they were observing. Harry didn't particularly like Trish calling so often--it made her seem needy. Still, he had a grudging respect for Trish, the way she had stood by Jake over the years, even when it was difficult for her.

"You ought to have that on silent," Harry whispered hoarsely. "Then I wouldn't know it was her," Jake pressed a button to stop the ring sound.

"Like it makes any difference," Harry muttered, as his partner started talking. "It's always her. You pick up every time it rings."

He wondered how they could find so many words, fill so much time, and yet never say anything of any importance that he could make out. He also wondered if he might be a little bit envious, remembering a different young woman, in a different world. Lara. He was getting that familiar, queasy feeling in the pit of his gut as he tried, for the millionth time, to distract himself from the memory of a series of events that, fourteen years ago, altered his life. Harry dabbed the sweat from his forehead with his lower arm, then rubbed the arm with his hand. Away from the ocean breezes now, but near enough to the slough to smell it, he felt the oppressive heat combined with the humidity that was no longer considered an anomaly for Southern California, now that millions of people had populated it, bringing water from wherever they could appropriate it, planting vegetation almost every place the water would reach. This location, though barren, felt muggy, and the stickiness of mid-August, sitting in a black vehicle with no air conditioner running, made him decidedly uncomfortable.

Harry's momentary lapse was interrupted by the sound of sirens in the distance. It had been about ten minutes since the original call. He wondered if it could be the officers sent to check out the truck—certainly they wouldn't use sirens. But there weren't many roads nearby, Jake had said. Harry's hearing was good, too. Whether Jake's was better, as Jake believed, was hard to quantify, hearing being so connected to other parts of the brain. It might be more about paying attention, concentrating, applying knowledge already stored than to the physicality of sound reaching tiny hairs on tiny drums inside a canal on the side of the head. With a sudden motion, he grabbed the phone from Jake's hand and spoke into it. "Say goodbye, Trish." He pressed the "end" button and handed it back to Jake.

Jake did not try to conceal his irritation, but he kept his voice low. "What the hell? What did you do that for?"

"Listen. Can you hear that?"

Jake was still scowling "Sirens," he said simply, then added, "They're not for us. There are always sirens."

"Around here?"

Jake's focus on the sound increased. He knew the area and the way sound carried. "They're getting closer," he stated. "What the--why in the hell would they use sirens on a call like that?"

Harry didn't answer, nor did he need to. Instinctively, both men went into a different mode, one of preparation, the way a cat becomes rigid and still when it sees a mouse or a bird. As they sat motionless, the sirens grew steadily louder. Harry and Jake watched the two Hispanic men stop unloading the truck and listen to the sirens. They started a series of actions that were perhaps rehearsed. First there was movement at the truck itself, behind or beside it, but because the van blocked Harry and Jake's view, difficult to determine.

Then the two men grabbed some cut branches and palm leaves from the floor of the truck's cab and threw them in the van on the boxes. They took a tarp from the same place and tossed it loosely over the branches so some stuck out. From the jump-seat in the cab, they pulled a rake, a broom and two shovels, which they placed over the tarp. All this happened within ninety seconds. Without appearing alarmed, they closed and locked the truck and got in the van, one with pruners in his hand, which he put on the dashboard.

Within a few seconds, a black and white pulled up in the driveway where the one-ton was parked. The cops stopped parallel to the street and just off the main lane, but situated their vehicle so there was no room for the van to exit between it and a four-foot high cement block wall that divided the business where the truck was parked from another commercial property. Suddenly, the van driver abandoned the ruse and stepped on the gas. To make enough space for an exit, he backed up to the building, then charged forward with all the speed the van was capable of. He plowed straight into the right front fender of the police car, spinning it enough so the van could escape. The police officers in their vehicle were immobilized. The driver had not yet unfastened his belt and sat there stunned between his seat and the airbag, but didn't appear injured. Harry could see, however, that the other officer, who had removed his seat belt the minute the car came to a stop and had been leaning toward the door or starting to open it, was thrown sideways in such a way that the airbag glanced off him, pushing him toward the impact. Harry had a bad feeling about it. Again without talking, he and Jake both sprang into action.

Harry grabbed a mini first-aid kit from under the seat and jumped out of the pickup, slamming the door and leaping out of the way just as Jake squealed into a U-turn and gave chase on northbound Hollister.

Harry guessed that the van did not have a super-charged racing engine, as their pickup did, and felt confident Jake would catch up to them. With a strong sensation of embarrassment, he realized how much he liked his partner and made a wish under his breath that Jake would not be harmed. The police officer opened his door, stood up dazed, then sat back down. There was no sign of movement on the other side. As Harry rounded the back of the black and white, he noticed that the passenger side door was open, but didn't know whether it had been sprung by the impact or if the police officer had managed open it before he slumped to the ground in a small pool of blood. He dialed 911 and ordered backup. Then he checked for a pulse and got one, weak and erratic. The man's head was on the asphalt of the parking lot, left side visible. When Harry turned it gently, he saw a large gash above his right eyebrow that appeared to be the source of most of the blood. Bad location.

Apparently the man's head had made contact with a G.P.S. device mounted on the car's dashboard. The cop moaned.

"Good, he's conscious and breathing," Harry thought.

Before he realized what was happening, the injured police officer had pulled away from him, half crawling, half running and got about fifteen feet away from the tiny bit of shade cast by the car before he collapsed again. Harry ran to him, carrying the kit that held compresses, disinfectant, and pain meds. The man did not seem to be in serious pain.

Harry raised him to a sitting position, half supporting him with his own body, so his head would be elevated and the bleeding would slow.

The sun was brutal, reflecting off the asphalt, and wouldn't be setting for hours. He scanned the horizon for the ambulance, hoping to see it arrive. But it wasn't an easy location, even for first responders. Harry talked to the officer calmly as he took out a compress and pressed it against the gaping wound.

The man asked, "Is there a lot of blood?"

"No, not much--just sweat." The cop put his hand to his own head, then in front of his eyes, which were apparently working fine. When he saw blood on his hand, he passed out cold, and suddenly became much more of a burden for Harry to keep in an upright sitting position. The guy wasn't likely to bleed to death, Harry knew, but there was the potential of dying from shock or from heat stroke. Missing from Harry's first-aid kit were the two things he needed most --water and shade. Just as he wondered what he would do next and wished that Jake were still there with him, he heard something. When he turned his direction to the source of the sound, he saw a vision. It couldn't be real, not in this little corner of Hell, surrounded by dirty asphalt and blood, but there was a young woman in a white gauze dress and leather sandals, fairly floating across the dusty street carrying a ruffled parasol, white with silk flowers.

He blinked twice and she was still there, coming closer.

Her hair was dark brown, not quite black, falling in loose waves below her shoulders, and her walk was like a dance. She was carrying a woven basket.

"Senor," she said. "Senor--" and he knew then she was an actual person, a female person, attractive, about thirty-five, maybe.

"Mister," she said. He must have been slow to respond and she tried in English. "Will this help?" She thrust the basket toward him and he could see that it contained a bag of ice from a store vending machine and two bottles of water.

"You're an angel." Harry said it, and he meant it literally. "I don't even know how to pray and God sent me an angel." "No. I just work in the store sometimes, help my mother."

Her English was good and there was just a trace of an accent. She crouched next to him on one knee, only the thin white fabric of her dress between her skin and the hot pavement. Because she had positioned herself to the west of him, facing away from the street, the sun silhouetted her, accenting the fluid form of her supple, brown body. Harry chastised himself for noticing, and turned to the task at hand. He asked her for the parasol and took it gently from her hand when she offered it.

Harry found a way to wedge the parasol, probably four feet across, between himself and the slumping cop, so that it cast shade on all three of them. Then he took the basket. After a quick drink of water for himself, he unfolded the large bandage from his kit and filled it with ice from the bag, which the woman had torn open with a table knife. Placing the ice pack against the wound where the compress had been, he again began talking to the man. He suggested the woman talk to him also and at the sound of her voice, the injured cop opened his eyes and asked where he was and what had happened. Harry answered and handed him a bottle of water, which he began to drink on his own. With the woman in white leaning over Harry in such a way that her breasts almost made contact with his face, he found himself repressing a wish that the ambulance wouldn't come, replacing the thought with a pang of guilt.

By the time the ambulance arrived five minutes later the cop had asked and got an answer to the same two questions five times. Harry asked the paramedic about that —"Did the man have brain injuries?"

The medic said such short-term memory loss was very normal in cases of even moderate head trauma, and that almost surely he would have a complete recovery. He would probably be fine by the time they got to the hospital. The other cop had been sitting in the patrol car with the engine running and the a/c on. He was checked out and given an okay. He had already called for a tow truck. The right door of the patrol car would not close. Harry wanted to get out of there before the uninjured officer started asking him questions, but he didn't want to be too far from the area or move the truck, because Jake would be coming back.. He offered to walk the woman back to the store.

As they walked, he asked her name.

"Elena Sanchez," she said. "And you?"

"Harry Dugan." He didn't know why he gave his last name, too. That was unusual for him. He knew he could get more information about her if he wanted. He already had the store phone number from the call to 911 about the truck, apparently made by her mother. Once inside, she introduced her mother, Lupe, who immediately excused herself and went to the back room to stock supplies. Did she think he was a cop? Was she scared? Maybe undocumented? But she made the call. She had to know the authorities would figure out who it was. Oh well, that probably wouldn't come up. But he did have to fill out an incident report just like a cop would, so he thought he might as well do that now, and he also might as well let Elena know who he was. He pulled a notebook out from a specially designed holster/vest under his light cotton short-sleeve shirt. He gave a quick thought to what else was in the vest.

Before he could explain why he was writing, she asked, "Are you hungry?"

All the action started just before he and Jake were about to find a place for a bite of lunch, but of course the thought of food had disappeared until now. He looked toward her, trying to think of the most polite way to say he was famished. "I can offer you almost anything," she said, with a slight gesture of her hand indicating the well-stocked shelves around her and with no awareness that her remark could be a double entendre..

Harry smiled. "Yes, I am hungry. I'll have whatever you're having." Then, "But a larger portion."

It was Elena who smiled then, grinning for the first time, like a shy schoolgirl, and he saw a gap in the center of her lower teeth that somehow added to her beauty. She didn't hesitate or ask any further questions, but found a package of chicken tenders, which she spread on a paper plate. While the chicken was heated in the microwave, she retrieved a ready-made salad from a waist-high refrigerator across from the counter.

"What dressing you want?"

"I like Thousand Island. Is that a possibility?"

"In here?" Her arm made a wide gesture toward the rows of stocked shelves. "No problem.'" She moved halfway down an aisle and came back with a new bottle. She divided the salad onto two plates, real plates, that also were stored underneath, and found silverware there, too. Apparently whoever "manned" the store was in the habit of having lunch right at the counter. Harry noticed one plate had two-thirds of the salad.

It got the same proportion of the chicken when the microwave bell rang; Elena then motioned for him to come behind the counter as she pulled out two stools.

"You're very trusting," said Harry.

"Whoever you are, Harry Dugan, I don't think there's much chance you sat in the boiling sun to save a man's life just so you could case our store to rob it."

"Good point."

"So, why the notebook?"

"Oh, that." He stalled a second, the tiniest hesitation while he made up his mind, again deciding to be straight with her.

"Well, I work for a police-affiliated agency, and they want a report whenever we're involved in some sort of incident."

"Oh," she said. Nothing more, but there was a discernible change in her expression and her demeanor. Elena was all to familiar with those who were willing to bend or even break the law, even those working directly or indirectly for law enforcement agencies. He wished he had lied to her, but it might be hard to explain Jake if he managed to catch up with the guys in the van and come back with them.

They ate in relative silence, and from that point on, it was like taking a report from an ordinary citizen. She answered his questions briskly, but not rudely. She did not volunteer any information.

"I'll go wait for my partner, I saw a bench in the shade half a block up." Harry said as he finished the report, folded it into the notebook and returned it to his vest.

"There will be cops coming, but I think I can answer all their questions and keep them from bothering you." He then offered his hand, and gave her an appreciative smile that came from his heart.

"Thank you for your part in this; it made a tremendous difference. I hope we will meet again, Elena."

He picked up on a softening of her voice, almost a return to the schoolgirl shyness, and a slight upturn to her lips just before she spoke. "That would be nice, Harry," she said, and he wanted to believe her.

Sign of the Shrimp

Jake knew how much power he had beneath the hood of his black truck. He was on a straight paved road with no traffic when he gave it full throttle. It wasn't more than a minute before he could see the van. He also knew how long Hollister Road was and that it ended at its north end in a "T" with Coronado Avenue. That intersection was approaching. He could tell by the speed of the van that it was unlikely the driver would be able to make the sharp turn. He also knew that along the north edge of Coronado ran a ditch, about two feet lower than the pavement, filled with sand, filtered and softened by years of winter rains.

The sand would bring the van to an abrupt and unpleasant stop. He checked Coronado Avenue in both directions and saw no traffic was approaching. He considered whether he could slip by the van on the shoulder, bearing right on Coronado and come to a normal stop, or use the oncoming lane and slide to the left. In the end his calculations, or his instincts, told him to hit the brakes quick and hard.

The simmering asphalt squealed under his tires and choking smoke rose into the lower parts of the cab. Miraculously, the seat belt had held him in place and the air bag had not deployed. His chest hurt a little, where the seat belt had dug in, but nothing to worry about. He could still see out the windshield. What Jake saw was the van, whose driver was attempting to turn right on Coronado, sliding sideways across the road, and then, with a last-minute endeavor to straighten it out, nosing into the ditch at right angles to the through street, a hundred yards to Jake's right. Jake's own vehicle had chewed through the asphalt and jerked to a safe stop in the middle of Coronado Avenue, blocking both lanes.

He didn't have time to move it. Jake reached into his vest and felt the relatively small . 45, one of two guns he had on his person. He didn't pull it out of the specially designed holster that was part of his vest, but reassured himself that it was there.

The van was so old it was not equipped with air bags, or they had worked once and not been replaced. The driver's face had hit the center of the steering wheel, causing a cut on his jaw and probably some loose teeth. The smaller, darker man at the wheel had his door halfway open and was about to run when he saw that he was face to face with Jake. As Jake looked him straight in the eye silently he noticed that it had the desired effect; he stopped in his tracks, froze for a second, a second which Jake used to look across the bench seat of the van to the passenger.

His head had apparently hit the windshield—there was some blood. There was a radiating crack in the window that looked like a big spider web with a tuft of black hair in the center.

Something on the van, near the back caught Jake's attention and registered in the back of his brain, but now the two men needed all his attention. The passenger reached for an item on the seat, and Jake's heart skipped a beat. He didn't have time to pull his own gun. He knew the vest under his shirt, thin and lightweight as it was, would keep the bullet from being fatal, but it would slow him down. Or the shot might be to his head. He should have had his gun in his hand.

Jake looked again, relieved that what the man in the passenger seat was pointing at him was an eight-inch long, spring-operated by-pass pruner, part of the landscaper ruse. Jake had to take advantage of the moment and act fast, because there almost surely was a gun nearby—it had probably slid off the seat and onto the floor when the van hit the low sage-covered sand dune on the other side of the ditch.

The driver had looked to his left, toward his partner, to see what Jake found so intriguing. When his startled face revealed that he too was aware the weapon wasn't a gun, Jake moved, swiftly and strongly. With his left arm, just as strong as his right, he grabbed the driver's right arm and pinned it against the open door while his right hand brought out a pair of strong plastic hand restraints from a pocket in his vest. Luckily, the driver's window had been rolled partway down, and it took only a second or two to secure his right hand to the door frame above the window. In another second he had his .45 out and pointed it at the passenger.

At the same instant that Jake aimed the gun, the passenger turned and bolted for the door. Jake wasn't about to shoot anybody in the back, not even a low-level drug runner. He re-holstered his gun and half-crawled, half-jumped through the van. Even with his big body, it was faster to go through than around. As he did so, he saw a glint of metal up under the dash, caught in the crack where the floorboards met the back wall. He grabbed it, made sure the safety was on and tucked it into his belt, all the while moving the direction the man had run. The other man, the driver, was screaming in Spanish— something Jake couldn't understand even though he was bilingual.

Scanning to the horizon, he spotted two little swirls of moving sand, like miniature dust devils. One was natural, the other was moving in a straight line, obviously made by the feet of a running human. Jake took an angle; with his longer strides and equally good endurance, it took only three or four minutes to catch up to him. The man got a second wind from somewhere, and squared off with fists in the air. He did not see his own gun sticking out from Jake's belt. Maybe he thought this was some kind of honor thing, a mano a mano moment. Jake approached to about fifteen feet away, pulled the newly-acquired gun from his waist, pointed it at the small man, then fired into the ground halfway between them, mainly to make sure the gun was loaded. The man's hands went immediately high into the air. Using the gun as a pointer, Jake motioned in the direction he wanted suspect number two to walk. They proceeded to Jake's truck, where the was secured with another plastic handcuff, in a seated position in the truck's bed, attached to part of the frame by both hands. Jake reached into the jump seat, procuring a hat and a bottle of water. He put the bottle in the man's hands, knowing he would find a way to get it to his mouth, and placed the hat on his head.

Somehow he felt a combination of pity and respect for the guy. Jake took the gun from his waist and placed it in a plastic bag and left it under his seat. He wasn't too worried about firing of the gun. For one thing, thee place was so desolate and hot, it was unlikely anyone would have been outside where they could have heard it; and for another, it wasn't his gun.

Meantime, the man who'd been secured earlier was screaming and cursing in two languages, mainly insisting that he was about to die of thirst or heat-stroke, and it would be Jake's fault, and his ghost was planning to come back and haunt Jake for the rest of his life or end it early, and maybe Jake better wish for the early death because the curse would be worse. Jake had to give the guy credit for some ingenuity. He grabbed another bottle of water, took a gulp and screwed the cap back on. He scrounged around and found another hat—an old one with a logo from the San Diego Padres baseball team across its brim, and walked to the van. He gripped the prisoner by both shoulders to settle him and stop him from struggling and squirming. He was bathed in sweat. The tired man acquiesced, and Jake tilted his head up and poured water slowly down his open mouth till he pulled away. Then, without rancor, he emptied the rest of the bottle over the guy's head and put the Padres cap on it.

Jake had taken the opportunity to pick up a few more plastic cuffs while stashing the gun and used one to attach himself to the driver before he cut away the ones from the top of the window. He knew the man was relieved to be able to lower his arms, which had probably lost feeling temporarily and were tingling. He also felt confident he could handle it if the guy put up a struggle and didn't see any need for a show of force.

After finally getting both perps settled and secured in the bed of his truck, Jake was relieved, but not too surprised, when he turned the key and it started right up. It was going to need new tires and brakes, but that wasn't anything for him to worry about.

There was something for him to worry about, though, a nagging thought in the back of his brain.

He put the truck in park, safely off the road, closed his eyes and thought for a minute, but nothing came to him. When he opened them, he was looking at the back window on the van's driver side. He saw a decal, and suddenly he knew. His whole body shivered. He remembered what he had noticed earlier, but to be sure, he drove up as close as he could get to the van, and sure enough, there it was.

He'd seen it before, in a training film or manual, the sign of the Shrimp. It stood for "El Cameron." This particular man had ties deep within federal, state and local anti - gang units as well as the local violent street gangs. Some say he even belongs to Al Qaeda. The most feared of the Mexican drug cartel leaders, El Cameron was a smaller than normal man who made up in guts and cruelty whatever he lacked in size. It was a decal on the window with only a picture, no words. The picture was of a bright red, slightly curled, segmented shrimp.

The man it stood for wanted people to know these men worked for him.

Jake knew he was onto something big. He snapped a photo of it, then got out and photographed both men in the back, just in case.

He got back in his truck and drove down Hollister to the only shade tree on the street, where he parked as the police came up from the other direction. He was happy to see Harry waiting for him on the faded bus-stop bench.

Home Base

After all the waiting, re-telling, report-taking, and waiting again, Harry and Jake were finally told they could leave the Hollister Street scene and head back to the compound. Their pickup had sustained minor damage, but was still drivable and the headlights worked, which was a good thing. It was already dark after 8:00 pm this time of year, when daylight savings time made the evenings stretch out longer. It had been a long day. Their immediate boss was not on site when they finally arrived at their facility, nor were any co-workers from the SCABS compound.

No one would have kept track of what time they checked in, anyway. They were pretty much considered big boys, able to account for their own time. Though they were paid hourly, it was almost unheard of for any of them to pad their time. If anything, the majority of the guys, and even the women who worked in administrative positions, were more likely to undercharge the department than to overcharge.

At the intersection of Hollister with Coronado Avenue, they had to negotiate around a tow truck whose workers were still laboring to extricate the van from the ditch, having already unloaded its contents and sent them to the Border Patrol's evidence room.

"There it is, Jake said as they passed close to the van.

"Yep," Harry answered. The symbol was small but it was unmistakable. "I can tell it's a shrimp. What did you say it stands for again?"

"My God, weren't you paying any attention?"

"I guess not." Harry answered. "It's not like I was sitting there with my thumb up my ass—I had some action of my own, you know, and a thousand questions to answer."

"Sorry, man, it's just that he's the Devil reborn, and it gives me the creeps".

"Oh, El Cameron," Harry scratched his head. "Yeah, now I remember you saying his name. Of course, I've heard about him. They say he's the leader of the biggest, or at least the cruelest, cartel. He even recruits kids from this side of the border—tells them horrific things he'll do to their moms if they don't cooperate. He gets kids to kill for him. Is that the lowlife you're talking about?"

"One and the same. He's one of those guys that scares the hell out of people just hearing his name. Makes you shiver and you don't even know you're shivering. People talk about him like he's the bogeyman. If you're a teenager and you ever want to scare the bejezus out of someone when you're in a dark place or out in the woods, you just mention his name. First time I've ever seen that, though."

He motioned with his left thumb back toward the van, now on solid ground, still attached to the umbilical cord of the tow truck. They could no longer see the half-curled red crustacean symbol, but Harry remembered it, indelibly etched on his brain, and he knew what Jake was pointing at. Now he had the creeps.

Immediately after turning east onto Coronado, they crossed under the I-5 and drove north to Palm on Beyer. Harry felt his heart beating while Jake guided their truck seamlessly through the traffic of Palm Avenue, taking the same route back that they had used in the morning. He wondered if Jake was as tense as he was, wound tight like a rubber band, vibrating. There weren't many vehicles, but they certainly didn't have the road to themselves. Harry wondered why Jake hadn't taken Beyer south to the 905 East, which would have been faster, but he withheld the question. Maybe Jake just needed some driving time to unwind from the day's activities and fears, or it was force of habit, more chance of interrupting or preventing criminal behavior.

They took the Ocean View Hills Parkway, which wound southeasterly around the base of bluffs between the 805 to the east and Brown Field to the west, a regional airport about a mile and a half due north of the Tijuana International. At Otay Mesa Road, instead of driving straight across onto Caliente and looking for the short, barely noticeable dirt side road that led to their gate, Jake made a sharp right and drove two blocks to a familiar corner where Otay Mesa became the 905. There were a couple other small businesses there, but the one best known to the SCABS crew members was the neighborhood bar called Lucky's.

They got out of the truck and walked directly into the bar. Harry wanted to ask what Jake was up to, but decided to just play nice and live in the moment. As they both sat down, a 40- something looking waitress who resembled a fashion model that had just stepped out of the Swiss Alps brought them two frosty beers in glasses before they could ask.

After some small talk that concerned whether or not they might like to spend a night with the woman who brought the beers, Jake looked directly into his glass and said, "I just can't believe he's got something going there. The new berm goes halfway from the border to Monument Road; that's the corner with the grocery store."

Harry got another shiver, and the face of Elena flashed in front of him. "And it's half a mile wide," Jake continued in a monotone, as if talking into his beer could make the whole day, or at least the Devil who called himself a shrimp, disappear. "It's just a stone's throw west and south of that intersection—the whole place down there is still crawling like a giant anthill with DHS and the contractors and sub- contractors that Homeland Security hired. Broke ground in April, '08. Even if they ever get it all finished, they'll still have to do constant upkeep because of our weather patterns. Don't know if they thought of that in the original plan, but down here we might get our whole year's quota of rain in two days. You know that. Lots of erosion, lots more dirt to move around, again. It's okay if it accomplishes what it's supposed to—I don't mind my taxes going to workers who keep our country safe. But," Jake paused to think, "if the shrimp is doing business right there, right under their noses, well then, maybe it's not working the way it should."

"Do you think you're in danger personally? Will he come after you? You know, for bustin' his guys." Harry finally expressed out loud what they were both thinking.

"Hell no!" Jake answered too strongly and too quickly. "He don't give a shit about those little pukes." He caught the eye of the waitress, who turned toward the bar to pour him another beer.

"But he lost a van-load of dope." Harry bit his lip, wishing he hadn't said that. Jake was thoughtful for a minute.

"There's that," he mused eventually, pushing the empty beer glass toward the far edge of the table. " It would piss him off, but just like a mosquito bite. He'll just swat it away and keep on working to make up for lost time. No use wasting energy on something so small. He's got bigger fish to fry. It was only weed, anyway—a freakin' van-load of white powder might catch his attention, might be worth doin' something about. Still, I think it would have to be more personal. Real revenge stuff."

"And the van itself probably belonged to the poor guys haulin' the boxes. I bet they get paid by the hour and have to buy their own gas."

"But they do get paid. From what I hear El Cameron has his own set of ethics, and he won't stiff the little guy. He'll slice the heads off ten of his competitors or next in line without wincing and hang them on a telephone wire, if he knows they purposely crossed him, but if they were loyal, did everything right and just got unlucky, he'll let it slide. I've even heard he runs free clinics for the poor down in Chiapas."

"No shit?"

"Yeah—not a whore with a heart of gold, but a gruesome Robin Hood who gives back. Quite a character."

Jake nodded toward the waitress again. He had finished his second beer faster than the first one. Harry stood up, shook his head at the girl and said, "No, cancel that, we gotta go."

"What the hell, man." Jake spat out the words. "After a day like today I need a few beers. You do too."

"Sorry, man," Harry said, putting a hand on Jake's shoulder as a father might, and relieved when Jake didn't shake it off. "It's just me--- I'm dead tired, and I still got a long drive home."

"Serves you right, you silly s.o.b., for renting a house all the way out in Santee." He was smiling when he said it.

They walked briskly to the pickup, and Jake got in the driver's side. He made no attempt to see if Harry wanted to drive. Harry knew he wouldn't, even if he'd had another beer or two. Once settled, Harry announced, "Santee isn't the boondocks, you know. It's all freeway."

"Yeah, how many?"

"Three or four, but one flows into the other. If it's not 7:30 a m or

5:00 p m, I can make it here in twenty-five minutes, thirty max." Harry seldom had to be on the road at those hours. They had assigned shifts, his

and Jake's both starting at 10:30 am and ending at 7:30 pm, with an hour for lunch. They never took a regular lunch—sometimes a granola bar in the car, other days two hours in a cafe, possibly doing some surveillance. And they often worked extra hours, which they got paid for.

It all worked out.

"Yeah, sure."

"No, really."

They entered the short side road off Caliente—the one that didn't show up on any maps; the gate opened for them. Harry hadn't figured out mechanically how that one worked. The other staff, some of the admin people and housekeeping, gardeners, all those had a key, and the gate had a grungy, old-fashioned padlock. They had to physically get out of their vehicle and open it every time. The ones who qualified with a thorough background check and a higher clearance from the government had devices on their vehicle that electronically sent a signal and the gate miraculously opened, the padlock sliding up and then back into place. For someone just sniffing around, it didn't look important enough to mess with. There was some scruffy brush around the gate, but not thick enough to hide anyone from the discreetly placed cameras, and it was always trimmed to exact specifications, while still looking natural.

Inside, more landscaping and a paved road that wound for three-quarters of a mile along another hill and then up the back of it to the buildings situated near the top. Most buildings had a full view of the border through south-facing walls of windows--bullet-proof, of course. Because there was only one way out, the place was equipped with a heliport and three choppers, in case of wildfires or other emergencies.

The pilots were security-cleared also and had strict orders to check in or return to base at any hint of such problems. There was a light on in Harry's office.

When he opened the door, he saw that Jill was at her desk.

He looked up at the clock. It was 9:15.

"You working overtime tonight?" he asked.

"No, they changed my hours. Twelve-thirty to nine-thirty now." "That's odd—you okay with that?"

"Yeah. I don't know why but they have their reasons. It's not like I've got a roaring social life. And they give me a differential. I'm okay with it."

Harry wasn't sure at first if he was okay with it, but after thinking about it a minute, it felt kind of nice—the idea of a light on and a woman waiting for him when he came in from the day. Not that she was a woman he'd be romantically involved with. He didn't know why he was so sure; she might have been older than he was, possible fifty-five, but she had taken very good care of herself, knew how to dress, and was intelligent enough to carry on a good conversation and know what subjects to avoid. It's just that she seemed like, well, maybe someone who watched out for him, or like family, maybe a sister. She was talking to him.

"Sorry. What's that again?"

"Harry, It's none of my business, I know, but I'm going to say it anyway, because I care about you."

"What's up?" This was unusual.

"Well, I'd never say this to anyone else, but you know how strict they are about drinking on the job."

Harry was mildly annoyed, but he didn't know if it was at her or at Jake. Anyway, he tried to hide it and sound normal.

"Thanks—I appreciate your caring, I really do. But our job was over for the day. It was a hot, dusty one. It was rough, especially for Jake. I figured he deserved a beer if he wanted one. No big deal."

"But you had one too."

"Oh, you know all, great Swami," he said with a grin and a little bow, hoping to diffuse the matter, for he knew it could be a big deal.

"Well, I know that because I can smell it." Harry had always heard that women had a better sense of smell than men. Something about cave-women protecting cave-babies from saber-toothed tigers.

"At least keep mints with you."

"It looks a little suspicious going around sucking on a mint, doesn't it?" "People thinking it is better than people knowing it."

"I only had one." He felt comfortable saying it, but it would have been kind of silly to deny. He knew they were in a secure room with no possibility of bugs. He also trusted Jill Kersey. If he were a Roman in an arena, he would want her to be the one in the audience the Emperor asked for thumbs up or thumbs down. She'd risk her own hide to protect his.

"Jake? He only have one too?"

Harry didn't answer.

"Just be careful." Harry nodded as he started towards his vehicle. Forty minutes later after a stop for dinner at his favorite fast-food café, Harry was in the living room of his small rental house in the suburbs —three bedrooms and two baths crammed into just over a thousand square feet. He was playing ball with his cat, amazed at how many games it could play.

"Good hit, Tiger Princess, that's at least a double," Harry said to the nine-pound ball of orneriness and loyalty hiding behind the back of the chair, with her left paw extended beyond it, in the direction of Harry. From his kneeling position, about ten feet away, he threw a wadded up ball of white paper an inch in diameter, like pitching a tiny softball. Without showing her face, the pet swatted the ball hard with her left paw. Of course, like any cat, she could use her four paws equally well when she wanted to, but in this game, she always batted left-handed. The next pitch went awkwardly to Harry's right and rolled under the table. He pulled out a spare ball. "Foul ball, that's okay."

Another pitch. This time the paper sailed over his head and straight down the hall. "Home run— good girl!"

The long thin cat with markings that made her look like a miniature leopard ducked behind the chair-back, playing hide and seek, then appeared at the top suddenly and pretended to strike Harry.

"Got me!" he said.

If he hadn't made sure her food dish was full before the game started, it wouldn't have been pretend. The cat then settled on the back of the chair and put her nose high in the air, waiting for her real reward, a pat on the head (or if he was absolutely sure no one could see him, an air kiss with a little squeaking sound). Harry didn't know whether to laugh or cringe. Years ago, he was the epitome of everything masculine, everything normal, with a wife in the kitchen cooking dinner, and him throwing a real ball for a golden retriever. A perfect Currier-and-Ives family in a picture-perfect New England setting, a hard-working cop with a vine-covered cottage in the country, a gorgeous loving woman, all his dreams come true.

As the cat lay sprawled out on the back of the chair, Harry disappeared into the bathroom. Harry poked his head through the doorway, "Good night, Tiger," he said, before taking a twenty-minute shower and falling into a deep restful sleep.

Mornings and Melli

The morning after the Hollister Street incident, Harry woke up refreshed. Mornings at the house was the most pleasant time of day, surprising him with a more relaxed kind of contentment than he'd ever felt in New Hampshire. The bed he'd picked up at the warehouse store when he moved in was still quite comfortable. Because the room he used was at the back of the house, with an east-facing window that let in some morning sun even with the blinds closed, he always woke gently with the changing light. With his typical work schedule, he didn't leave the house until 9:45 am. There weren't many days that being up early was imperative, but he was usually awake by 7:00 am. and used the time to read or run personal errands. He owned an alarm clock but had hardly ever heard it ring. Even without the stimulus of the sun, he was equipped with an internal clock that allowed him to tell himself what time he wanted to rise before he fell asleep; and he automatically awakened at that time. It never failed him.

Harry always went to the room he used as an office and opened the door for the cat, before showering and having breakfast---cereal, milk and fresh fruit. The office was basically the cat's room; he put her there with a bowl of crunchies when he retired for the night, and put her outside for her morning romp when he woke. He knew there was some risk to allowing her out in the large backyard, which, even though fenced, included part of a canyon. In her first two years, some freedom was a lesser evil than attempting to co-exist with a half-wild feline, mean as a badger and determined to be outside. The compromise was daytime only, backyard only, as if she agreed. The fence was not an obstacle, but at least she touched home base often and was always waiting when he came home.

At night, he locked the small cat door, which only one time had been breached. He had fallen asleep on the couch and woke to a rustling sound beside him. Looking down, he'd discovered a young skunk. With considerable apprehension, Harry had opened the sliding patio door, then made a wide circle and walked a respectful distance behind the cute black-and-white stench factory, making gentle shooing motions with his arms.

Harry and the "princess" had, over time, learned a lot about each other. She became aware that he didn't hate cats or want to hurt her, but he could be a bit clumsy or forgetful. He found that she loved to play and had immense energy that subsided only slightly as she matured, and that she did not tolerate an empty food bowl, always leaving the last ten pieces.

She demanded fresh water every day in the same place, and wouldn't drink unless she heard the faucet running. She would often nip playfully, but it took a number of bites deep enough to leave marks on his wrists before he fully grasped her rules.

The twin bed in the study, besides being the cat's, was for the occasional guest, or for Harry if he ever had more than one person stay over. His bedroom was not the master, but the bathroom was just down the hall, and it allowed him to rent out the master, which had its own exit to the front yard. He wasn't sure, when he first arrived in San Diego, whether he would find work right away or what kind of job he would have to take, so the boarder helped cover the cost of his rent and make the money he had borrowed last a little longer. The fact that the tenant was then a late-twenties single woman, pleasant but quiet, didn't hurt. Anyway, like the cat, the boarder came with the house—Harry didn't have any say in the matter. Harry drifted into nostalgia as he watched the cat attempting to sneak up on a scrub jay, a bird that was more likely to do her harm than be eaten. He recalled the first time he told anyone about Tiger Princess. He had called his mother in Dover to let her know he had landed safely in southernmost California and that he had a kitten.

****Flashback Late May, 2007, Santee, California****

Harry had not heard his mother laugh like that since before his father died. Loud, natural, uninhibited, subsiding after thirty seconds or so into soft giggles.

"Did I hear you right?-- You said you adopted a KITTEN? And named it Princess? Harold Samuel Dugan, whatever has come over you?" The giggles continued between the questions.

Harry didn't answer immediately because it felt so good just to listen to her being herself, being at ease and happy. If anyone deserved happiness, it was Ann Dugan. She was fifty- nine the last time he saw her, eight years prior, a little plump and a little gray, but still a beauty. She usually wore her hair in a loose bun at the back of her head, and it had enough natural wave to look full and lovely that way. He thought her beauty shone even more when she relaxed at the end of a day, or early on a Saturday morning, those times long ago when he had visited his folks at home. Ann Dugan had been strikingly attractive, not a line in her face, not a wisp of gray in her hair, before that day in 1995 when the uniformed officer knocked on her door. Thank God that Dover, New Hampshire, was a small enough town that someone knew someone who knew Harry, and he had been contacted and told to get over to his parents' place immediately. Nothing else. He was there in the kitchen, pouring a glass of

water for himself and his mother when they both saw the car pull up.

It could have been something less serious, but Harry knew it wasn't. He reached under the counter, behind the phone books and pulled out the bottle of blackberry brandy that he knew his mother kept there, then got to the front door in time to hold her while they both cried. It was the only time in all his adult years that Harry had shed tears, though there had been many times he felt so empty he wanted to cry but couldn't.

He missed his father more than he could ever tell anyone. He felt guilty, three years later, for leaving the place he'd lived all his life, for leaving his mother alone. But he didn't have much choice and his mother knew that.

She had been the only thread that held his life together during the two lost years, when she was essentially his only connection to the town that had been home to generations of his family. And he knew what she had lived for was that he would find himself.

"Ma, it wasn't me that named her," he said into the telephone, quickly jerking himself back to reality. "It's the only way they'd rent the house to me."

"Well, I'm glad you're in a house. I know things will work out, now that you're settled in San Diego and in touch with that guy John told you about. Who is they?"

"The Nelsons. The judge and his wife. They're retiring and moving to someplace smaller--nice people. They remind me of you and--" he continued, trying to smooth over the hesitation--"Dad."

"And they wouldn't rent to you unless you adopted the cat?" "That's about it. The place came with this tiny striped menace.

They had already made an offer on the condo they're moving to when Her Majesty showed up at their neighbor's house, a barely weaned fur-ball looking half the size it should be, but eight or ten weeks old, the vet told them. They'd always loved animals, the girl says, but planned for the move and found homes for everything, including the last three chickens and the two peacocks. But of course, they took in the kitten."

"But of course. People do that. But, oh my God, peacocks. I never knew anyone that had peacocks, except at the zoo, naturally. Wait a minute. The girl? What girl?"

"Oh yeah, I meant to tell you."

"What, son, you had to adopt a girl, too?"

"Well, she's not a girl, really, she's a woman. And a very attractive one I might add. She was renting a room from them and they didn't want to just throw her out. The location works out so well for her, and it's not that easy to find a room to rent out here in the East County. She's a very good tenant, they said."

"Sounds too complicated. Was this the only house you could get?"

"No, but I didn't want to waste any time. I went and saw that guy Phillip—John Saunders' cousin, the second day I was here, while I was still at the hotel room. He referred me to the Nelsons—like I said, sometimes a rental can be hard to find around here especially for what I had to spend."

"Yes, and did Phillip give you a job?"

"It's not that simple, Ma. He said he'd do what he can, and I think he really meant it. I'm supposed to see him in two weeks. But I don't exactly have a resume, you know."

"You were a good cop!"

"Maybe I should have him talk to you."

"Don't get smart with me."

"Ma, how many years you been saying' that to me?

I'm sorry, really. You've helped me so much, I don't have any right to be sarcastic with you. The truth is, I don't know if John's recommendation will be enough. I sure hope it is. He's a good friend and he went out on a limb for me." The words caught in his mouth, but he couldn't tell his mother what he knew about John Saunders and his two-sided friendship. And now, visualizing himself treading water in a wide river, about to slide over the falls without even a barrel, he saw John's referral as his only lifeline.

"I don't have anything else going for me now, career-wise. This guy Phillip, he said that it would help if I had an address, other than a hotel room, and someone had told him about the judge needing a tenant. Maybe the old guy will be able to go to bat for me, too. I think both of them like me. I just want to do all I can 'cause I'm thirty-eight years old and not too many more chances left to start over. The sooner I can get set up, the better. And the sooner I can start paying you back."

"That's not important."

"It is to me."

"Okay, so tell me about this woman in your life."

"Ma, it's not like I'm dating her. I've become her landlord, I guess, and it's important for us, for me, to keep it on a professional level."

"Is she nice?"

"Yes, what I get to see of her. She's pretty much kept to herself in the month I've been here. She's about thirty, give or take, maybe a little younger. Her name is Melita Freeman. Her mom is Irish and her dad is Native American."

"Hmmm. I don't think I ever knew any Indians. What's she like?"

"Well, she doesn't go around in buckskin and feathers, and she's certainly no savage.. Very pretty--long, straight hair, almost black, but her eyes are blue. Usually wears a ponytail and glasses, when she's using her laptop on the patio.. She's a bit too geekish for me--or maybe I should say

intellectual. She belongs to the Audubon Society and knows everything about birds, about nature in general, I think. This is what I hear from the Nelsons. I only met her once, when they introduced us."

"Does she have a job?"

"Oh, yes, she writes grants, and I think she's a graduate student or researcher, too. She does most of her work at home, in her room or on her private patio adjoining it."

"So, a writer. Didn't Lara always want to be a writer?" Harry swallowed hard. "She talked about it now and then." "You should give her a call and let her know you're okay."

"Ma, I trust you to fill Lara in on everything in my life. I'm glad you two have stayed in touch—more than you can know."

"Nevertheless," his mother insisted, you should check in with her." Harry held the earpiece away from his ear. "She and"— She paused for a moment, as if she caught herself almost saying something that she would regret. "Well, she asks about you all the time." Harry had noticed the pause, so he realized that his mom knew, but it was still too soon to tell her that he knew. "And you might want to get a hold of John," Ann Dugan continued---let him know you saw the guy. Have you been in touch at all since you left Dover?

"Yeah, I talked to him a couple of times."

"Well, I know you'll be busy after you get this job." He loved the way she could sound so certain, in an off-hand way. I hope you'll have time to call your dear old Ma once in a while."

"I'll call you more than I did when I was on the road, I promise." "I suppose once a week would be too much to hope for?"

****

After he'd wrapped up the phone call, Harry pulled a white t-shirt on and, wearing his plaid pajama pants, took a stroll out front to pick up the morning paper. It was just past eight. He'd wanted to get the call in early---he knew his mother often had lunch plans, and it was three hours later in New Hampshire. Recently retired from her job at the phone company, she had no relatives nearby, unless she counted Lara, but lots of friends. It eased Harry's conscience a little that she was so active.

Between the house and the sidewalk was a lattice trellis, completely enveloped by a fast-growing cape honeysuckle, that made the front yard feel like one of those walled gardens in the deep south, in Charleston, perhaps. One of Harry's jobs was to keep it trimmed at the top. He didn't mind—it would take only ten minutes with the garage-sale trimmer that the owners had left for him, and it made it possible for him to go get the paper in his pj's.

Walking back to the front door, he heard a rustle and, squinting into the shade, he caught a glimpse through another wall of lattice, left unpainted and weathered to a pleasant grayish brown that blended into the background. It separated the main part of the front yard from the tenant's patio. He softened his step on the smooth blue beach pebbles that made up the path, but it was too little, too late. She had already heard him, he could tell. She was placing a marker of some kind in the book she'd been reading.

Through the diamonds of wood, he saw her stash the book on a small round table and rise from her position on the padded bench, where she had been half-sitting, half-lying, propped up by two little cushions, colorful and tasseled. Before he realized she had moved, part of the lattice was creaking apart—he hadn't known there was a door built into the semi-wall, and it startled him.

"Whoops, sorry if I scared you. I know you weren't expecting this to open. I kind of like it that no one can tell--somehow it makes me feel safer in my space." She was wearing faded jeans, but he was happy to see they had no holes in them. He hated that, even if they were bought that way on purpose because it was supposed to be stylish. She had on two layered cotton tops. One had a round neckline, sort of low, with fake diamonds edging it and short ruffled sleeves over the shoulders with wide gaps under the arms that were filled in by the sleeveless undershirt. Tank top, they called it; Harry had no idea why. She wore them well.

The "door" was barely over a foot wide, but an average woman could slip through easily by turning sideways. So, the pretty young woman actually did talk.

"Good morning," he said. Caught off guard, he thought it best to go with the most basic phrase. Through the open door, he caught a glimpse of some sort of flowers, hanging in pots along the back fence, on the property line. They were weird and amazingly beautiful at the same time. Instead of leaves, there were pale green flat paddles, awkwardly jointed like so many extra-terrestrial puppets, but they bore flowers, two or three on each plant, some about to open, others fully formed and the size of saucers-- brilliant fiery hot pinks, soft pinks, creamy white-with-a hint-of-pinks. Her gaze followed his.

"Oh, I see you noticed the epiphyliums," she said, in a most un-self-conscious way, apparently not the least bit aware that a strip of his slightly out-of- shape belly was showing between the thin t-shirt and the pajama bottoms. Nor did she seem to notice his bare feet or unshaven face. "Orchid cactus, most people call them. May is their best month.

Come, take a closer look." She pushed the lattice panel further open, toward him, stretching the spring close to its limit.

Harry heard a little creaking noise. He followed her inside, mainly because it was apparent she expected him to, and to do anything else might appear rude. As he did, the tie-string on his pajamas scraped against the frame piece of the entrance- way. He thought, "Note to self—start working out again." "Melita. Right?" Harry started to extend his hand, but thought it might seem foolish since they'd already been introduced. Instead, he just smiled a foolish grin.

"Yes, Harry. But most of my friends call me Melli." "I like that. I've never known anyone named Melli."

She smiled and Harry felt a sense of relief, like the ice was broken. He was surveying the blooming plants, all hung so their six or eight-inch pots were close to eye level. They were truly intriguing.

"Orchids, huh?

"Well, botanically, they're neither orchids nor cacti. They're in a different family--all get their nourishment directly from the surrounding air, in their natural state. Usually they live in hot humid climates and grow best in the crotches and crevices of tree branches. We grow some of them in pots. Here's another epi."

Hanging above the colorful plants was something Harry recognized from scenes in movies of the Old South, but he had never seen it in person. Spanish moss, hanging from massive oak trees over shadowy, narrow roads or beside waterways where alligators lurk or festooned in creepy night scenes in a cemetery. It was totally unexpected in this setting. He stared without comment.

"Most people call it Spanish moss," she was saying, after having given another unpronounceable Latin name. It fares better in more humid climates, although San Diego, and all of Southern California, is becoming more humid each year as population levels of humans increase, and they import more water for their manufacturing, agricultural, and personal landscape needs. Here it grows pretty well when grouped near other plants and where it is in substantial amounts, not just a strand or two. It likes regular misting and airflow--hanging on trees or open fences, but not metal or solid ones. She smiled, "Oh, good, here's a bloom."

Harry was already having a hard time grasping the fact that Spanish moss could live here; now she says it's blooming. He bent closer to look, and sure enough, there was a flower. Tiny and lime green—half a dozen of them would have fit on his pinkie fingernail.

"Wow, that's neat," he said, and was surprised to find that he really meant it. He looked around with fascination. He didn't know what he expected to find behind these airy walls, if indeed he had any expectations at all, but this was like entering another realm. As he looked down the fence-line, along the side of the house, he caught a glimpse of what appeared to be a small but complete outdoor kitchen, shaded by the neighbor's tree, with a green and white striped awning extending from the fence to keep its leaves off her work surface. He looked up at the tree--must be forty feet tall and perfectly rounded, resplendent now with the mellow light of morning filtering through its leaves. He began to smell coffee, a deep, rich aroma.

Again, she was watching him to see what he was looking at. "White ash," she said simply. We have two kinds around here--not native, of course. The Shamel Ash is seen too, but less often. The pollens of both cause allergies in a lot of people. Glad I'm not one of them."

He followed her back from the fence and realized they were standing near the door—a real door, this time, that led to her room, left fully open. There was no screen.

"Aren't you worried about flies?"

"Not this time of day. They are most active at 4:00 pm, and not this month. We may start seeing some in June, when I'll hang my deterrent. A bag of water with pennies in it. Works pretty well."

Harry was fairly sure Melli could explain in scientific terms why the fly-chaser worked, but he chose not to ask.

"Coffee?" she asked. "I grind my own beans and I have a two-cup French press. It's ready now."

Harry couldn't think of a good reason to refuse, so he nodded his head. As she stepped through the doorway, he remained where he was. He figured she'd bring the coffee out. His eyes started to focus and he could see that the room, though only about twelve feet square, was laid out as neatly and efficiently as the garden. On the back wall was a closet with mirrored doors like his. The left wall held a deep, wooden cabinet, four or five feet tall and six feet wide. It had glass doors with wire behind them, like you'd see at a lawyer's office, and was packed to the brim with books. At the top was a rail. Two smaller chests stood to the right of it, like stair-steps. Across from the cabinet, under the window, was a padded bench with more storage under it, he presumed and two baskets of folded clothes on top. A relatively small recliner sat in the corner left of the closet, blocking the door to the hall.

"Come here," Melli called, holding a vase in her hand. "Look at these--these are real orchids, cymbidiums."

There were five stems, each with six or eight fully opened orchids as big as a fist, in shades of yellow, beige and pinkish brown, with tall ferns interspersed. He wondered who had brought her a bouquet so elegant.

"Gorgeous," said Harry. As he stepped foot inside and turned toward her, he saw that the front wall, just to his right, held a counter with cabinets over part of it, and, closer to the side on his right, the one with the window, a keyboard and monitor, a printer, a phone and a small T.V.

That part of the counter was lower and open underneath so it could function as a desk; it had an office chair rolled under it. Next to his arm was a microwave, and what may have been a hot plate, with a shallow wooden box over it and a toaster oven on top. To his left, a bright bathroom.

Melli reached under the counter and pulled out a quart of milk from a short refrigerator, showing it to Harry. He declined the milk but accepted the mug she offered, and they walked outside to the bench. Directly across from them was an old country-looking cupboard, with peeling paint, fitted out to use as a potting bench. "I think the shabby chic works perfectly here, and I coated it all with water-seal. The curtains under the lower part hide my supply of firewood."

"Firewood?" asked Harry.

Melli tapped on the table in front of them, three feet in diameter, and Harry noticed it had metal legs, tile, and a wooden top that lifted off. It didn't take him long to figure out that the coffee table served a dual purpose. Which reminded him of a question that had come to his mind in his brief moment inside.

"I hope this isn't too personal," he ventured, "but when I stepped into your room, I don't remember seeing a bed."

He hoped he wasn't blushing, having coffee in his nightclothes and talking about beds to a near-stranger.

Melli laughed, a low, natural sound. "It's a legitimate question. Did you notice that bookcase?"

"Yes, it was a beauty with those wire-glass doors."

"I had it custom-built to my needs. By a friend. It's got secrets-- you probably didn't notice but it's deep enough to hold two rows of books. Those doors have shelves on their backs, and when you open them, one row of books swings out to reveal the others in back. Pretty neat, huh?"

"Yeah, but it doesn't explain where you sleep, not that it's any of my business."

"That's the other secret. Those units that look like steps really are. I have a thin mattress on top and a duvet in the bottom step. The rail makes it safe. There's a light-blocking curtain on the wall that looks like a decorative panel, but it moves on a track, so my tiny cave can be dark even in the middle of the day."

"Do you do much sleeping in the middle of the day?"

"Not usually, but sometimes research or a field trip has me up all night. And sometimes I just feel like a nap. Plus, at night it blocks any glare from the streetlight out front that strays into my room. Next time you visit, I'll show you."

He offered his cup and toasted, "To neighborliness."

Points East

There was no sign of the sun on that early August day as the two border patrolmen wound their way east on Jamacha Road, just past noon. The thick marine layer felt like light rain. It was unusual this far east at this time of year, but maybe there was some monsoon activity coming up the Gulf of California, the narrow sea that separates the peninsula of Baja from the rest of Mexico. They had traveled north from their headquarters, using the 125 freeway, the same route Harry took to go to and from work most days.

"I've done this hundreds of times and it still feels funny to be going north to get to the border," Harry offered, just to make conversation.

"I know what you mean. Makes more sense if you think of the border in its entirety. More than just the International Crossings."

Harry knew that what most people thought of when they heard the word "border" was the international crossing point from the U. S. into Mexico, at San Ysidro, almost directly south of their headquarters. It consisted of dozens of lanes, where the 5 freeway and the border meet, and the northbound lanes on the Tijuana side sometimes backed up for miles--and hours-- especially on the last evening of a long week-end. Radio traffic reports routinely included the wait time at the border. There was another crossing a few miles east, where the 905 met the border, and a separate truck crossing. Harry remembered the time, shortly after he had started the job, when Jake brought him there and they sat in an air-conditioned room looking at a screen that showed the inside of every truck they wanted to check, like a hospital x-ray machine on steroids, with an instant read-out.

Twenty-five or thirty miles further in was the sleepy community of Tecate, with its one-lane crossing. It was in this rugged stretch of land, from the main crossing to Tecate, which the SCABS referred to as "The Edge," that most of the successful illegal border crossings took place.

Despite serious patrolling above and to the sides of it, regularly-spaced towers that constituted an "electronic fence" further east, where the Interstate dropped close to the border, and a real fence from the ocean to Tijuana's eastern environs, this no-man's-land was hostile. It was nearly impenetrable, almost certain death to those who entered unprepared, and the best opportunity for those desperate enough to do anything for a shot at a better life or money to send their anxious families. Only the most fit or the most foolish would consider entry.

"The border's not just one place, you know. It runs for a couple thousand miles, one hundred and fifty of which are at the bottom of California. That's the part we're responsible for." Harry repeated the mantra that both of them had heard from Phillip Bradshaw, the man who Harry had first reported to that tense day in June of 2007.

Phil was now the one who conducted their morning check-in and today had assigned them to patrol the two-lane Highway 94, east from the Spring Valley area to the point where it met up with Interstate 8, which ran almost parallel to it, a little further north.

"Enough of the 'Phil-the-mill' shit," complained Jake good-naturedly. The guys on patrol called him that because he was a paper mill generating stacks of forms they had to fill out, requiring them to log in details that no one could possibly care about.

"Can you believe that guy?" Harry questioned. "Not wanting us to follow up on all that crap that went down yesterday on Hollister. There's got to be something major going on. There's no way those guys would have the sign of the Shrimp on their van if they weren't connected to the s.o.b. It might be our best chance to get him if we strike while the iron's hot."

"That isn't how government does things."

"Maybe it's how they should--they're always yelling at us for going off half-cocked, but they just sit on their asses and do nothing. And it's business as usual for the cartels."

Jake agreed. "I don't know if they're really trying to get their evidence in order-- irrefutable evidence that will stand up in court, or maybe they just don't want to get caught up in all that trial stuff. Can you imagine the paperwork for everybody if they tried to prosecute El Cameron here?"

"Like that would ever happen," Harry snorted.

Jake continued, as he was in the habit of doing, in what consisted of a monologue with an occasional remark from Harry. "There's more to it than that, though. It's common knowledge that a lot of loads of contraband--drugs and people--are pre- greased and cross the border without any worry. The poor bastards that stand out on the hot asphalt all day waving cars through, or into secondary? They don't get paid enough to make them invulnerable to offers. Sometimes they get offers they can't refuse. It can happen to our guys, too."

"I guess it's always a concern."

"The low-lifes that aren't connected are the ones you hear about. They stash a couple people under the car, or hide a big bag of cocaine in the gas tank and use a coffee can re-piped to the carburetor; but the people at the gate know all the tricks and have access now to a world of information at their fingertips. Probably the guy that sold him the coffee- can contraption got a kickback for calling the border as soon as the poor bastard got off his property. Unless the piper has been paid, they'll get caught and we'll hear about them on the news."

On their right, to the south, Harry caught a glimpse of a large lake, beautiful to look at, the county's largest reservoir, which they would skirt for only about a mile. He always felt cooler when he saw it.

"Sometime we ought to stop and sneak in a swim," Harry suggested.

"Good ole' Sweetwater Lake," Jake answered. "Only the water's not as sweet as it sounds. I, for one, wouldn't swim in it or drink it."

"But isn't it used for our drinking? It must be pretty clean?"

"Yeah, after they doctor it up with chlorine and ammonia, it's clean, I guess. I'll still take my bottle." He lifted his drinking water as if to toast. "There's cows grazing and walking all around the reservoir and into it. You know what cows do."

"They do it in your bottled water, too."

Jake ignored Harry's comment. "Anyway, what you get out of your tap is partly water from the Colorado River, our border with Arizona, as you well know. That gets here by irrigation ditches--have you ever been out to the dunes, by Gordon's well? Seen the canals?"

"No. I think Melli goes out there sometimes, to rescue desert tortoises." Jake expanded the lesson. "The irrigation canals--everyone calls them ditches, and that's exactly what they are. V- shaped cement troughs that make a nice place to cool off for the local population, mostly migrant workers. There's some of that in your tap water, too, and more from the Metro District in Los Angeles. They get it from the Sierras around Bishop and a small amount of rain and runoff that the reservoirs catch. We just don't have enough water on our own to support the number of people that live here."

"Well, good old' Sweetwater looks pretty refreshing from here. Could we swim in it if we wanted to?"

"Can't get near it. There's no swimming, legally anyway, in any of the so-called lakes around here. Quite a few allow boating and fishing. I don't know how many of the fishermen actually eat what they catch, but I've never heard of anyone getting sick from them. Just the same--" Jake interrupted himself to point out a location of interest on their left. "See that small mountain over there--that's Dictionary Hill. Named that because the developer gave away sets of encyclopedias as an enticement for people to buy lots there. Strange place, though. He got the roads and water pipes in, then ran out of money, so it just stayed like that a long time—a place for the juvenile delinquents to hang out or drag race. There are people that have seen things roll uphill out there. They even did it on the T.V. News one night, with a beach ball."

Jake seemed to relish his role as tour-guide and trainer, possibly because his audience was older than he was by a decade. Now, their roles were starting to reverse, and Harry sensed it bothered Jake a little. Jake never said anything. Still, it amazed Harry that his partner could come up with new stories or descriptions every time they drove this route.

"We're on Jamacha road now. You know that. But on the other side of the 125, going west, it's called Paradise Valley Road. Again, a misnomer-- deceptive. It takes you to an area you probably wouldn't want to live in. Quite a bit of crime—gang stuff." In a few minutes they came to Rancho San Diego, another typical suburban community, where they would pick up the 94. If they took it the other direction it would lead straight to downtown San Diego. Due north was El Cajon, with Interstate 8 running through it. The 94, also called Campo Road, took them southeast. In another ten miles, they'd begin to skim the border, from Tecate to the town of Campo.

"So what do you know about Campo?" Jake asked, always digging for an opportunity to show his older friend how much he knew.

"That it's way out there—pretty much the end of civilization," Harry answered.

"That's about it," Jake said, then got uncharacteristically quiet and drove silently for miles, traffic thinning considerably on the two-lane 94. They passed through the small community of Jamul, quaint in a rustic, back-country sort of way, a town where it appeared most people owned a horse or a swimming pool or both. Maybe like Santee used to be, Harry thought. Moving on, trees were smaller and houses fewer. Sagebrush lined the road as they wound their way east through the barely-there town of Dulzura and beyond. There was scrub oak, some quite large, wherever a little run-off collected from the surrounding hills.

Harry knew SCABS didn't usually go much farther than the town of Jacumba, where the 94 met the 8. He remembered that there was a 4000 foot pass just beyond it and then a steep drop into the desert of Imperial county, a desert transformed by irrigation into a veritable garden. The valley regularly racked up temperatures well above 110 degrees most days this time of year. Torture when it was dry, he'd been told, but pure hell with the humidity of monsoon season, especially if the thunderstorms that threatened didn't materialize. He noticed that the drizzle of the morning had turned to brightness just short of sunlight.

As if hearing his partner's unspoken question, Jake announced, "It's almost always clear out here, even when it's gloomy at the coast. Even there, it usually brightens up by late afternoon. They get enough precipitation this side of the summit to grow these beautiful oaks. Some trees have died from the recent drought years and blights. Or fire, of course. They get a bad one out here every few years."

"Tell me about it. I'd only been in my house a few months when they had a firestorm. October of '07. One hit Chula Vista, another up on Palomar, one in Rancho Bernardo. So dry you couldn't touch a car door handle without getting knocked on your butt by static electricity. Humidity around 5%. Nobody in Santee was worried. My neighbor was having his house painted. The outside. Everyone was talking about the Cedars fire four years earlier, almost to the day. The whole city evacuated for that one. The town was saved mainly by a guy running his personal bulldozer all day to make a firebreak on the north edge of town. At dark, fire-fighters set a backfire and it worked, amazingly."

"Half the friggin" county was burning, " Jake added, "and it's one of the biggest counties in the country. People were calling friends to evacuate just as the same friends were calling to ask if they should evacuate. Scary. I could see flames in three different directions one time. They lost three thousand houses that year. Dozens of people burned up in their houses or their cars. And of course, there were people out here in the desolate stretches, undocumented immigrants. Some never got found, or if they did, no one knew who they were."

Harry could not think of a fitting comment; they drove in silence for a while.

"We're coming' up on Barrett now. Barrett Junction, a lot of people call it, only there's no other road for a few more miles. Then you can drop down into Mexico at Tecate or stay on the 94 East to Portrero. See that fish fry sign? They been doin' that for forty-some yeas now. Maybe more. Used to go out there when I was in high school, with my parents, believe it or not. Might have been before I got a driver's license, or just after, but it was a while before I got my own car. There were always a bunch of people who knew each other, and some who didn't--- rednecks, mostly, I guess you'd call them." He paused a few minutes. "I got my first good feel there." Jake went on. "A girl I sort of knew 'cause I hung around with her brother, but she was still in middle school. In the back seat of her parents' car. There wasn't much there except the fish-fry roadhouse, and a few houses. Still isn't, as you see. We were hangin' out down by the creek, six or eight of us. Every once in a while a parent would yell, and one of us would yell back. Of course we had beer. We snuck it out in the plastic cups we were supposed to be drinking soda from. Sometimes we had to pour cola in it so it looked the right color, but it got us a little bit high if we drank enough of it. Couldn't do pot there."

"So what happened with the girl?"

"Well, I'm not sure. All of a sudden we were a little bit separated from the others. She pulled on my arm and said she had something to show me, something she made in class, I think she said, and it was in the car. So I went to the car with her. The next thing I know, I was unsnapping her bra and she was letting me. And then I had my hand down her pants. Oh my God, I still get horny thinking about that night. When was your first feel?"

"Too long ago to remember."

Jake pulled in at the roadhouse and they both got out. "Good a place as any for lunch," Jake said as he opened the screen door, equipped with a spring to pull it back into place. "The only place, pretty much," he added as the door smacked closed behind them.

A couple of flies that had slipped in buzzed around the entrance, trying to keep their distance fromnthe blades of the Casablanca-style fan that rotated placidly near the wood-plank ceiling.

"Hi, guys," said the perky waitress.

She was wearing jeans, a t- shirt and a pony-tail as her uniform. Harry was surprised that she didn't call Jake by name. It certainly wasn't his first visit. "What can I get you?"

"Two beers," Jake answered, without consulting Harry. "And two fish sandwiches with cole slaw, I guess." Then, turning to Harry, "That

okay?"

"Yeah, I guess."

It had taken Harry years to get accustomed to this degree of casualness on the job, but since he was not in a police uniform, he didn't feel quite as awkward when Jake ordered a beer for him. He would never have had a beer on his previous job.

The room was huge and almost empty.

"Get any moisture out your way?" Jake asked the waitress, letting her know, if she didn't already, that they had come from the city.

"Six drops," she answered, then moved away.

Jake stopped talking while they ate. He tipped the server generously, Harry noticed, and when they stepped back outside, he pulled a baseball cap from his back pocket. "Did it get ten degrees hotter while we were in there?" he asked.

Harry had noticed the heat even on the way in--muggy, like he was used to in New England, not dry like it was in Fort Stockton. "Aren't we supposed to have a dry heat?"

"Usually is. This is a bit out of the ordinary."

On hot days, and especially humid ones like today, the SCABS uniform was uncomfortable. It consisted of dark blue cotton pants and any solid color short-sleeve shirt other than white, as long as it fit over the vest and looked normal. Long sleeves were not required, except for guys with tattoos. The jackets had pockets inside and out for things they might need on the job, but today they both left their jackets in the truck. A specially designed "smart phone" hung from a belt was standard issue. The vest was amazing—made of a Kevlar fabric to protect them from most bullets and sewn intricately with pockets for the paraphernalia of their trade. And, of course, the holster and revolver completed the uniform.

Harry remembered their first trip out this way, when Jake had asked if he had his full uniform. He had patted his vest with a smile, signifying that his gun was present in its built-into-place holster.

"I highly recommend you add your own as back-up," Jake had offered. Harry remembered him reaching down and sliding up the lower part of his pant leg, revealing the handle of a second smaller gun tucked into his sock. "I can tell you where to shop."

"I might take you up on that," Harry had answered, and indeed he had. "Wave to Mexico," Jake joked a few minutes later, and

they passed the sign reading, "Tecate, two miles." "Strange, isn't it?" Jake said. "What?"

"How one town can be in two countries. Same name on both sides of the border. You know that little guard shack that sits on the road that comes through?"

"Yeah. Been to it a few times, but never beyond it."

"Well, it's always manned. But even now, it's pretty laid back. Before 9/11, it was too relaxed. One time I came back from San Felipe with some friends on Super Bowl Sunday and they were all watching the game on a little portable television. Barely nodded as we drove through. Are you a football fan?"

"Who isn't?"

"I don't know. No one I know. Season's coming up soon. The real season, I mean. I don't pay much attention to the exhibition games. I don't think the coaches and managers take them seriously. The Chargers are pretty popular around here. Not that it matters. They always manage to snatch defeat from the mouth of victory late in the season, even if they make it to the play-offs."

"So I've noticed."

"People are loyal. Even though their home team has only been to the one Super Bowl and got the shit kicked out of them. But they did play what Sports Illustrated calls the best game ever played, in any sport. Back in the early'90's. It was against Miami--in Miami--Went into two overtimes 'cause it was a playoff game. The Dolphins had it won at least twice, kicking the winning field goal, and both times it was blocked. Both times by a guy named Kellen Winslow, who spent the time in between lyin' on a bench writhing in pain. Cramps. The humidity and the temperature were both about 98, and you can imagine, down in a stadium with no breeze. Anyway, the Chargers pulled that one out of their butts. Shame they sold out and changed the stadium name. Jack Murphy, he was a helluva guy, according to my dad, who was a friend of his. You ought to look him up sometime if you are ever bored."

They passed another town, smaller than Dulzura, which meant there was only a sign designating it as Portrero, and a gas station. Then, he gazed off in the distance. "I guess everybody knows it by now—used to be hush-hush," Jake said in a conspiratorial whisper.

"You talking about Earth-ops?"

"Yeah, right over there."

"I know. Sometimes you can hear the sound of small arms. Or not-so-small. They aren't too keen on publicity—try to keep a low profile, but

all that's been blown to hell now. Even so, they still have a lot of freedom, if you know what I mean."

"That's for sure. People think they're something like us, or we're something like them, but I tell you--it's a whole different animal. For one thing, they're more international. Or I should say, overseas—wherever we're not supposed to be at war."

"But we don't do any foreign operations, do we?" "Not officially. But yes."

After a few more quiet minutes, Harry said, "Man, this really is a God-forsaken place, isn't it? From here all the way to Arizona, nothing' on the border? No trees, no water, no people?"

"If there are people, they're probably going to die. Very few roads, except this and the interstate. The ones there are, you need a good 4-wheel drive and God help you if you have a flat or break down. Nothin' but rocks and cactus. Big, round, moon-scape boulders. You ever see them?"

"Yeah, out by Scissors Crossing—the badlands."

"There are worse places. Down on the other side, there's Highway 2 that sort of parallels the border like the 94 and the 8 do on this side. Starts down at Rosarito, fifty miles south of Tijuana on the Baja coast. Comes up to the border at Tecate and close again at La Rumerosa. They're building a major road across the top of Baja; don't know if it's done yet. But when I used to go down to the hot springs at Guadelupe, we had to take the 2, or go to Mexicali on the 8 and 94, then cut back. It's bad-ass around the town of La Rumerosa, on top of the Sierra Madres. Name means "The Sorrows." A lot of people don't realize that mountain range extends into Mexico. High altitude, but it's just a huge rock pile. I was on that two-lane highway once in February and saw a Mexican family building a snowman. That was after a wild horse jumped in front of our van and almost killed us. There are no guard rails on the hairpin curves. Lots of trucks and cars passing the trucks whether it's safe or not. Drops of hundreds of feet into crevasses filled with more huge round boulders and rusting hunks of all the cars that didn't make it. No way even to get the bodies out. Don't know how that road ever got built—prisoners, I guess. Welcome to San Diego County East, new guy."

"I been here six years now."

They passed through Campo, and a little later entered the Indian Reservation of the same name.

"What was that bump?" Harry asked.

"A cattle guard," Jake explained. "Haven't you noticed them before?" Jake asked with a big grin.

"No. I'm east coast, not exactly an expert on cows. How do they work?"

"On the res they let the cattle run free," Jake answered. "And there's no fences to keep 'em from getting on the road. Makes driving risky—we lost one of our best agents that way. Usually in a car versus cow, both lose."

Harry noticed that Jake had slowed from 70 mph to 60, which was still five miles over the posted speed limit.

"There are spaces just far enough apart for the cow's feet to slip into if it tries to walk there. They never do try, but they do come up onto the road, especially at night or on cool days. So it's driver beware."

Harry wasn't a nervous passenger but he found himself feeling glad that Jake had slowed down.

"Good thing we won't be on the reservation very long," Jake was saying. "It's narrow here but it stretches ten miles north, up beyond the 8. You might notice that the land we gave the Indians was not exactly ideal."

"Ideal for sidewinders, scorpions and tarantulas, I'd say." "Wow, I'm impressed. You been studying the flora and

fauna of the area?"

"No, but I hear a lot about it from Melli, my tenant. And about the reservations and all the politics involved in whether or not to hook up with the gambling promoters. She's half Indian, and she's against it, because it's more non- natives making money off the Indians. They get half or more, the promoters do. Most of them are from Nevada—not native, of course. There was a bit of controversy on the councils of some tribes, but most couldn't resist the luster of white man's gold. Maybe I should say white woman's. The casino buses come to the assisted living and senior places the day after the old ladies get their social security checks. Never seen so many people in such a hurry to give their money away."

"Yeah, I guess the natives feel that half of a lot is better than nothing," Jake said. "I bet they'll all have casinos in a dozen years. Even in

Jamul, they're determined to have one, and that's a very small band. Some huge Minnesota corporation is backing the fight against the townspeople, who don't want the traffic or pollution or lights. The big places out in Pauma Valley, you go there any time of night and those parking lots, acres of parking lots, are full-up."

Harry shook his head. "Casinos in every town will ruin the back-country. Maybe already have. This land may be rugged and mean, but it has it's own beauty."

"Agreed. We're comin' up on our turn-around in a few miles. We'll head back the way we came, staying vigilant for suspicious activity." His tone bordered on mocking. "Did you know Jacumba used to be called Boulevard? Still is on some maps. A bit of an identity problem. The real Jacumba is, or used to be, a few shacks right on the border, on a dirt road that runs south and east along the 8 out of Live Oak Springs, where the 8 drops down close to Mexico. That happens again at the sand hills just before Winterhaven and the bridge to Yuma. Not much activity that concerns us out that far—just a lot of desert rats with their dune buggies and quads—always ridin' 'em drunk, or just careless. Sometimes they go up a long, gradual hill that turns out to be one sided, and they get a sudden drop--over a sand cliff. A few die. What bothers me most is the kids--What the Hell?"

Harry was relaxing after his meal, lulled almost to sleep by Jake's hypnotic tour-guide speech, but he snapped to when he heard the change in tone. "What. I don't see anything."

"That's because you're not supposed to see anything out of the ordinary, new guy," Jake said as he executed a quick but not tire-squealing u-turn. Those words again—Harry was beginning to consciously dislike them, but he could hardly complain since Jake usually accompanied them with a smile. Not this time. "Did you see that van?"

"Sure, I saw the van. One guy in it, driving the speed limit. Looked pretty normal to me. It said Ace Floral Delivery."

"I'll give you points for observation, but think about it, do you see any flowers around here Harry?"

"Not that I can see, but maybe there's a place that grows them further east."

"Not even in the next thousand miles; maybe somewhere in east Texas." Jake was headed west now, gaining speed on the van, but not so quickly as to be noticed. "There's irrigation on the other side of the mountain, of course, most of the Valley, but far as I know they grow only food crops. It's pretty fascinating how they can coax so much out of such a barren place. That's where most of the water from the Colorado goes— that and San Diego. Nothing left for poor Mexico. Like I said before, that river forms our border with Arizona, and a little bit of border at Arizona's

southwestern tip. Their border with Baja, below most of Arizona, is the state of Sonora. We don't do much work over there. The Zonies and their politicians don't appreciate us as much as California does. They're pretty independent."

"More like ornery and staunchly conservative."

By now they were following the van, at a discreet distance, but keeping their speed identical to his.

"So, I still don't see why you're so sure it isn't flowers. Couldn't they fly them in to Yuma and deliver them?"

"San Diego's closer. Wouldn't make much sense to schlep them over that mountain pass. It's an ass-kicker. Besides, I don't think many people in El Centro can afford a bouquet on the table at all times.

They were going slower now, 60 instead of 70.

"And one more thing." Jake added, "White van, pastel colors, Ace? They're trying too hard to look American. Something's up."

The van maintained a steady but slower pace for about a mile.

"He wants me to pass him. But I'm not going to." Jake stated the obvious. "He'll start going 75 in a minute." The van responded on cue. Jake kept the gap even. Suddenly a burst of blue-gray smoke came from the exhaust pipe and it jerked up to about 90, then the driver braked hard and guided the van onto a short side road that skirted a seasonal creek, apparently with enough winter or monsoon water to support a good stand of vegetation. Somehow he made the sharp turn without overturning. Before Jake could stop behind him, he had jumped out and stood facing them. The agents pulled out their wallets to show their authority, but the man kept his eyes on their eyes. His gaze was direct, almost pleading.

"Better cuff him," Jake directed Harry, who was one step closer to the driver.

"How can I do that? He hasn't broken any law. He's co-operating," Harry muttered back, but pulled out the plastic handcuffs in case. The man then spoke, uttering a loud whine without taking his strong gaze off them.

"Ooooh. Mi amigos."

Before he finished, doors on the opposite side burst open from a center seam, and like a geyser sending a fountain of water and foam into the air, the van spewed its contents of lithe, wriggling, dark-skinned humans into the shrubby high desert. Like sparks from a popping log, they went in all directions at once--fast. For a split second, the agents' attention was drawn to the mass exodus, then Jake yelled,

"Quick, get the cuffs on him! " But it was too late. The driver vanished before their eyes. Harry stood stunned.

"Don't worry, we'll get them all," Jake said, as he reached behind the seat. Harry, in that tense moment, appreciated Jake's confidence.

"Sure glad we have the technology," Jake said, referring to their portable infrared heat sensors. They were relatively accurate over distances up to two hundred feet and easy to carry. Not only could they indicate that some warm-blooded creature was in a certain location, but the visual readout showed its approximate shape.

"We might have a little trouble after dark, if we don't get them right away," Harry guessed. He knew their equipment would still function, but the smarter illegals and their coyotes knew how to pick a big, south-facing boulder and trick the screen. The boulders absorbed so much heat from the sun all day that the sensor just showed a big blob, not people hiding behind it. He knew this because Jake had taught him.

He repeated, "If we don't get all these guys by sunset, we'll have to check the south side of every big rock."

Jake cut him off. "Bad juju. We may be here all night." "We've done it before," Harry reminded him. "Think we

should call for help?"

"Let's just see how it goes. We'll separate. More than likely these guys are unarmed. They would have been checked by their handlers. There's a possibility the coyote is carrying but probably just for snakes or javelinas. Just the same, be on your toes and keep your hand on your weapon. Do one at a time. Walk them back to the van and cuff 'em to something or to each other. Whistle if you need help, or dial. They usually co-operate. They're weak, hungry, thirsty. They know they'll die out here if they don't come with us. That coyote isn't going to come back and risk jail to save their hides. The only reason they bolted is that's how they've been instructed. In this case it made a good distraction and he got away. Maybe how he planned it."

"How many do you think?" Harry asked.

"I'm pretty sure I saw nine, not counting wily coyote. One's a woman. I didn't get a real good look. I was nervous about that driver."

"With good cause."

It took until the sun was hovering over the western horizon for the SCABS agents to get seven men and two women back into the van.

"Got 'em all except the coyote," said Harry, physically exhausted.

"We aren't gonna get him. Not this time. He knows every inch of this area, has water hidden, probably blankets. But I got a good

look. I'll get him one of these days." Jake placed a call for the mobile processor, which would most likely just take photos of each and escort

them back to Mexico. The van would be impounded. Then he turned to Harry. "Come here. Something I want to show you."

Harry had made four trips to the van with detainees, each from farther way from the previous hiding place. He just wanted to drop, but he would rather not let Jake know that.

"Sure," he said. "Whatcha got?"

"Just be a good boy and follow your leader." They traversed a steep hill, following a path that may have been made by something other than humans and giving wide berth to a particular type of plant. "Chollas," Jake said, pointing it out, "a.k.a. jumping cactus or cow-blinder." Harry thought it would be dark before they got back to their vehicle and was glad his cellular phone was equipped with a high-intensity flashlight and a battery.

"There, take a look," Jake said as he crested the outcropping. Harry pulled himself up and stood tall, looking in the direction Jake pointed, due west. He was awe-struck. The view seemed to go on forever, with a big, red ball in the center—a magnificent canvas with oranges, reds and purples highlighting the thin, horizontal clouds in white and

charcoal gray. "See that tiny silver thread under the sun?" "Yeah, what causes that?"

"It's the ocean."

"Holy God. You can see the Pacific Ocean from here?" "That's it, my man."

"This is amazing. What makes the sky so red?

"Smog. You should see it when there's a wildfire. Sky's the color of blood. Let's get our asses back."

"Yeah. Uh, Jake, thanks for this visual treat. It's my first time seeing the Pacific. I won't forget it."

The ride back was uneventful, but passed faster than the eastbound leg. Jake only had one story.

"Remember I when I was talking about Jacumba?" "Yeah. Anything there?"

"Well, most people wouldn't think so. But it's got a history. I think one person owns the whole town, or did. Used to be operated as a spa. Now there's a nudist colony, uh, resort."

"You been there?"

"No, not that one. I don't see how people could be comfortable there, especially naked. The wind is blowing all the time. Blowing dust."

"You said not there. You been to a different nudist colony?"

"Well, it's not something I brag about, but there was one time, sort of a dare." "Well, go on, by all means."

"There were three couples. We got to drinking and talking one night and this guy who had been working a short time for the gas and electric company, well, he said he got sent out there on a job."

"Yeah, I never though about it, but I guess places like that need electricity, too."

"So, this guy, he said we should all go out the next day, which was a Sunday, and once one person agreed, we sort of all had to, or seem like wimps. I remember we all rode out in the same car, so we wouldn't change our minds."

"Where was this?"

"A place out east of El Cajon, under the edge of Shadow Mountain, a pretty nice area. Lots of oak trees. Not sure if it's still there or not."

"So, what was it like?"

"We talked all the way there, about how embarrassing it would be if we got a hard-on seeing all those naked women. But the brochure said that doesn't happen. You know what? They were right. Can't explain it, but as soon as you see everybody--I mean all kinds of people kids and old women and men and they're just walkin' around so natural and at ease and playing ball or swimming or having a lunch—it just made us feel like it was okay. In fact, it seemed odd to have clothes on. Our women (barely women—I think we were all about nineteen) were allowed to keep their clothes on if they wanted to, but none of them did. I didn't ever feel like I wanted to go back, but it wasn't a bad experience."

Harry had nothing to say.

Beautiful Exhaustion

Harry arrived home, on the brink of total exhaustion. He got out a bottle of Glen Livet Scotch whiskey, a gift from his buddy John Saunders when he left his other life. He thought about opening it to celebrate the capture of all the illegals, as well as his first view of the Pacific, but it somehow just didn't feel right. Maybe he'd just have a beer and hit the sack. Behind the Scotch bottle, in the last unpacked box, one he had left that way on purpose because it had too many painful memories, was a photo in a cheap 8" by 10" frame. As if compelled by a force that was separate from him, Harry's hands reached for the photo. He didn't want to look at it. But he did.

It depicted three smiling people, cheeks ruddy with wind-induced color, hair just slightly disheveled, innocent smiles on their faces. Charmed and charming. They were on a dock, two men with a woman between them. A very good-looking woman. Harry was one of the men— the other was John Saunders. Behind them, miles of blue sky and deeper blue ocean. The Atlantic—the only ocean Harry knew, or had seen for that matter, until today. Until a couple of hours ago. He had been so busy getting settled, trying to pick up loose ends, and working, that he hadn't found time to go sight-seeing. He guessed that he had been within a few miles of the Pacific a number of times, and was sure he could smell it sometimes. Then there was yesterday--only yesterday?-- when they were about to be in the middle of the sandcastle contest when the call about the truck came in, and all he saw was bicycles and streets with sand in the gutters. Yes, technically, until today, he hadn't laid eyes on the world's largest ocean. Harry held the photo at arm's length and stared at it, working to hold back the wave of emotion, marginally close to nausea, that was attempting to overtake him. What he held in his hands was the only reminder, other than the travel brochure with the castle on it, of his previous life--that and his memories. Too many of them. Before putting the picture back in the box, he turned it over, as if he thought the envelope taped to the back of it might have somehow come undone.

Reassured that it was still there, he sat down on his big, cushy but not-so-fashionable sofa (courtesy of the Nelsons) and popped open a cold beer from the refrigerator. Before he had a chance to put it to his lips, he heard an unusual sound. His doorbell was ringing. At ten fifteen on a weekday? Out of habit, he picked up his revolver, which had the safety on but was not yet unloaded. Fortunately, the door had a peephole in it, and enough light shone through the living room window beside him for him to recognize the person standing on the stoop. It was his tenant. And she was carrying a towel.

Harry and Melli had shared coffee on her patio a few times, and he had told her to come visit and even soak in the hot tub sometime, offering to stay inside or leave so she'd have total privacy.

"I just might take you up on that some day," she had answered, "after a long hike or a lot of lifting. It's funny what we have to do on the job sometimes. Did I tell you I work for the college—UCSD? I'm supposed to be a writer, but somehow I end up moving entire libraries or furniture from one room to another. It's whatever needs to be done. A Jacuzzi might feel good sometime, and you wouldn't have to stay away; in fact, I might appreciate your company."

Of course, she would have heard his truck and seen him come in if she were on her patio, and she would know she wasn't waking him.

"Hold on a minute," Harry smiled at her, realizing sheepishly that she couldn't see anything but his right eye. "Be right there," he mumbled, hoping she heard him and that she wouldn't have second thoughts and disappear before he could get his wits about him and open the door. First, of course, he secured the gun as he was supposed to do, unloading it and storing it out of sight. He looked around and saw a room that looked normal for a suburban house; he wasn't a secret slob. The morning newspaper, almost covering a men's magazine, and a freshly opened beer on the coffee table probably wouldn't frighten her away.

The minute Harry opened the door his nervousness disappeared. "You said this morning that you were expecting a busy day today, following up on all of yesterday's excitement. I thought I might just see how it went," she began.

Harry told her as much as he could, without breaching his security regulations, about yesterday's events. Now she seemed like she wanted to be chatty. At first, he thought he should just back off, but she looked so interested, and--interesting. He found himself forgetting how weary he had felt moments before.

"Sorry, I can't tell you anything about my work or I'd have to kill you." Immediately, he regretted the joke.

"That's all right. I'm not on the need-to-know list," she said with a genuine laugh, and Harry was relieved. After a moment, she added, "Hey, maybe I should go get the bottle of champagne I have in the back of my refrigerator. We can celebrate the fact we both have jobs when so many don't."

"I have another idea," offered Harry, "if you're the type of person who would drink Scotch."

"Maybe I am."

"It's a bottle I've been saving for over two years, waiting for just the right occasion."

"Well, in that case, I'll definitely give it a try. I have to admit to you, I haven't ever had Scotch before."

Harry was already opening the bottle and pouring the amber liquid over two ice cubes in each of two short glasses. He passed one to her and they clinked, wishing each other success on their jobs. Melli took a sip and made a most unusual facial expression, trying to smile, Harry thought, when her impulse was to spit it out.

"Not too fond of it?" he ventured.

"Hard to tell," she answered. "Maybe it's like a good cabernet. You have to develop a taste for it."

"Could be. I poured two glasses of water, for chasers. You could drink that while I get you something else." He started to rise.

"No, sit down." It was not an order, but an invitation. He did. They chatted easily, more easily than Harry imagined he could with a woman, even more comfortable than--no, he wasn't going there tonight.

Melli finished most of her drink, then picked up the towel. No, don't leave, Harry thought, but didn't say it.

She hesitated with a shy smile on her face.

"The real reason I came over was to take advantage of your facilities. Is the offer for the hot tub still open? I played three hours of volleyball today, first time in a year. I could sure use a good, steamy soak."

It's a good thing that's all she wanted, he thought. If she had said she wanted his body, he might have had to ask for a rain check. Harry started to refill their glasses, but she raised a hand.

"No more for me, thanks. I would rather take my water to the hot tub, if it's all right to have glass there."

"Absolutely. There's a deck, and if the sky's clear enough, we can look south, over the riverbed, beyond El Cajon, and see where I was working today. I'll just go get my suit."

He felt a little ashamed that Melli had reminded him that he didn't need to continue drinking scotch all night.

Harry was glad the hot tub was the self-contained kind, with a well-insulated lid and walls. It easily maintained the temperature he set, and it only cost about twenty dollars a month. The best part was that the spa, like the cat and Melli, came with the house. Rummaging around for his bathing suit, not worn since a motel room two years ago somewhere on the old Route 66, he thought how lucky he was to have a home, a job and a couple friends. After sitting in 103-degree water for ten minutes, he lifted his water glass to meet hers, and toasted: "Here's to our first six years of friendship."

Hunch

"Ten bucks says we don't get out of this room till noon."

Jake was nudging Harry's elbow as they sat in adjoining chairs, along with about a dozen other agents, and listened to Phil-the-mill's droning voice.

Trying hard not to be impolite, and to catch a little of what was being said, in case it turned out to be important, Harry leaned to his left and whispered, "You're on."

About forty minutes after the briefing began, Phil was wrapping it up, in plenty of time for Harry to win his bet. "You guys have a slow day today." Harry couldn't help chuckling under his breath, realizing how hard it had been for him to lose the New England expressions that were the fabric of his childhood and so much a part of him as a young adult that it took years of hearing nothing but West Texas drawls to wipe them out of his speech patterns. Even then, he sometimes had slip-ups. Phil appeared to be beyond help when it came to accents.

"So there shouldn't be any problem. You can work on them at your leisure, but just don't forget to turn them in at the end of the day."

Harry was thinking, "Did I miss something?"

Someone on his right handed him a sheaf of papers. Moving by rote, he took one and passed them to Jake. As he did so, he saw Phil move to the blackboard at the front of the room.

"Like I said, there are three sheets of paper coming around for you. They look alike at first glance, with these three columns. He printed three words across the board in traditional white chalk: Objective-- Purpose— Action. The only difference is a single word at the top of each page, on the line above where the columns start. You are to fill out your thoughts or plans for each of these words regarding SCABS on the first sheet, regarding today's job--or yesterday's--and finally, your life. Please try to be as accurate and complete as you can be."

Groans and barely audible comments such as "this sucks" were heard throughout the room.

"It's a bunch of gobbledygook." Harry said to Jake, who happened also to be his main partner.

"That's not the word I would use," Jake responded sharply.

Harry's thoughts drifted back to the open, untouched beer sitting on his coffee table when he woke. Before the reel in his mind rewound the scene of him pouring it into the sink and smiling as he did so, the third paper had been disseminated and everyone waited to get their assignments before they left.

"As I said, slow day. Just be available, find a public place where you can watch for any suspicious activity, and get your comments on these." He held up his copies of the three questionnaires.

Harry could see Jake's body go rigid. Once they were in the truck, he slammed the papers onto the dash.

"What the Hell do they want from us?" Why do they make us do bullshit like this? It's not like we're studying to be shrinks."

It's nothin' but words," Harry answered, although he was feeling a lot like Jake. "They just want to make us write something. They don't care what we scribble down—it could be most anything—just as long as they know we're paying attention, so they have something to turn in to their bosses--who probably just look to see it's filled out and never read it.

Everybody has a job and a paycheck. Anyway, we get paid by the hour. 'Marchin' or 'fightin,' my friend used to say about his job after he got out of the Navy. In our case, 'workin' or 'writin'."

"Okay, I'll fill out their goddamn papers, but I say we do our writin' at the beach."

"Sorry, Jake—we're desert rats, back-country bums. We're not golden-haired surfer boys."

"Speak for yourself, old man," Jake headed the truck west.

"I think I liked 'New Guy' better. But, actually--the beach sounds good," said Harry. "In fact, that will fit right in with what I was hoping to get accomplished today."

"Okay, I'll bite. What is it you want to do at the beach—you who have only seen the Pacific once, from fifty miles away?"

"It can't be just any beach," Harry clarified. "It has to be Imperial Beach. And it has to be after we make a little stop."

"You want to go pick up the pretty Senorita in the white dress and take her to the back room and make whoopee, or however they say it in Spanish." Jake knew very well how to say it. He was fluent in the language, but he spared Harry, who was still trying to pick up the basics by listening to the Mexican cable channels whenever he had spare time at home.

"Yes, of course, but you're confusing fantasy with reality. What I really want to do is take another look at that parking lot."

"Where we saw the truck?"

"Yeah. Something is nagging at me; can't quite put my finger on it, but I know it has to do with that lot. With squares."

"Squares?"

"Squares—areas on that lot with something different about them--color, texture, height, I don't know. Squares or rectangles I saw in a dream. That's what I was seeing when I first woke this morning, and it seemed important, like a vision, but more of a hunch. I didn't look at the parking lot while I was there, not consciously, but I saw it clearly this morning. Those squares. I just have a feeling something's going on. I wonder if the truck's still there."

"Visions and hunches. You're having visions and hunches?" "Visions not so much. I've always had hunches; you do, too."

Jake measured his words. "Whatever you saw in your vision, I don't know. But I can answer that other question. I asked Phil this morning and he says the truck got moved out yesterday. They took it to the yard and went through it pretty good—didn't find anything, not even pot residue or fingerprints. Looks like a pretty clean, well-run operation."

"They can trace the plates."

"No can do. They're fake.

"You got to be shittin' me. Fake plates? As in counterfeit? You don't mean stolen?"

"Counterfeit—almost like someone who makes them in prison made an extra set—or sets. Very realistic-looking. They may be able to narrow it down, but it won't be easy. There are quite a few prisons, in this state and others, that do that job. Or it could have been made somewhere else, with stolen forms, or with a pattern someone made. Pretty good job, though, Phil said."

"You and Phil are pretty close, aren't you?"

Jake looked puzzled, then laughed and said, "Sure, we got a thing

going."

Harry knew that Phil had pulled some major strings to help him get hired, and Harry appreciated it; but he had a feeling, just a nagging thought in the back of his head that Jake knew more about that than he let on. Someday, he would ask him, but just not right now.

"Well at least we've got the van. It's got to be crawling with evidence that will lead back to the Shrimp."

"Should be a gold mine. Phil tells me they haven't even started to check it out yet. May get to it tomorrow or the day after. It's in a different impound yard, with lots of security."

"Better be."

"So you dreamed something and now you want to follow up on it?" "Kinda like that," said Harry. "If we go there, I'll know in a minute

or two whether I dreamed it or saw it. Remember how it was a hunch that made you take us on Mr. Toad's wild ride across the slough? And because of your hunch, we caught the two dudes pretty much red-handed. Two dudes that are going to lead us to bust the biggest drug lord in a decade."

"Biggest? I thought he was a shrimpy guy."

"Smart ass. Small in stature only. Anyhow, so now it's my turn. Humor me. After that, we'll go to IB and I'll get a good look at the ocean. I'll even help you with your homework."

Jake's irritation returned, somewhat mitigated. "Damn—they must think we're still in junior high. I didn't like it then and I don't like now."

As Jake maneuvered the truck onto 5 South, Harry pulled out his electronic tablet and started tapping, mostly with his index fingers. The action was accompanied by hissing and guttural sounds, interspersed with occasional low-volume curses and a few electronic beeps.

"What the heck you tryin' to do?" inquired Jake as he drove.

"You know how much I hate computers. Just looking something up on this machine drives me nuts."

"Get used to it; it's what the world is all about now and there ain't no goin' back." "I'll get it eventually," Harry said, calmer, "but by then, they'll have a new model."

"The learning gets easier every time. But we all have to go through it." "Okay, if you say so, Jake." But maybe you should be the one

doing this."

"Well, it might help if I knew what 'this' is."

Harry put the tablet down and looked as serious as any man could be.

"Remember when that 911 call came in, you know, the one that got it all started?" Jake nodded his head. "I know the woman said something about the boxes—too many. Like they were re-loading the truck in the middle of the night, then unloading it again. But that doesn't make any sense."

"What does make sense?" Jake asked.

"You're gonna think I've been watching too much television, but I was wondering--I want to see what the woman said first, but do you suppose there could be a tunnel under that truck?"

"I doubt that. They would have noticed it for sure when they moved the truck. Anyway, it couldn't be done here. Besides, the ground's to unstable, with so much drainage from the Mexico side, the T.J. River going through, and hardly any vegetation to hold the soil."

Harry tried to interject a thought, "Anything's poss--."

Jake cut him off. "And right under the noses of the Feds. You know that they own all of Spooner's Mesa now, the Department of Homeland Security. And they're working on it constantly—always at least one construction crew, day or night. It would take a pretty ballsy guy to pull something like that off right under the noses of DHS."

He looked at his partner and saw the eager joy of discovery drained from his face. "But, hey, it's worth looking at," he added. "Put that thing down, we're almost there." Harry still clung to the tablet, as Jake pulled up in front of, not in, the lot. He looked around to see if anyone was nearby, but the place appeared deserted. Jake reached out his right hand towards Harry, "Gimme that," he said, and Harry handed over the tablet. Within two minutes, Jake had brought up the transcript of the 911 call: ". . . take boxes off. . . all day . . . too many . . . truck can no hold, but still more. . . ."

"Wow," Jake said under his breath. "Sure sounds like a tunnel when you read it again, but it does seem impossible. Let's go take a look." "What would we do without computers?" Harry put his tablet back into the pocket of his light jacket and left his jacket in the truck.

"We'd go see the woman," Jake answered nonchalantly as he locked the truck." "We'll do that too."

"Yeah, you just want to pick up on the girl. I know." Harry only smiled.

"So, are these the squares you dreamed about?" Jake pointed to half a dozen areas of darker asphalt scattered around the lot, rectangular in shape, not square.

"Exactly," Harry answered. "I guess I must have seen them." He was walking to the one where the truck was parked. "But not this one."

"These all look pretty new. They're all over the place. The city can't afford to re- pave anywhere, and most owners of private parking lots just patch the asphalt. Maybe use the same companies and coordinate times. I bet there's some in the street out front."

"Yeah, but look at the edges." Harry knelt and examined the patch. "It's like there's a tiny gap around this one. No hinges, but if it's lightweight, like if they made it with compressed styrofoam and only a coating of asphalt on top."

"Two men with a couple of pry-bars might be able to lift it off."

"Hmm." Jake said no more but walked away, toward a fence. Harry followed. Twenty yards down there was a rusty piece of iron. Long and narrow. They started walking faster, but Harry asked Jake to stop.

"I want to think about this first. We should use gloves, in case we could get fingerprints off it."

They stood a minute in the sun, already baking the area. It was noon.

"If we went and got gloves, it would be like putting a neon sign on our heads—people would notice. If that is a tunnel, they're probably watching the place."

"Sure didn't look like anyone around. But--what if they've got cameras on that old warehouse? We may be on someone's screen right now. I have an idea. Just in case, can you go over toward the fence, the other direction from the bar, where that puny sage bush is? Look around you like you're nervous, and then take a piss. I'll look the other way and wait."

While waiting, Harry took out his phone and moved it to the camera setting, which for the agents was a separate built-in unit of much higher quality than most, and asked it for the highest resolution. With his back to the building, he took a zoom close-up of the steel bar that lay parallel to the fence. He then sauntered nonchalantly over to Jake.

"Let's go check the other patches, then stroll past the possible trap-door again," he gestured. "Look natural but discreetly check around the building and the edges for another bar like the one we saw. They'd need two. Try to spot a camera without looking at it, and I'll see if I can sneak a photo of the crack. Then we'll look for patches in the street, like we're interested in asphalt. Maybe it won't seem too suspicious. I'm sure glad we didn't drive into the parking lot."

Back on the road, Harry looked at the camera read-out, which included the clandestine shot of the crack around the edge of the trap door, and sent it to his home computer so the photo could be enlarged.

"So what did you see?" Harry asked.

"You were right about one thing--there was another bar. Exactly like the one we saw— it was layin' close to the warehouse door, near a thirsty natal plum. Pretty plant, but you don't want to get close to its thorns. There were a few other metal scraps, but the bar was unmistakable."

"Yeah, I hate to say it but I was right about the camera too. A small one, looked old, but that might be by plan. It's not that unusual, though, even in this area. Seems like every guy that thinks he's got anything to protect has one put in. But still, when you add it up--"

"I can't wait to take an enhanced look at that crack. Did you take pictures of the others for comparison?"

"One of them—didn't want to be obvious. Shall I send them both to your home unit?"

Harry knew Jake was a computer aficionado and would have a better PC. There seemed to be an unspoken agreement that they would not tell their superiors, yet, what they thought they were on to.

"Naw, send it to my tablet. I can look at it back at the compound. Their equipment's ten times better than mine. Not that mine's bad, but our

employer is nothing if not state-of- the-art. And the art of technology—it's enough to blow your mind. No one questions what I do with the computers in there. They trust me."

Harry didn't ask why. Instead, he noted that Jake had missed the turn-off to Imperial Beach. "Hey, where you going?"

"There's a better place—to fully experience the ocean, then we'll get some lunch."

Harry could already see the ocean. It was on both sides of them, only a stone's throw away. On their left, midday sun glinted on waves two to four feet high, giving them a metallic glow as they flowed in from a distant horizon and gently lapped the sand. On the right was still water and low industrial buildings near it, with a chain-link fence around them.

"That's the desalinization plant. Hold up, the bay will be a lot prettier to look at in a minute." Jake was right. In the distance were boats, and beyond them, at the blurry edge of Harry's vision, something white, like clouds but on the ground, with red caps. Before he knew what he was seeing, Jake engaged the four-wheel drive and made an abrupt left, heading straight into sand, toward the water. "Lifeguard trail," he announced. "Usually deserted. Get your shoes off and roll up your pant legs. You're about to step into the Pacific."

It was a feeling Harry would remember all his life. Sand slipping from under his feet, tingling the bottoms like a thousand tiny bird pecks. He'd felt it before. But this ocean was cold, even in August. He shuddered, as the immensity of what lay before him sank in. Ahead, only water.

All the way to eternity, all the same, shimmering. Everywhere else, the sparkling sand appeared to be moving. Behind was the highway, but an embankment of soil barely darker than the sand raised it out of their view.

Squawking cheers of seagulls were the only sounds besides the surf. No other person was in sight. Harry had not known there could be secluded beaches in Southern California so devoid of activity.

"Nothin' but ocean, all the way to Japan," Jake said.

Harry uttered one word: "Thanks." "The water was freezing," he told Jake as they edged back to the highway. "What is it—in the sixties?"

"That's about right. It usually takes till the end of August to hit 70 degrees. Gets down to 50 in the winter. The lifeguards are allowed to wear wet suits if it's below 55, but most of them don't. They're tough."

"My God, that would freeze their balls off!"

"According to what I hear from the chicks, that never happens." "Over there's the state park entrance. Silver Strand State Beach,"

Jake pointed ahead and to the left. Camping or day use. No dogs. Ten bucks just to drive in and come back out. Very crowded this time of year."

"Yeah, I see."

"On the right a ways down is a nice marina and restaurant. Not too expensive for lunch."

Harry checked his phone for the time: 1:45. They usually ate between two and three and sometimes grabbed a bite just before or after they clocked out. "I guess we'll miss the crowd?"

"It won't be empty."

After the waitress seated them in their booth, Harry took a long look out the window and thought he had entered another dimension. It was other-worldly, but it was also familiar. He had to take a minute, draw a deep breath, and think. Then he knew where he was. He was in the picture, in the brochure that had remained on the seat of his Datsun for the ride across the country. Only when he moved into the Santee house did he bring the worn folder, about the size of a map, complete with its faded picture of paradise, inside his new home and put it on his dresser. The photo on the map matched the world before his eyes, a fairytale view of white castles with red roofed cupolas and cones of different sizes, and the bluest sky. No clouds but a faint mist over the red tile. In the foreground, part of the conical roof of a boathouse, darker blue.

"Wake up, Harry, we have to order."

Harry didn't know how long the waitress had been standing patiently at his side, or how long he had been gazing, mesmerized, into his past. He placed his order and made small talk with Jake until it came. They ate their burgers, complete with bacon, avocado and bleu cheese, in relative silence. Harry was afraid to let himself look again at the brochure come to life.

A busboy took their plates and refilled their soda glasses. He was pleasant and professional and they did not feel rushed.

"So, I was thinking," said Jake, "maybe when we leave here, we could swing by the impound yard where the van is and see what they've found. Or look at it ourselves if they'll let us. They have to let us in with our credentials."

"If it wasn't for you, Jake, they wouldn't have the freakin' van."
"True, but you know how those investigators are."

"So where is it."

Jake had his phone in his hand. "Okay, it's down off of Market Street in South San Diego—just above National City. Not a nice neighborhood to be in after dark, or for

the unprepared. But we'll be there before dark." "Yeah, unless we decide to fill out our paperwork first." Harry felt bad bringing up what he knew was a sore subject.

"Oh, God, that," Jake answered. "You know what—I can't think of a better place to do that crap. Outside on the patio—we can watch people get in and out of the gondolas."

"You gotta be shittin' me. I knew this was a high class place, but gondolas?"

"They give the tourist what he wants. But there are residences here on this little peninsula, too. A lot of them have water frontage—enough to tie up a fifty- foot boat, for some. It's a lot closer than Coronado, from anywhere in the South Bay, and a lot nicer than IB. Quite a few people come here for a break from the city, too."

"I can see why."

"Another thing," Jake mentioned after they found a nice outdoor table and broke out their "objective" papers, "if we wait till five to check out the van, the evening shift

might be a little more lax. It'll still be light." "Whatever you say." Harry was bothered somewhat by

Jake's casual approach to his police work.

Halfway through the paperwork, the two took a walk around the compound, enjoying the manicured gardens and views of the San Diego bay and, in the distance, "Crown City," Coronado.

"The Hotel Del is a pretty special place," Jake explained, when they had finished printing all their answers and could draw a breath. "Built in 1888. Had bath houses and tents all along the beach in the early days. Edison himself supervised the installation of electricity, and they had signs by the switches, assuring people it would not blow them up. They've had a bunch of presidents stay there and filmed a few movies. Marilyn Monroe movies.""Beautiful. No place in the world like it. No place like home. Hey, I think Frank Baum stayed at the Hotel Del. He wrote The Wizard of Oz. Am I right?"

"You already have a connection to it—almost like you've been here before--but I know you haven't."

"Came close."

"Care to elaborate?"

For some reason, here under the protective blue dome and with the backdrop of misty red roofs over white linear forms, Harry felt safer with Jake than he ever had before. If he were ever going to open up about his past, this was the place to do it.

"How much time have you got?" he asked.

"As much time as it takes, my friend. As much as it takes."

BBQ Sauce

Harry drew a deep breath. He had never told anyone about his love for Lara, not even to the woman in Texas, and how everything was destroyed in one night by one well-meaning gesture. Maybe he wouldn't now, either, but he felt like this was the time to start. "You knew I was married."

"Yeah, but that's about all. Was it a good marriage?" "The best." Harry examined his left hand. "That's it? That's all you're saying?"

"You don't want to hear all this."

"Actually, I do, and we have some time to kill anyway. I thought the papers would take hours."

Starting slowly, and with intense emotion that showed in his face, Harry said, "It was a dream marriage—honest, playful, good sex, as much as I could handle. We weren't rich, money-wise anyway—lived in a flat above a pizza parlor at first. But neither of us cared. We had enough to make us happy."

"Where?"

"Dover, New Hampshire. She was still in college when I met her; I was twenty-three. Married a year later. She never did graduate, but I don't see that as my fault. She got a good job, at a high-end furniture store, arranging the window displays. She loved it, and she loved me. Still does, if I'm to believe the last thing she said before I left."

"But she left you?"

"Yeah. She had a reason."

"For a guy?"

"No."

Jake sensed Harry's reluctance but was genuinely interested. He changed his line of questioning. "Were you a cop then?"

Harry nodded. "Yeah. A good one. I was also doing an in-service training at the college. I was twenty-four. She was twenty. I don't remember our first date, or the second, but on the third we went to one of those art movie houses and saw Dr. Zhivago. That night, back at her condo, we just couldn't get enough of each other. Good thing her roommate was out. After the second time, neither of us could move--or even talk. She was purring like a cat. After that, whenever I wanted to remember, I called her "Kitty-Lou." Her real name was Lara. Just like in the movie.

"That's quite a coincidence. Was she pretty?"

"The night of our ninth anniversary, in September, '95, she was the prettiest woman in the world. I got home before she did. Instead of opening a beer, I found a bottle of wine from Pauli, the pizza shop owner. We always had good wine available for guests, but seldom drank it by ourselves. I wanted that night to be special. I had found her the perfect gift."

"What was it?"

"It was a music box, about as big as a cereal bowl. I can still see it sitting on our oval coffee table, wrapped kind of messy 'cause I did it myself. It was shining in the glow of the yellow street lamp and the flashing red neon of the word Pizza. I'd thought about going out for lobster or clam chowder— there were good restaurants in walking distance. But I chose to stage my little celebration right in our living room. There was a corkscrew next to the wine, Pinot Noir it was, and two glasses, and a plate of apple slices and cheese and some round crackers. I got real fancy.

When she came in the door, with that glow hitting her light brown hair it looked like when the sun rises over the Atlantic—shimmering liquid gold. And she smiled this Mona Lisa look. Well, there could have been no woman prettier."

"Was she surprised you remembered your anniversary?"

"She said she'd have forgiven me if I hadn't. But there were things she couldn't forgive." Something about the way Harry cut off the sentence and got immediately quiet made Jake decide not to pursue that yet.

"Did she like the gift?"

"Oh, the music box. She still has it and plays it, that I know. Even though she's with--. The reason it was perfect is because, well, you'll never guess what song it played."

Jake was thoughtful, but puzzled.

"For Lara—what song for Lara?"

"'Lara's Theme'? No way. The one from Dr. Zhivago?" "The very one—I still can't believe I found it."

Harry seemed to really enjoy talking about his past with Lara.

"I mean the movie and the name, all like it was meant to be. The unbelievable part is that I happened upon it at a garage sale. The little old blue-haired lady let me have it for $3.00 when I told her Lara was my wife's name."

"Did she like it? - She asked me if I remembered the night of the movie—"before the sex," she said, and she giggled--she was kind of shy. She said the only part of the movie she remembered was at their little cottage in the country, when the hard winter was finally over and the fields came alive with wildflowers, and that she remembered the music from that one particular scene, and said, 'Now we'll always have it.' And you know what she said next?"

"What?"

"She said it brought up a dream. She didn't know why because the movie was set in Russia and this was somewhere in the U.S., maybe

California, she said. It was like a fantasy but she knew it was a real hotel because she saw it on a brochure from Pauli, and she wanted to go there for vacation."

"Did you?"

"We were going to, the next September, for our tenth anniversary. Funny thing, that's when I got the papers, in Fort Stockton, Texas. It wasn't planned that way, just took them a while to catch up, but they came the very day that would have been our tenth."

"Ooh, that must have hurt."

"You have no idea."

"So what was this vision from the brochure?"

"It was a group of cottages with red-spired roofs, floating on a cloud. We saw it today." For once Jake had no comment.

Harry took a deep breath and looked at his phone to check the time. "Whoa! We sure don't have to worry about getting to that impound yard before five. It's already 6:20."

"We could just hang out if you want. The sun sets in about an hour."

"No, we been here long enough to wear out our welcome. There will be plenty of time for gorgeous sunsets now that this ocean and I are friends."

They tucked away their paperwork and got in the truck, headed east. On the way to the southern edge of the city of San Diego, just before

they reached the 5 freeway, their speaker crackled with a report from the police radio. It connected to their phones but was mounted in the truck for their convenience while driving. It was a sound that couldn't be missed or mistaken, unless they had it on silent or vibrate, sort of like a sped-up air raid siren. Both men listened intently.

The 911 operator gave the address on Gamma, near the corner of Highland and Division, and also listed 43rd as one of the cross streets. Vehicle fire, possible explosion.

"Holy shit," Jake said, his face changing color. "That's where we're going! 43rd and Highland are the same street. Name changes at the border between National City and San Diego.

Harry, suddenly on high alert, looked at the screen of the GPS device built into their dash. It confirmed what Jake had just announced.   "You don't suppose--."

"Don't know, but we can't waste time," Jake answered, as he reached under the left front edge of his seat and pulled out a battery- powered flashing dome light that was activated by the touch of his hand, and tossed it to Harry, who pressed his window button and reached as far out as he could to secure the suction flasher to the roof. Jake was already increasing his speed and passing cars.

They saw it before they reached Highland Avenue. To their left, there was a rosy-orange glow in the darkening skies, beautiful if you didn't know what it was. As soon as they had made the two left turns, onto 43rd, and then, almost immediately, another left on Gamma, they smelled it, and knew. The unmistakable, thick, sweet, smoky aroma of marijuana, sort of like oak wood mixed with BBQ sauce, with some oregano thrown in.

"Not a good sign," sighed Jake.

Harry, who had never indulged in the herb, though he suspected Jake had, and maybe still did, recognized it, nevertheless.

"This is looking more and more professional--big time," he announced. "You're preachin' to the choir. I knew that the minute I saw the decal."

The gate was open and Jake pulled in right behind the fire- truck, which had apparently arrived only minutes earlier. There was a flurry of activity around it by the three fire-fighters, one of whom appeared to be a woman. Two of them picked up a hose which had been thrown out on the tarmac and held it near the business end, while another operated some electronic devices inside a panel on the outside of the truck. A river of white water came bursting forth.

Harry and Jake were outside their truck, ready to break into a run when an armed guard approached and asked to see their badges. At the same time, they heard more sirens approaching. The guard pointed to their truck, then to a spot near a building and farther from the burning van. No words were needed.

"Not much we can do, Harry," Jake groused as he moved the truck. "Nope, unless we're needed and asked. Meantime, maybe say a prayer that something will be left for us."

"Doubt it would be heard." They watched the flames burning high into the air, sparks splitting off the top ones, having some resemblance to orange-red rattlesnake tongues. Water hissed and sent up plumes of steam to blend with the black smoke and the flames. The second fire rig had set up and was spraying white foam which didn't reach the top layer of the fire. The smell had become more toxic than a mixture of metal and petroleum. Jake asked to speak to the manager of the storage facility. When the man got there, after a ten-minute wait, he motioned toward one of the several small buildings, the one with a sign reading "office" over the door. Settled inside, Harry flashed his badge asked if the manager knew how the fire started.

"Spontaneous combustion is my guess," said the man, an African-American of indeterminate age with some gray in his natural hair and mustache. He appeared to be as fit as the firefighters and quite sure of himself, in a polite sort of way.

"We've had it happen before, mainly on warm days. People leave oily rags in their cars--more so with vans and trucks." With no other movement, Jake's and Harry's eyebrows both lifted as if they were one set. The manager continued, "Can't be arson, that's for sure."

"How do you know?" Harry asked.

"Cuz there isn't anyone allowed inside but a small crew, all with security clearances. No one gets in that gate without being checked for a badge. Period. Someone's on watch 24-7. No fences have been compromised. This is a very secure facility. We know there's evidence in these vehicles.

No one came and set fire to that van—I'll stake my life on it. I trust my people." "Could someone, like, throw a Molotov cocktail over the fence?".

"Have to be a damn good shot --and have an arm better than Rivers at his best," the manager said, referring to the local NFL team's star quarterback. "There's a double fence all the way around. We store some things in the space between, but no vehicles." Noting that his two questioners still appeared somewhat skeptical, and thinking they had probably been sent by their superiors on official business, he offered confirmation. "We can look at the video right now if you like."

The two agents looked at each other. Harry spoke for them.   "Yeah, that would be good."

By now darkness had set in and the van had become a glowing ember, sort of like coal from a campfire, magnified a thousand times. Apparently the crews had kept fire from spreading to any other vehicles, but the van appeared to be a total loss.

"Not much evidence to be retrieved from that," Harry thought to himself.

"How far back you want to go? The call came in at 6:52," announced the newly arrived man whose name-tag read Darren Jenkins.

"Thanks for being so helpful, Mr. Jenkins," said Jake.

Harry thought he was about to decline, but instead he said, "Start at six, maybe—could we do that? In case, you know, it smoldered a while first."

"Sure. Possible it cooked a bit before it got noticed. But you ain't gonna find no hand-propelled rocket comin' over--that I guarantee."

The monitor had eight small screens, for the two wide-angle cameras mounted on each of the four sides, high on the barb-wire-topped, chain-link fences. With four sets of eyes, and fairly light vehicle traffic on Gamma, the men could track it easily; there was definitely no suspicious pedestrian activity.

"We really appreciate this, Mr. Jenkins. You can call us if anything new comes up that might be of interest. We should be going--need to check in down at Otay. Oh one more thing—how hard would it be for us to get a copy of that disc? " Harry asked.

"If you can wait another ten or fifteen minutes, I can do it. But let me warn you, you won't be finishing it in an hour if you don't have one of these monitors. The two cameras from each side go together on your monitor, so you're talking four times as long."

"That's why we have grunts," said Jake. "Doubt if anything will turn up, but doesn't hurt to be thorough. Do you have cameras inside?"

"Yeah, but I'm not authorized to show anyone. You'd have to have a subpoena."

"No need for that," Harry answered. "Just curious." Then, deciding Jenkins was someone he could trust, offered his hand and his business card. You call us if you think of anything, or have any questions, or when you have further information. Please. We think that van might be connected to some major organized drug crime."

"You didn't have to tell me the second part. I knew it was pot before the fire. Wait here, I'll get you your copy."

As they got in their truck, Jake said, "You didn't ask who found the fire."

"Thought about it," said Harry, "but I didn't want to push Mr. Jenkins too far. He was pretty helpful and might be again. I think he actually likes us."

"Who wouldn't? Anyway, we can get to that later. So, you really think it was spontaneous?"

"No," said Harry. "Not much chance of that. Just too much of a coincidence. It has to be an inside job."

"Not necessarily." Jake smiled, his techno-nerd, know-it-all smile. "There is one other possibility."

"And what would that be, Mr. Johnny Quasar?" "Remote detonation."

Harry scowled. "Didn't think about that. It's pretty state-of-the-art, but I guess they coulda done it. That would mean they have an office or something, or access to one. They're only good for a few hundred feet. There was no one on the sidewalk pushing a plunger."

"Not so far-fetched. And no plungers, nowadays. A cell phone, or something smaller, in a pocket would do it. And no 200 feet; that's only the cheap ones. They got stuff that can send a signal a half a mile. And that's just what any jerk can go buy at the corner electronics store. Military's a cat of a different color—halfway around the globe, I bet."

"No shit?"

"You remember out on the 8 a few weeks ago," Jake said, "there was that guy that got stopped by a border patrol, and before he could get out of his car or do anything, the car caught fire?"

"Yeah, I heard about it. The border patrolman got burned so bad he had to go to the hospital by life flight. Lucky somebody called it in. He's gonna survive. The dope smuggler, or whatever, in the car, poor chump, he wasn't so lucky." Harry pondered a minute, then asked: "You think the fire was intentionally set, from a distance?"

"It's not out of the realm, with good equipment. A small charge planted in the car, wrapped in something combustible. Close to the driver, so he can't get out and talk to La Migra or the cops. Only goes down if the

unfortunate driver gets pulled over. Someone would have had to be monitoring the car in some way, eyes or ears, or the gear would register when the vehicle stops moving. It would have to be triggered from that place, or from a relay along the highway. It's a stretch, but--."

"Or another car. So, the van fire at the impound yard-- you think it could have been done by a relay or a passing car? Could that happen?"

"I don't know. But maybe. That's why I was glad you asked for a copy. We can go over it with a fine tooth comb, one fence at a time, even separate the cameras if we have to."

"Who is 'we'? And what grunts were you talking about?"

"We're the grunts. 'We' is me, because I can get to the good monitors, with enhancers. Those at SCABS. Don't see how you can be with me, unless you want to let Phil in on what we did today and what we suspect."

"Not sure about that," Harry said. "I'm leaning to reporting our visit to the yard, even though it may seem like too much coincidence. It's what really happened. But I'm thinking not to mention the tunnel idea till we know more."

"My thoughts exactly. We may want to find out what they discovered in the van, but I bet it's nothing. The only way we're gonna find our anything about El Cameron is to go shake up those two dudes who were in the van."

"Yeah, that's our best bet, and that's another thing I don't think we ought to mention to Phil just yet. What do you think about going by the lock-up tonight?"

"A little late for visiting hours," Harry answered. "But mainly, it's been a long day and we're already on overtime. We'll be brighter in the

morning. Maybe our little snitches will be, too. Let's get an early start. Around 10 am sound good?"

"That works for me" Jake said, "Trish was hoping for dinner out tonight, so I better give her a call."

Brotherhood

The morning after the van fire, Harry woke up early, eager to get on the trail of the Shrimp before it got cold. No point in getting to work early, though. This was something he wanted to do together with his partner, and Jake wasn't likely to arrive before ten-thirty. Harry did some yard chores, then went in and fixed his breakfast.

He looked at Princess, sitting on a round blue hassock, one of the few items of furniture that he had brought across the country with him. It was too big to bring, but Harry rationalized that it could serve both as a sofa and a nightstand to his drop-down bunk. He could picture the trailer, being pulled by his Datsun hatchback, probably the last one still running, even in 1996. It made quite a spectacle: the car was a fire orange color that almost bordered on neon, and the trailer had been painted by its previous owners with a woodsy scene, a lake and a rainbow trout on a line. The two together were an incongruous sight. He missed the car a little, nothing compared to how he missed what it represented.

The cat looked small, almost lost in the center of the hassock. Harry thought about how it used to be Rusty, his beloved golden retriever, who curled up on that very piece, and how he and Lara had always referred to it as "Rusty's Throne." How ironic that the throne was now a resting place for a cat named Princess before he even made her acquaintance. He hadn't been notified when Rusty died, but he knew the dog couldn't be alive anymore. It was fourteen years since those days in the front yard, throwing a tennis ball for his ever-eager pup, looking every bit, he was sure, like a television commercial. Rusty was one of Harry's fondest memories of Dover, and there was no doubt the dog had been loved and cared for since, because Lara promised. Harry went back in his mind to before they got Rusty, allowing himself a rare few moments of reverie. He'd come in late from work one night, a few months before his life collapsed. Lara was waiting up, prepared to play one of her favorite games. They sat in soft living room chairs, facing each other and, between sips of blackberry brandy, asked and answered questions. "Truth Serum," she called it, referring to a game not the drink. She poured two shots of the deep claret-colored liquid into small crystal snifters. It wasn't his favorite drink; he preferred a good Scotch if he was going to drink hard liquor. Not his favorite game, either, but they did get to know each others deepest feelings, and he had nothing to hide. No subject was taboo—family, politics, religion--but respect was one of the rules. Her first question had been how long since he'd visited his mother and he'd said "too long" and they should plan a visit. Lara's own mother had died from cancer and her dad had moved to Florida, where her brother lived. Lara wasn't the type for self-pity and never felt lonely. Besides work and Harry, she had plenty of friends and loved photography. He recalled bits and pieces of that conversation:

"Do you ever wish I wasn't a cop?"

"Of course, all the time." He'd been surprised by the quickness and intensity of her answer. "The part of me that worries," she had added. "The part that loves you is glad you're doing what makes you happy."

"My mom worried about my dad," he had confessed, "all the time. That's why she was so set against me following in his footsteps. But it couldn't have been any other way." He'd made a strange half- smile, half-scowl." It's ironic that with all her concern over his occupation, he died in

a boating accident, happy as could be. And both of his own parents still alive. The gods have a funny sense of humor."

"You miss him, don't you." Lara had asked one more question, starting, "I'm glad you're a cop and I know you're a good one--."

"But?"

"Well, the usual. I worry about your safety." "And?"

"I don't quite know how to say this--you're exposed to so much. From the perps, but also from the other cops. We don't mention it much but some of your brothers on the force can get pretty hardened and mean---start hitting their wives, drinking too much, going corrupt--."

"It's what the job does, to some guys. Do you really think it will happen to me?" "No, it just crosses my mind sometimes," she had answered. "I'm

sorry."

"No apologies." He had taken her in his arms. "The only one I think of as a brother is John, and he doesn't have a wife. But if he did, he'd treat her well; he's about the most honorable guy I know."

"We know." John had a sailboat and Lara loved sailing as much as Harry did. The three sailed together often when their days off coincided.

Funny what twists the road takes, Harry mused, thinking about John Saunders and how close they had been. John probably wondered why they weren't still. Harry's mind took him back to the time in New Hampshire six months before he left, when he had taken a day off after a particularly violent day on the force, and he had asked Lara, on a whim, to call in sick and spend the day with him. Of course she couldn't lie, but her boss gave her a personal day. They decided to drive down the coast to a quaint restaurant for the daily special and a steaming bowl of clam chowder. It was January and quite nippy, but no snow or sleet was falling. They took a different route to the coast highway, just to see some new territory, and as they passed a little unincorporated area that looked more country than suburban, yet was just a few miles from a major expressway, Lara had gasped audibly. "Oh, look at that little house. Can't you just imagine us living there. See the roses and the newly mowed lawn, and you throwing the ball for Rusty."

Not a romantic, Harry had almost spoiled the moment: "I don't see any roses, just dead vines all over the roof of the porch."

"That's not just any dead vine," Lara reminded him. "It's a Cecil Brunner rose—a pink miniature. It's very fragrant. Just wait until April. Then you'll see that dead vine covered with green leaves and tiny roses."

"I'll take your word for it."

"And I'd be inside cooking roast beef with braised root vegetables and a berry pie, and maybe there would be little crib in a nursery."

That caught Harry's attention. He had always hoped to have children, but was afraid to broach the subject with Lara, since she had never brought it up and seemed content with their life as it was. But they had been married over eight years and Lara had passed her thirtieth birthday.

"Well, you sure do paint a pretty picture," Harry had finally chosen as his reply.

They'd found a corner table in a little cafe, a spot close enough to the great Atlantic to see waves crashing on rocks, and when they looked out the other window, there was a pond encircled with snow and large, dark, rounded boulders and with a few skiffs of ice floating on it. The sun sliding low into the sky at an early hour had created rosy dark pink streaks on the black water, and near the center, looking as regal as if it were part of an oil painting. A solitary white swan floated lazily.

Harry had returned to purchase the cottage, even though it didn't have a For Sale sign on it. He had managed it all without telling Lara, and now all that needed was her signature on the papers. She almost passed out when he told her the reason he had brought her to the little cottage. For six months, life for him--for them--had been heaven on earth. The only thing that could have made it better was for Lara to have announced she was pregnant. Before that could happen, Harry blindly walked off a cliff that ended the world he knew.

There on his Santee sofa, he re-lived his last few days in Dover, seeing them just as clearly as when they had happened in real time. He saw himself as Lara had seen him, putting away the lawn-mower and throwing the ball for their rambunctious golden retriever.

With climbing roses blooming profusely behind him, a white picket fence in front, and Lara coming out to the porch with two cool glasses of lemonade—the scene was picture perfect. A few hours later, arriving at work for the swing shift, he was given two assignments. The first had to be finished by 10 pm, because at precisely 10:45, he was to be at a certain address, in a dangerous part of town, to make a brief acquaintance with a man who had been described to him as a snitch in a very important case that Harry would be heading up if all went well.

Because he was hoping to be considered for assistant chief-of-police, and because it was in his nature to do his job right, Harry accepted the assignment without question. He stood on a dark corner in front of a brick building, watching. A man in a pin-stripe suit, somewhat unusual for the time and the place, appeared out of the shadows, wearing dark glasses. Harry walked nonchalantly toward the man, as instructed. As they passed, they paused briefly, the man in the suit nodded and then continued on. A moment later Harry passed a Cadillac on the one-way street and heard the sound of an automatic window opening. He stopped, turned to face the car and saw another man, also wearing tinted glasses. With no fanfare, the man handed Harry an envelope, then started the car and left Harry turned left to go to his own car. But just before he reached it, he heard something.

A little whimpering sound like an animal, then nothing. He strained to see in the darkness and could make out a form, but it was deep in shadow. He closed his eyes for a moment. When he re-opened them he could see a woman, of slight build, wearing a tank top and shorts. Her body was quivering as if she were cold, though the July night was just cool. Her body seemed to be vibrating, with occasionally an involuntary convulsion, but she was not sobbing. Her arms were folded across her chest and she rocked back and forth ever so slightly. This was a part of town where it was not unusual to see prostitutes, but this woman did not fit the picture. Harry stepped closer and realized she was injured— scratches and scrapes on her arms, bleeding slightly, puffiness around one eye, a tuft of hair dangling where it shouldn't be, like it had recently been pulled from her scalp.

Harry tucked the envelope safely into an inside pocket and moved closer. She looked at him with a blank stare that showed no friendliness and no fear.

"Did someone hurt you?" Henry asked. She nodded.

"Your husband?"

"For the first time she seemed to realize someone was there and responded normally. "No, we're not married. We've been together for five years."

"Any kids?" As a cop, he wondered if there might be children left alone in a nearby tenement or taken by the man, or hurt.

"No, I had a miscarriage once."

Harry could only imagine why. "It's not good for you to be alone out here like this, at this time of night."

She became a bit defensive, irritated, but he could tell she wasn't drunk. "Where am I supposed to go? I don't have a car or any money." "You're hurt. Do you think you should go to a hospital?" "No. Can't afford it, and this is nothing, really."

Harry decided not to tell her he was a cop. She seemed to trust him. "Maybe I could take you somewhere where you could get cleaned up, loan you a bit of money. Do you live near here?"

"Yeah, right there." She pointed to the next building. "I can clean up there." "I don't think that's a good idea. He might come back and hurt you worse."

"He said he would kill me—that I should be gone and never come back. But he doesn't mean that. And not to touch anything there—it's all his stuff. But I got my purse in there and some special stuff of mine I put in a bag behind the sofa."

"How 'bout I stand by out front while you go in and get your stuff, then I'll take you to a place you can spend the night and give you the address of an agency that can help? I'm sort of in social work myself."

She must have thought the devil she knew was worse than the one she didn't know, and agreed. Harry found out which unit was hers, on the ground floor, and stood by the door listening for any sound of disturbance.

When it took longer than he expected, he began to second-guess himself, but she appeared, and it looked like she had washed off the blood

and combed her hair. She was around twenty-five with a nice body and, he realized, quite pretty. She had a canvas bag, a small satchel and her purse over her shoulder. She had put on a light jacket and shoes. Harry drove a short distance to a motel he knew of and accompanied her to the lobby after giving her a handful of bills so she could pay for her room and looking in all directions to make sure no one was approaching them.

Once there, he put down her items, and was sitting in the only chair, rummaging through his wallet for a card from the city's main shelter, when the woman spoke to him.

"My name's Carrie- Jo, and I want to thank you. You're a kind man, I can tell. I also have a favor to ask. I want to know if you can stay a while with me tonight. I'm not a whore, so it's nothing like that. I just, well, I'm feeling so scared and I just don't want to be alone. At least have a drink with me." Now tears were forming.

Harry didn't know if she had noticed his wedding band. He made no attempt to hide it. He didn't expect this. He also didn't know how to say no to a vulnerable, confused girl —or to a drink after an emotional day. Why she had trusted him this far was beyond his reckoning, but now it was like he had an investment in her.

He excused himself to the bathroom, called work to officially check out, and called Lara to tell her that his special meeting had turned into an all-night stake-out but that he was safe. Then he spent the next six hours protecting and comforting a woman who was a complete stranger to him.

Two men in a car had watched him after he took the envelope, followed slowly with no lights on as he made the short and predictable trip to the nearby hotel, which catered to prostitutes and their clients.

"What do you think's going on in there?" one of the men in the car asked.

"Can't say for sure, but it must be against the rules," said the other. "Well, I'd break the rules for that."

"Then we'd be investigating you. Don't know—she looked a little

straggly to me." "Some hookers do." Well, looks like he's settled in. Did we get any good pictures?

"You bet. He turned and looked right at the camera, the name of the hotel clearly visible."

"That should do it. Looks like we got ourselves a bonus. Now let's get the fuck out of here."

Harry got the woman checked in at the shelter and got home in time to kiss Lara goodbye as she left for her 10 a.m shift at the furniture store. He did some yard work, watched some silly daytime television, then got showered and dressed for work. Immediately upon arrival he was sent to talk to the Chief. "IA?--You've got to be freakin' joking. I haven't done anything wrong. I did exactly what I was asked to do."

"You have the envelope?"

"Not with me," Harry lied.

"Well, that probably doesn't even matter, not now with the other."
"Other, what other?"

"Well, I don't see anywhere in your orders that you were supposed to spend the night with a hooker in a seedy hotel."

"That wasn't a hooker. I offered assistance to a stranger. Wait a minute—you were watching me? What the hell? Why?"

The chief ignored the question. "Looks like you got mighty careless. They'll give you a lawyer and he'll fight to save your pension, but I doubt if he'll win. You'll be lucky if you're not charged."

The next day was Harry's day off. Lara came home with take-out, and while Harry was in the kitchen setting the table, she went to the liquor cabinet in the living room and got out the brandy and two glasses. Harry was wondering how he would tell her that he was being investigated, but when he saw the brandy, his heart raced so fast, he thought he would pass out.

"Are you up for a game of 'truth serum,'" she asked, almost too pleasantly. Harry went cold, every muscle taut and stiff, hoping that she wouldn't notice the change in demeanor.

"How 'bout we eat first?" he said as light-heartedly as he could. "Good idea."

The questions, as he expected, were mostly hers. After a few innocuous inquiries, she asked how the stake-out went and he said okay, hoping she would consider it police business and probe no further. The next question came like a swift blow: "It wasn't a normal stake-out, was it?"

He decided to be truthful but not informative. He offered a simple

"No."

With eyes wide open and focused on him, she said, "Last question —
did you touch her?" Her face was desperately pleading, hoping to hear the
word "no" again, but Harry could not lie. Not to Lara.

"Yes. But it's not like you think--nothing happened." By then her face
had crumbled and she made a little moaning sound, barely audible.

"Okay, I have a question," he continued. "How did you know?"

"Shampoo. When you hugged me goodbye this morning there was the
smell of shampoo on your hair and your neck. A brand I used to use but I
don't anymore. And neither do you." "Honey, let me explain, please. I felt
caught up in a situation, but it wasn't physical, I swear. If anything, it was an
emotional lapse on my part. I don't even understand it."

Lara interrupted him by putting her hand up in front of her face.
"Please, Harry, I don't want to hear this. I can't. I have to go."

Harry didn't follow her, just sat a minute stunned. He could take
anything they threw at him at work, even losing his career if it came to that,
but he couldn't lose Lara. What had he done? He picked up the bottle of
brandy from the coffee table in front of him, stood and looked at his reflection
in the mirror behind the liquor cabinet, standing there with his heart shattered,
and his hurt turned to anger.

"You goddamn stupid son of a bitch!" he yelled at himself. "How
could you do this to yourself?" He threw the bottle full force at the mirror. The
reflection remained intact, but shimmering slivers of glass went flying in a
radius from the point of impact and thick maroon liquid ran down the glass in
vertical streamlets. Lara was speechless, but he could feel her cringe. Her
shoulders shaking, she got up and went into their bedroom.

Later, Harry knocked gently on the door, even though it was open.
Lara had two suitcases lying open on the bed and was placing slacks and

blouses into one of them, carefully and slowly, almost as if she wanted to prolong the process. Crumpled tissues littered the bed and the dresser top.

Harry spoke first. "I know I can't change your mind, and I know it's my fault. I got everything cleaned up in the other room."

"Thanks."

"Where will you go?"

After a long pause, Lara answered, "Tonight a motel, then I'll decide."

"I'll do anything I can to help you. You know I love you. Even if I can't have you or get you back, I have to know you're okay or I can't live."

She dropped a blouse, moved toward him and hugged him quickly. Then, even more quickly, she backed away. "I'm not going to change my number and I'll stay right in Dover. I won't stop loving you, don't worry." A man from the policeman's union sat next to Harry. Harry guessed he was a lawyer, but he might have been a paralegal. He was young, about twenty-five, and Harry'd never seen him before. He took notes, but said nothing to the investigator. Harry's appointment had been set for 8:30 a.m, an odd hour for him as he usually worked a swing shift. The Internal Affairs rep seemed to take sadistic delight in his job.

"Well, well, look what we have here. He spread out a group of photos in a fan shape as if they were a deck of cards. How do you explain this?" Harry recognized himself—a good front facial shot, with the hotel in the background and the woman, who was slightly more shadowed and hard to recognize, on his arm. In another shot, it was clear that he was handing her money. Still another photo showed them entering the lobby door. He realized the man was waiting for an answer.

"I don't know."

"Neither do I," said the investigator. "Neither do I. Look, I think you're a nice guy and a helluva cop, but the evidence speaks for itself. You might as well go home now, come back tomorrow and get your things. They can let you know tomorrow whether any charges will be filed about the bribe."

"Bribe—what the hell are you talking about?"

"Right here—this photo. You're seen taking money from a known crime figure." That was the first inkling that Harry had that he was being set up. Seventeen years later he still didn't know who or why.

That morning Harry was home before ten, wondering how things could possibly get any worse but afraid to even follow that thought, because each time he thought he'd hit bottom, another blow dropped him lower. He had a strong desire to talk to his mother, and another compulsion to get out the "special occasion" bottle of Scotch under the bar. He knew better than to do either. The right-shoulder angel beat out the left-shoulder devil, and he made the call to his mother.

She wished it could be in person but he was glad to have distance and phone lines between them. Maybe she wouldn't know he was shedding some decidedly unmanly tears. He did get the whole story out, and in return, her sympathy and support. Her unconditional love buoyed his spirits, if ever so slightly. He then opened a cold beer, and followed it with two more, and took a long nap.

Upon waking, Harry found the world to still be there. Afternoon sun filtered through the blinds, highlighting tiny motes of dust, and little brown birds flitted through the rose vines above the big window in the living room. Rusty wiggled his back end, lowered his head and stretched out his front paws in a gesture that begged Harry to come play with him. T.V news was blaring something about Iran-Contra, and a plane with a cargo of weapons crashing in Columbia. He heard it but registered nothing. He wanted to call Lara at work, but what would he say. Would she even talk to him or just hang up? Half-buried under magazines on the coffee table, he noticed the corner of a brochure, and picked it up, staring at a castle in the clouds with red-tiled roof spires. He couldn't remember how long he looked at it or whether that influenced his next decision. On an impulse, he picked up the phone and called his partner and friend, John Saunders, expecting to leave a message. Instead, John answered and invited Harry to come over.

Rusty, who was always welcome at John's, jumped out of Harry's truck first, getting a big hug from Harry's best human friend, then all three settled down on the porch.

"So, that's it," Harry said. "What's next?"

"I thought I might head out West. You know, get a fresh start. I'm thinking about San Diego."

"Geez, man, are you sure you couldn't get any farther away?" Harry smiled. After a couple of minutes in comfortable silence,

Harry announced, "Yeah, I just don't want to stay around here. Found out today there won't be any trial. One little ray of sunshine, huh? But I still feel betrayed."

"Life just sucks sometimes. Sure isn't fair. That's a pretty big move you're making. You know I'm going to have a tough time around here without you bustin' my chops every damn afternoon." John tried to laugh, but his voice was cracking, and he turned away a few seconds to regain his composure.

"So, California, huh. A little part of me envies you. Not sure I even know where San Diego is—sort of like a suburb of L.A, right?"

"No, it's a hundred and thirty miles south, almost on the Mexican border."

"Wow, now that you mention it, I got a cousin lives down there— he works for some kind of border agency. Hey, maybe he can help you get

set up with a job or something. Hold on, I'll go look up his info." A few minutes later John came back with a slip of paper and handed it to Harry.

"Yep, I'll be packing and moving down the road soon as I can find someone to take care of my house till it sells."

"You can count on me for that, buddy." "Thanks, man" "You gonna be driving?"

"Yeah, but I'm taking the car—this truck guzzles too much gas for a cross-country trip. I'm gonna pull that old teardrop we were gonna to fix up. It'll hold everything I need and give me a place to sleep along the way if I need it. Don't know what Lara will do with the truck—probably sell it. I think I've got everything signed that I need to and I'm gonna try to be ready by tomorrow—get outta here early the next morning."

"If she needs to get rid of it quick, I'll buy it from her. Can I come by tomorrow and help you pack before work?"

"That would be great."

The next morning early, Harry carried his personal effects from the Dover police station in a cardboard box. As he passed through the automatic door with the burden in his arms, he caught a glimpse of a newspaper stand, with a glaring headline on the top paper: High-ranking Detective Steps Down"; and in smaller lettering under it, "Harry Dugan to resign; No Reason Given." Further down the block just before climbing into the Datsun, he overheard voices: "No trial—he must have some good connections." "Or enemies."

An hour after arriving at the cottage for the last time, John's ten-year-old Toyota pickup rolled into Harry's driveway.

"I'm here to help with the heavy lifting."

"Did you bring some Scotch?" Harry joked. "That's the heaviest thing I want to lift." When Harry's few important possessions, and the hassock, were loaded into the trailer, leaving just enough room for Harry to crawl into the bunk high on one side, the two men shook hands, then embraced.

"Gonna miss you, friend," said John.

"Me, too." And that was that.

Weeks later, John probably wondered why he had become so cold, had distanced himself in ways other than geographically. John evidently had gone on with his life, the life that should have been Harry's, without giving too much thought to his old friend out West. What John didn't know was that Harry had heard Rusty bark in the background when he called John at home, soon after leaving.

Harry remembered his last night in Dover, after John left. He had been going through the pictures in the house—the ones that were left after Lara took her half. He was surprised to see she had left him the one of the three of them on the dock, after a great day of sailing. It became his most important possession, and the place he decided to tuck the envelope that had caused all their problems, still unopened. It fit securely under the wire that stretched across the back of the frame, and he wrapped it several times in butcher paper, then a layer of bubble wrap and put it in a manila envelope. As he was wrapping the other pictures, or removing them from their frames, he got a call on his cell phone and was caught off guard to hear Lara's voice on the other end.

"I heard you were leaving town."

"Wow, news travels fast among friends." There was an undeniable note of sarcasm in the words, but Lara ignored it.

"Are you sure it's what you really want, Harry?"

"Maybe not, but it's best to let the dust settle a little. I'll be staying in touch, and of course, my mom will be hearing from me regularly. If you need anything at all, give John a call. He will be watching the house until it sells."

"Okay."

"Lara, John's a good guy. You can trust him. Oh, one other thing-- a very important thing. Can you please take care of Rusty temporarily until you can find him a good home?" Harry was glad she couldn't see his face.

"Harry, Rusty has a good home and always will. With me. That's one thing you can count on, no matter what." Because of that, Harry knew. He talked to Lara occasionally along the way south and west, and she talked about the dog in every call. She would have certainly let Harry know if she'd given him to John. Yes, he could have been mistaken about it being Rusty, or there could have been a legitimate reason for Rusty to be at John's house, but his first suspicions were confirmed a few months later, when he again called John. That time it was not a dog's bark. That time it was a song he heard, vaguely, in the background. There was a subconscious sense of familiarity, then sharp recognition when he woke in the middle of the night realizing what he'd heard faintly in the background was the theme from Dr. Zhivago, coming from Lara's music box. There were quite a few sleepless nights in the years after that. Harry still had a some polite conversations with John from time to time, but the bonds of brotherhood had been broken.

Harry interrupted his daydream to look at the clock. Almost 9:30. Still time to meet Jake at ten. Once settled, he looked around for Jake, becoming a little anxious as ten-thirty came and went. Finally at eleven-fifteen, his phone rang. It was Jake, and Jake was telling him he'd be a

little late. That part was obvious, but there was something else, a rolling sing-song quality to the voice that Harry recognized instantly. He could understand a guy being a little bit tipsy late at night, or at an afternoon BBQ, but eleven in the morning? He was conveniently forgetting a few of his own mornings.

"You're already a little late, but never mind that. Are you okay, buddy? Is something wrong?"

"Naw, I'm alright. I am just tired."

"Jake, I know you. You're not okay." Harry was careful not to mention the slur he detected, or the word drinking. "You gotta tell me what's wrong."

"Nothing, I said." Jake's tone was out of character.

"I'm not tryin' to make trouble for you, partner," Harry tried to soothe him. "I'm tryin' to save your butt. What's goin' on?"

"Nothing. Trish and I had a little fi---no we had a dis---a dis-agreement is all. Or dis-argument." He laughed at his joke. "She'll get over it. So tell Phil I'll be there in an hour."

"Listen to me, my friend. You are not coming in today. Got that? I'm gonna tell Phil you got the creeping crud. A horrible sinus infection— that I could tell by your voice. He'll believe me. Now, go back to bed and get some rest. Or call Trish. Or do whatever the hell you want to do, but don't come here. Don't call here, either. You got that. If you do, we're both fired. I'm goin' out on a limb and you owe me that—got it?"

"Yeah."

" I want your word of honor."

" Okay, word of honor. Shit, I didn't wanna work today anyhow."

When Harry told Phil, he muttered something under his breath that Harry thought sounded like, "Sure. Last time it was the Monday flu. He'll be in tomorrow." He looked more sad than angry.

Phil handed Harry a stack of paperwork, "If you are going to be alone today, take a look through these and see if you can prepare a list of businesses to check in with."

Harry read the top sheet "IMAGE, what is this all about, I though that was Homeland Security Investigations Program"

"Just be glad it is a smaller stack." Phil said with a smile as he walked out of the room. Harry was wise enough to be grateful that he had a job and he knew that Homeland Security was probably overloaded with this new program designed to strengthen hiring practices and combat the unlawful employment of illegal aliens.

Witness Defection

Phil was right about Jake returning the next morning, right on time, his normal bright and cheerful self. Harry wasn't sure how, or if, to bring up the previous day's absence. Anyhow, they had bigger fish to fry, and that was the first thing he mentioned after the morning meeting.

"Still want to stop by the detention center and see what we can find out from those two drug-runners in the van? They've had plenty of time to get their stories straight, but we're not getting any info from the investigators, and those two scum-bags might just tell us something."

"Nothing we could offer them in exchange, but it's worth a try." Jake was picking up right where he left off. "It's not much out of the way and we just have routine patrol today."

The immigrant detention facility they went to was made up mostly of holding cells for those who were in the country without documentation and had been involved in petty crimes. Sometimes, perpetrators accused of more serious crime were also held till their arraignments. It was unlikely these two had been arraigned; it was routine for these people to waive their right to a speedy resolution because that gave them more time in country to arrange for legal help, or for their bosses to do so. Jake had their names in his computer, or at least the ones they had given when apprehended—they had carried no I.D.

The administrative person took the names and looked them up on her screen.

"Sanchez and Gonzales, yes, they're in B-26. Hold on, I'll call someone to bring them. Meantime, let's see your badges." She compared their photos to their actual features, then asked them to stand with toes on a line, where a photo was snapped. As an added precaution, each agent placed a thumb on an ink-pad and left an imprint where required.

After a fifteen-minute wait, a uniformed guard came to the doorway and motioned to the clerk. They both stepped away from the desk, into a doorway, but Harry could hear part of the conversation.

"That's what came up when I entered their names." Then, "Today, why wouldn't it be?" Other words followed, but the two prison employees had stepped back into a hall and Harry could no longer hear them. When the woman finally returned, ten minutes later, she had a sheet of paper.

"It seems our computers were down for a while during the night," she explained, " and I didn't have the most current information. This paper shows that Mr. Gonzales and Mr. Sanchez have been released as of, um, let's see-- 6:30 am. August 28th. That's today." She took a quick glance at her computer monitor to confirm that she had the date right.

"Released!" Harry almost shouted the question. "How can that be? They were in here for some serious crimes and possible connection to a cartel."

"That I know nothing about. It says here: 'release approved, fine paid.' They'll be reporting back in on September 15th."

"Sure they will." Jake's sarcasm cut like a knife. "I thought we didn't give bail to illegals. Who ordered this and who paid the bail?"

"It wasn't bail. It was a fine. Looks like they dropped most of the charges." "Who ordered this?" Jake's voice boomed.

"There's a signature here, but no typed name. I can't make it out." Harry stepped forward. "We're going to need to speak to your

supervisor."

Another fifteen minutes elapsed before the supervisor arrived. It was another woman, Hispanic but fluent in English. She gave her name and wore a nameplate, but the SCABS agents were immediately frustrated with her manner. Neither would forget her face. "What is it you want to know?" She asked in a pleasant but business-like tone.

"Who in the hell let these guys go? They were material witnesses in a major drug bust." By now Harry's patience had worn thin.

"Well, sir, I can assure you it was not me. I can also tell you that whoever did so had a valid reason."

"Who would that be?" asked Jake.

"That would be Mr. Rutgers—he's in a meeting right now."

"Of course he is." Harry was seething but remained calm on the outside. "We'll wait. Tell Mr. Rutgers, if it's more than ten minutes, we will go away. But his problem won't go away. Mention the name Abraham Fox. He's our supervisor and he isn't going to like this one bit. Tell him he doesn't want to be messing with the DHS big-shots."

After the Hispanic woman left, Jake leaned toward Harry to remind him in a whisper that they didn't have a direct connection to Homeland Security.

"You know that, and I know that," Harry whispered back. Then there was a buzz at the desk.

"Thank you." said the clerk. Then, to Harry and Jake, very professionally, Mr. Rutgers will see you now." It had been about five minutes.

"There was no point in keeping them here," said the man behind the desk, a round-looking guy with a fringe of hair so black it looked unnatural. It costs money every day we house them, and there's always someone breathing down our necks about over-crowding, or immigrant rights."

"But these were witnesses in a crime—a major crime with even higher level implications. How do you just let them walk?"

"No chance of getting a conviction. It wasn't our call, you can ask your boss. Without evidence--it looks like all the evidence was contained in a vehicle that had not yet been searched."

"Yeah, they took their sweet time on that," interjected Harry.

"That vehicle was, unfortunately, destroyed by fire on August 25, 2012." "How convenient."

"Look, guys, I feel as bad about this as you do. But some, you win, others, well we just have to know when to cut our losses. This was not a case we could prosecute—you know that."

"We could have squeezed them for info," Jake suggested.

"What were we going to offer them—an early release?"

"We had my testimony." Jake was like a badger digging out his prey—he would not be placated. "I saw the jerks. They had weapons. There was a gun. There were boxes of pot—big boxes, lots of boxes."

"The only weapon mentioned was a set of pruning shears. You say there was a gun— did you see it?"

"I know there was a gun—I saw him reach for it." Jake had not told anyone, even Harry, that he had pocketed the gun that he found on the floorboards. He never knew when an extra might come in handy, for him or his partner, especially if it couldn't be traced. He planned to check into that. And now, with the fire, no one could question the absence of a gun.

"And the pot—you could testify that's what it was?" "Yeah, I know pot when I see it," "But wasn't it in boxes?"

"It was pot—I could smell it. I know what pot smells like." "Rutgers voice became kinder. "Picture yourself on a witness stand, convincing a jury you could identify pot unequivocally by its scent." "Works for dogs."

"Come on," Harry said. "He's right--we're wasting our time here." He did not want to make an enemy of a guy who was on the same side as they were and just doing his job. "Maybe they'll try a quick turnaround and we'll pick 'em up again—maybe we'll find a new weapon."

"Fat chance."

Harry's hand was out. "Thank you for your time, Mr. Rutgers." "Well," said Jake, "let's head for Campo Road. We might as well

go through the motions. We seem to stay one step behind El Cameron, and I don't think that's accidental." He knew there was a chance, but a slim one, that the gun he'd stashed away had been used in a crime in the U.S. and a bullet would be found that could be matched and linked to the Shrimp. He couldn't do that himself, though; he'd need to confide in someone at CSI. Right now, he didn't want anyone to know he'd found the gun. Too many questions and not enough discretion.

"Yeah, the more of these roadblocks we run into, the more I want this guy," Harry muttered.

"Tell me about it."

"For the present, we just watch and wait, I guess. Meantime, there's a lot of back country to patrol."

They stopped in Jamul for a bite and a sandwich-to-go for later, and Jake got beverages and a bag of ice for their cooler. Then they took some off-road trails out of Dulzura.

They Spent most of the afternoon in the shade of a large live oak, with a pair of top-of-the-line binoculars passing between them.

"What's our next move regarding El Cameron?" Jake asked.

"Like I said, patience. See what the detectives find, see if the truck comes back."

"I'd like to go poke around that trapdoor," said Jake.

"If that's what it is."

"Oh, meant to tell you—I got a good look at it on our best equipment, and it's definitely not sealed, like a patch would be. It's a thin line, but it's loose. The other picture, the patch from same parking lot, is made to look like there's a slight gap in it, too; that's what I get out of it. Probably they all are, but it's not the same."

"Think we should go see if it opens?"

" No—too dangerous, with cameras," Jake shook his head.

"What about telling Phil—or Abe?" Abraham Fox was the manager of their compound, a guy Harry had felt respect for since the day he hired on. He had asked Harry to call him Abe, but suggested dire consequences if he ever used Abraham.

"Don't know if they'd believe us, for one thing. I just kinda want to wait a bit—maybe those two that we just missed will reappear, or we'll get some news from the detectives. Oh, by the way, I'm sorry I messed up yesterday. I know that's what cost us the chance to question them. The more you get to know me, the more things you'll find out. Some aren't so pretty."

"We all have our vices," Harry said. "Anyway, it was me and my sob story about lost love that made us miss getting a look at the van."

"Nobody's fault—just timing."

"Yeah."

"Let's go out to the point and take a look with the OTIS before we head back," Jake suggested. "The light ought to be just about right."

"Good idea. Seems like we've been sitting under this tree all day."
"We have."

The OTIS, which stands for "Observer's Thermal Imaging System," took some time to set up, but they finished before dark.

Jake took a look first, then turned it over to Harry.

"I don't see anything."

Harry took his turn. Their shift was going to end in about an hour, allowing time to get back and clock out by 10:30. Sometimes in the summer, they worked twelve-hour shifts, because having eyes after dark could be beneficial. His partner, Harry noticed, was on his personal phone, talking in a tone that meant he and Trish had made up. He didn't interrupt, but he was watching a group of individuals that were moving from bush to bush and every so often hiding behind a large boulder. Jake was oblivious for the moment to the movement in the distance. Without the scope, he probably couldn't have seen even if he hadn't been on the phone.

The huddled bodies were close to border, just on the north edge, though there was no way to for the average person to tell. Harry had only one hour to decide what he was going to do about the bold people creeping across the ravine, people he secretly sympathized with and admired. He continued watching. They looked as if they thought they had a chance. They moved closer. Harry had to make a decision.

"Anything interesting happening out there?" Jake had wrapped up his phone call.

"Nope," replied Harry. "Just a few hot spots. Some nights every rock looks like a human and the other way around."

A little later, as they made their way back on to Campo Road, they saw a group of Hispanics being detained by Border Patrol agents on the highway. "Wonder who they are," mused Jake.

"I guess they're the 'hot spots.' They must be pretty good if we missed them." "Or lucky."

"Well, even if we didn't get 'em, the Border Patrol did. I see they got the coyote this time, too--different guy than the one that slipped away from us. Guess we know where he'll be going. The rest—they'll be headed the same place we're headed—home. They'll be a lot poorer. No refunds on the smuggler's fee."

The Shrimp's Sting

Harry was on his own the next day. Jake had let him know he was going to hang around the compound because there was an opportunity to follow up on some of the meager info they'd gathered and to see if anything else had turned up from different sources about their quarry. Harry asked for and got permission to do a little patrolling out near Spooner's Mesa. A force, like gravity or magnetism, compelled him back to the grocery on Hollister. When he walked in, Elena smiled, but it was a wan smile, nothing like before. She looked tired, haggard, older than he knew her to be. He didn't comment directly on her appearance.

"Pretty busy, huh?"

"Oh, Harry, it's so nice to see you. But I don't have any time to talk—it's just so backed up and so--." She wanted to say more, he could tell, but her lip was trembling. He also knew she wanted, maybe needed, someone to talk to. He asked, "What can I do to help?"

"You mean it?" Her dull eyes brightened. "Wait a minute, I'll show you." When the last of the three customers in the store left, she took his hand and led him to the storage room in back. "See these boxes, they're

heavy. With frijoles—cans of refried beans. They need to go on shelves all the way in the front corner." She turned and pointed towards the back wall. "There's a dolly, but they're very heavy. My brother Rudy usually does this, he's very strong, but he's with my mother."

"Your mother, is she okay?"

"Yes, at least I hope so. She went to Puerto Nuevo, down in Baja, south of Rosarito Beach. My sister's baby is one year tomorrow—Mama wanted to be there for the birthday, and she couldn't go alone. Lupe doesn't want to come up here without her husband and he can't come." Harry did not comment, hoping the silence would induce her to continue. Finally, she said, "She's afraid."

"What is she afraid of. Isn't she legal?"

"She is, but not her husband. They--they had some trouble. Oh, you don't want to hear this."

A customer entered and Harry moved the boxes to the front. When Elena finished at the cash register, she joined him and they stacked cans on empty shelves, bottom to top. "Elena, I don't want to pry, but I promise I won't say or do anything to get you in trouble with Immigration. Maybe I can even help you. You can trust me."

"It's not 'La Migra' now. It's something worse. I don't want to make things bad for her. This man, he wants the money she owes him."

"Is he on the up and up? Does she really owe the money."

"No. I don't think she does, but he thinks so. And she doesn't have it. That's why she won't come here. She left right after Margharita was born, to be with Arturo. Then that man, that awful man, he started calling us. He said the check she gave him for papers didn't cash. I think he's lying."

"Was he making false papers for Arturo?"

"Si. He does that, he says they are correct and legal, but people get caught anyway, or sometimes he takes the money and doesn't give the papers. He has an office. It looks very proper. He's a big man, seems very nice at the beginning, but then he takes money and does nothing. Or does it wrong. He has hurt many people; no one dares to complain."

Harry waited and worked as she answered a phone call that sounded routine then helped some new customers. When she came back, she looked more composed. "I shouldn't be telling you this, but there's no way to hurt them now, I guess. It was early last year Lupe met Arturo, at the city college in Chula Vista. He's had a student visa from Uruguay. When they fell in love, he asked to have his visa extended. They wouldn't do it. He appealed it, but they said he could not live in this country while he waited, so he moved to Tijuana. She moved in with him but kept going to school, crossing every day. Mama, she worried, and Papa just grumbled. Then Lupe she got pregnant and Arturo snuck back in so they could marry here."

"Does your father live nearby?"

"Si. Yes." She pointed toward the back of the store. "In that little house. We all do. He watches television. His back, it hurts him so much from all the years of working with the short shovel and hoe. He can hardly walk. But he took care of his family and he studied and got his papers. Not from someone like El Gato, from the judge."

"Did they marry—Lupe and Arturo?"

"Yes, the whole family was here. It was beautiful. Then he tried to come in a second time and they arrested him. Said he could never come back. He doesn't even feel safe in Tijuana. And Lupe, she stopped her classes and moved there to Puerto Nuevo. She came here to have the baby but he could not be with her."

"I don't see why there was a problem. Didn't he automatically become a citizen as her spouse?"

"No. No, senor. That's what so many people think, but it isn't true. Many more papers, many more fees. Things like affidavits from people not related, from 'employer.' We cannot figure out. The man, his name is Leonardo Delgato, but he is called El Gato Grande, the big cat. Or El Gato Gordo. I should not say what that means."

"It's okay, I know."

She smiled her shy grin.

"He says he can make it easier. 'Streamline the process.' He uses big English words, dresses sharply, but he is not a cat, he is a weasel." She started to tremble, almost beginning to cry. Harry put his arms out and she stepped into them for comfort and strength. He found a tissue and pressed it gently under her eyes.

"How much does this human rat say your family owes him?" "One thousand, five hundred dollars."

Harry pulled out his wallet and started counting hundreds and fifties. Elena pushed his hands away. "No, senor Harry, we cannot take your money. You work hard, like we do."

"It's all right. I have a special fund for situations exactly like this. I would be wrong not to give it to you."

"But I have no way to get it to him now. I cannot leave till Mama and Rudy return."

"Take it. You will have it if he comes looking for you. It could save you some trouble. If he doesn't come, buy your father a good television set. In the meantime, maybe I can change his mind. Do you know where his office is?"

"Si. I can give you the number—on the street, not the telephone." Harry took the address Elena found for him, then lifted her hand

and kissed it. "I will come tomorrow from 8 am until 10. Have some work ready for me." It was a statement, not a question.

Harry found the office with no trouble. Near 9th and C, right downtown. Not on Banker's Hill but not in a bad area, either. He had left his vest in his locked truck, in a secret compartment. He wanted to look as "civilian" as possible. The rugged boots helped. The signs for the business were neatly lettered, one over the door and one in gold lettering painted on the window. Harry saw a man inside and stepped back into the early-afternoon shadow cast by a small street- side tree. He couldn't see the features, but the guy was big, all right. Harry had parked around the corner, after clocking in at work and letting Phil know where he'd be. He carried only his small phone in one pants pocket and an equally small but superior quality camera in the other. He adjusted the camera for its highest level zoom with automatic focus correction and activated the anti-glare feature. He moved it as close to the window as possible, leaving room for the lens to advance and snapped the man's picture.

Harry walked straight up to the man, who stood up and took Harry's outstretched hand. Harry gave his name, and so did Mr. Delgato. The big man gestured to a chair, and smiled a big, toothy smile that flashed "insincere" like a neon sign.

"What can I do for you, Mr. Dugan?

"I'm here on behalf of a friend, Senor Arturo Garcia Martinez. You know him, right? Originally from Uruguay, more recently residing in San Diego. I'll get right to the point, Mr Delgato. Mr. Garcia Martinez has many friends, in both countries. He's a man of honor, but he does not like people who treat him wrongly. He has already changed his mind about permanent U.S. citizenship because of mistakes you made, and he has nothing to fear. You, on the other hand, should be worried. Mr. Garcia wields a fair amount of power even as a visiting consultant." He pointed the face of his camera at the "cat" so he could see his own likeness.

"You can't do that."

"I just did, and I already sent it to my home computer. Why should it matter? What are you hiding?" Harry looked around the office.

"I run a legitimate business—everything is above-board and fair," El Gato protested. When the man started to elaborate, Harry interrupted him: "That is a matter of some dissent. But I'm not here to investigate your business or cause you any trouble. I only want what's fair, like you just said." Harry was not worried the man would try to start a fight or call out a couple of goons. That wouldn't be his style. Anyway, he knew he could take care of himself if necessary, even without all the accouterments of his job. "In short, you did not provide the service for Mr. Garcia that you promised, and you are lucky he is not taking you to court. Or hunting you down like the big cat you pretend to be. He owes you nothing, but as a gesture of his good will, he has authorized me to offer you $250 for your trouble. Your part of the bargain would be to stop harassing all members of his family. I strongly recommend you accept his offer. There will not be a second opportunity."

Mr. Delgato mulled over what Harry said for a full minute. Then he stood up, offered one hand to shake while he reached with the other for the envelope and said, "Mr. Garcia's offer sounds reasonable."

The next morning, at eight o'clock on the dot, Harry's personal truck, a small-bed, older model pulled up in front of the grocery on Hollister. Something didn't feel right. The sign said open, but the lights inside were dim. He rushed in, calling her name, and was relieved to hear her voice from one of the aisles near the back. She was bent over, stuffing four-roll packages of toilet paper on to shelves, and he lowered his own body so he could help her. Even in the natural light filtering through the small dusty window on that side of the store, he could tell there were bruises on her face. "My God, Elena, what happened?" His stomach tightened in fear.

She lowered her chin as far as she could, but turned her body to face his. "Someone came to see me," she stated simply. "Two men."

"No, it couldn't be," Harry thought aloud. He would have sworn Delgato wasn't the type to order this.

"It wasn't El Gato," she stated, and just as he was about to breathe a sigh of partial relief, she went on, "but it was about you. I'm so sorry, Senor Harry."

"You're sorry," he almost shouted, astonished that she could possibly blame herself. "It's me that needs to be sorry. Who were they? What did they want?"

"They gave me this." She pulled something out of her apron pocket —a photograph. It was black and white, five inches by seven.

"Let's go where there's better light."

His legs ached from only a few minutes of squatting the way she did. As they walked into the back room, he turned on a light and he saw her flinch. He took a good look at the picture. Fortunately no customers came in the front door. Harry stared at the photo, of him alone, standing in the parking lot across the street, and he shuddered. He knew who "they" were.

"They brought me back here," she said, her voice barely audible, tears just a heartbeat away.

"Did they--uh--hurt you?"

"Only this." She pointed to her face and he could see they had roughed her up pretty bad. Bruises, mostly. A few scratches and scrapes— no deep cuts. It would all heal.

"But they showed me other pictures." Elena's eyes watered up a bit, "Very bad-- horrifying. It made me vomit. Pictures of women. Hurt in such awful ways. I can't even say--."

"You don't have to. The pictures were probably staged—like acting, and make-up." He wished he could convince himself.

"Oh." she said. "They said you have to leave them alone—don't come back to this street ever. If you stay away, they won't hurt me any more, that's what they said. I didn't want to make trouble for you, Harry."

"Elena, it's me that made trouble for you." "But you have to do your job."

"Not if it means you getting hurt. You have my word I will not come snooping around this street again. Or even visit you."

"But, Senor Harry, I was hoping we could, you know, be friends."
"So was I. You're a very special woman, Elena, much too good for me, but I was looking for a chance to prove to you I'm a decent guy and

maybe you would find something to like about me."

"I already found that."

He held her again, and said, " I wish it weren't so, but this is very serious stuff. You can bet the people I work with and the other agencies will do everything in their power to find the very bad man who's responsible for this and put him away for a long time. But I'm the one he knows, and that means it's too dangerous for me to be around you at all. Until he's taken care of."

"Is it El Cameron?"

He put his index finger to her lips, as if preventing her from saying the name could lessen the evil. "We will have our time, believe it." He kissed her on the forehead and backed away. "Now I'm going to call my partner to come and stay with you the rest of the day. If I can, I'll have you watched and protected, but the best thing I can do is stay away. You understand, don't you?"

She nodded, then looked away from him. Harry wasted no time.

"You got to get here as quick as you can, Jake. I'll leave when I see your car. Don't go anywhere near their parking lot. Just go in the store like you're a customer. I don't think El Cameron has anyone out here on full-time watch, just the cameras. And I don't think they got enough of a shot of you for facial recognition, but I'm there, clear as day. I don't know how much they can find out about me, about SCABS, if they start looking electronically."

"I can fix that. Do you want me to do it before I head out there."
"Yeah, I guess that would be good. But nothing else. Jake, I'm

going to talk to Abe Fox, the sooner the better. Maybe you can let Phil know. I think I need to tell him our suspicions, about the tunnel, okay?"

"Of course. Whatever it takes to resolve this situation."

"We gotta get him, Jake."

"We will."

Less than an hour later, Harry was in Abe Fox's spectacular office. Last time he'd seen it was his interview in 2007. It hadn't changed much, but it didn't need to. Harry remembered Phil Bradshaw telling him about Abe just before Harry met him six years ago when he hired on. "Then, if it goes that far, you'll talk to Abe Fox. Whatever you do, don't call him Abraham. He hates it. He's the director of this entire department, and he personally wants to meet all new hires and talk to them, make the final call. He can be intimidating. He's a big guy—not fat, just strong. He's African-American, shaved head. I wouldn't want to get on his bad side or be in a physical confrontation with him. Main thing is he's the smartest person in this building." Phil had then handed Harry his application form.

Abe still held the same position he'd been in the last time Harry was here, reading something that apparently wasn't very important because he dropped it the minute Harry entered his office, as he had done before. It was quite a location—not a corner but a wide window in the center of the room that curved, sort of like a bay window with clear glass in large vertical panes that encompassed most of the west-facing wall. If a person stood near it and looked to his left, he would see the border. Although you couldn't quite see the ocean, the sunsets would be amazing. It was common knowledge that Abe seldom left his office before sunset. Mr. Fox apologized for the brightness, saying he had thought it might remain gray most of the day. Harry thought it was just an excuse to play with his toy—a button on his desk which could dim the huge windows to any desired level of darkening, as they filled with liquid. He suspected that everyone who entered the room got the same apology.

"Okay, let's skip small talk and get right to it. I know you wouldn't have asked for this visit if it weren't important."

Harry reviewed the Hollister street bust briefly, then told him what happened to Elena.

"Sounds like El Cameron all right. He's been getting more and more brazen, doing business almost openly in this country; but he always manages to disappear into the shadows and all we get is the riff-raff if anything. Don't think we're not on it, though."

With some embarrassment, Harry shared his and Jacob's suspicions about the tunnel.

"Sounds impossible," said Abe, "but I've learned from years on this job that I have to remove that word from my vocabulary. Sounds like something we should look into, right away."

Harry was distraught. "No, you don't understand. I'm sorry, with all due respect, sir—" "What did I teach you six years ago?

"With all due respect, Abe, that's exactly what I was hoping to ask you not to do. Can't we just leave it alone for a little while, until this dust

settles, a few weeks? Maybe there's a different way to look for that bastard. And I was hoping to get some protection—24-hour protection for the woman."

"You don't want much, do you?" said Abe, with a natural smile and a chuckle. "Why is this woman important to you?"

Harry opted for the truth. "I haven't known her long, but I care about her. She can't leave the store right now--it's the family's livelihood. She's been victimized so much already. I'm sorry, s...uh, Abe, I know you don't have time to hear every immigrant's tale of woe."

Suddenly, Harry thought back on the night he comforted the woman in Dover. He almost second-guessed his own professional judgment. Was this another emotional lapse, he wondered, that could alter his future? No. Perhaps, aside from his professional duties, he had a real emotional connection with Elena.

"No, I don't. But if you can summarize hers in five minutes, I'll listen." Harry added the details about the family's problems with Delgato.

"Ah yes, El Gato Grande. I know of him. His list of victims is in the hundreds, maybe lots more. Can't touch him 'cause none of them will testify. Can't blame 'em—it would destroy their lives. I'd like nothing better than to put him away. Maybe your Elena can help, maybe she can't. But this is what I can do for you: her brother-in-law will get a pass. I'll defer his criminal case indefinitely so if he stays clean and out of trouble, he won't get deported. Maybe citizenship."

"But did you realize I said he's in Mexico now—how will he get here?"

"I'll see to that. Tell her to notify the sister to get their things packed—four suitcases, no more. To go to the bullring in Tijuana, all three of them on, let's see," he leafed through his calendar, "September 4th—

that's a Tuesday. She should wear a good-sized name-tag on her right lapel, first name only, and wait on the right of the main entrance. Our team will take it from there. I'll put this into your tablet."

"I don't think I should even talk to her," Harry said.

"Oh, yeah, right. Have Jake do it."

"And about the protection?"

"I can do three days, no more. I have a crew in mind for this situation, and we can have eyes on the parking lot with no suspicion." Harry was skeptical but he didn't want to question what Abe sounded so sure of. "I see your concern," the supervisor added. This always works, ask Jake about it. If something goes down where the truck was, though, we will act on it. You have to know that."

"Yes, I understand. I appreciate this, Abe." "Don't tell me, show me."

Harry stayed around the compound for the day, catching up on paperwork and worrying. He was anxious to talk with Jake.

"I knew I'd find you in the break room," Jake said on returning from Hollister Street. "So how did everything go?"

"No problems. I told her about your little visit with El Gato. She tried to give me some money she had in an envelope under the nickels. Said it was from you. I wouldn't let her. You gave her your own cash?"

"Yeah, in case I couldn't make the big cat go away. Abe said something about a crew."

"Yeah, one of our best sets of under-cover guys." Jake looked around to make sure no one was in earshot. There's three of them. With construction skills. They come in and set up a scene at her house: they will dig out some sewer pipe and replace it. They do it for real, so she gets the benefit of a minor bathroom remodel in the store. There will be boxes with a new sink and toilet, then the old toilet sitting out front till they leave. No one would entertain even the slightest idea that it's anything else. They'll be doing two other things: protecting her and watching the parking lot."

"I guess that's the most I could hope for."

"We could hope for—I like her, too." He saw Harry shoot him a glance. "Like a sister, don't worry. Now, go home and be sure you get a good night's rest. We're goin' to Yuma tomorrow."

"Who are you, the activities coordinator?" They walked out the door together and headed to their separate vehicles.

Splashdown

Phil-the-Mill's briefing room was a very noisy place at 10:45 am. Many of the patrol agents worked the same shift that Harry and Jake did. Phil signaled Harry and Jake to wait. After the others had cleared the room, he asked them how they felt about another trip to Yuma.

"No problem," said Jake. "Marchin' or fightin'." Harry was pleased to hear him use the expression. "Was it a few weeks ago we went there?"

"Yeah," said Phil, "you'll be going to the same place—our offices on the west end.

Across the 8 from Wintergarden and just a block from the Arizona Port of Entry.

Corner 8th and B. You've been there once, Jake.

You don't need a map, do you?"

"No sir." "This time I've got something bigger than a packet of papers for you to deliver."

Phil had brought out a fairly ordinary looking ice chest, red with white sides. "There's an electronic key that opens this, and you don't have it. It's in the Yuma office. Abe has a back-up key. I need you guys to treat this with absolute respect---and don't let it out of sight. It has something in it that is indispensable and irreplaceable. You don't need to know what it is, but this much I can say. It's not a bomb or anything that can hurt you physically. Just take good care of it and turn it over to this woman and everything will be okay." He showed them a photo. "I'll program her picture and info into your tablet. Just make good and sure you do an eye-scan and get a signature before you turn it over. Make it look as routine as possible."

"Boss, this is an ice- chest. How can it be routine to get a signature for an ice-chest?" Jake looked directly at Abe.

"It would be if you were delivering human organs. Which, by the way, you're not. You don't have any problem with this, do you?"

He didn't wait for an answer. "You still do your regular vigilance and pursuit after the drop. If you spot something before then, contact dispatch. Got it?"

"Yes, sir," said Jake, and Harry nodded.

The three-hour trip across the bottom of the state was uncomfortably warm going up the grade to the summit, because drivers were instructed to turn off their air conditioners. This was no time to overheat the engine.

"Not many steep grades in New Hampshire," Harry said.

"You ever been in the Imperial Valley before?" Jake asked.

"No. Well, just once, coming here from Texas. But I think it was night."

"It's where large portion of the country's produce originates. Part of the "bread basket". This and the San Joaquin Valley in central California. Nothing but poor people here, except the growers and a few others."

"Does it go all the way to Arizona?

"No, there's the sand hills just before Winterhaven, then the river, then Yuma. Looks like the Sahara when we get to the dunes—probably the only place in the country like it, except maybe in New Mexico."

"We got dunes at the coast in New England."

"Not like these, I bet. Speakin' of Texas, been meaning to ask you how long you were there. Fort Stockton, was it?"

"Yeah, I was there about eight years.""What was it like?"

"Typical small town, only worse 'cause it's west Texas. A few thousand people. Hot, dry, dusty, and nothin' good about it except the interstate."

"What would make a guy stay in a town like that for a decade?"

"A hard dick. At first anyway. Then it was a good place to hide. And watch the world go by." Jake was silent, so Harry continued.

"Met this girl that worked at the Paradise Motel. She had the night shift. Got off at one am. Cute and nice, and didn't ask any questions. She wasn't planning to stay long, probably saving up a few checks and taking a bus to San Antone or Amarillo. And I, of course, was just passing through on my way to California. There was a physical attraction, no doubt about that. Not like with Lara. With Lara it was on all levels. With Bonnie, it was satisfying a need, for both of us, and then we became friends. Not soul-mates."

"Wha'd you do there?"

" Mostly hung around her place. Helped her fix things. Made a few bucks now and then doing security work. Swam in the pool at her motel. It was a huge indoor complex in a garden—had a two-story spa if you can believe that. You'd be surprised how many people come through that little cow town and what stories they can tell. I did a lot of listening. When I got bored, I'd go home and drink myself to sleep. Never got rowdy. On my 40th birthday, in 2006, I got a present from my mom. It was a journal with the words "My Life" on the front. It made me think-- which is probably what she had in mind."

"And that's when you decided to move on?"

"Yep. To finish the trip I started eight years earlier. Maybe get on with my life." "How was Bonnie about it?"

"She'd been talkin' to this guy online, an old boyfriend from Des Moines, Iowa, where she grew up. He sounded like he wanted to get together, have a kid. She was still young enough, decided to give it a try. I hope it worked out for her."

They arrived at the dunes that Jake had described. Harry had to admit that they weren't anything like the dunes in New Hampshire. "Yours have ours beat—bigger and all golden, not grayish," he said, "and not a sign of vegetation."

When they crossed the bridge over the Colorado River dividing California from Arizona, Jake commented that the water on the Mexico side was unusually high.

"Meaning, it's moving," he said. "Usually it's sluggish and muddy. They must have had some good monsoon rains last month."

"What do you think's in our box?"

"Not the foggiest. We'll probably never know. Could be cash, but I doubt it. I think last time was a test, and now we might be doing this every once in a while. It's on a need-to-know basis, and you know where we fit on that totem pole."

The drop-off was a piece of cake. They stopped to fill up for the trip back at a gas station just a couple blocks from what was the I-95, but what looked like an ordinary suburban artery. Next to them at the adjacent pump was a pickup truck with a make-shift stake-bed, like farmers installed for carrying hay. They had already seen numerous hay trucks, but there was something about this one that made them take notice. It had a small jump-seat, not a true crew cab and there were two men in it, who did not get out. A third man was pumping gas and another returned from the mini-market and said something to him, then got in the truck, on the passenger side All four men were small and wiry, with dark tan, leathery skin. That wasn't so unusual, but they seemed nervous, and the driver made a circle around the back after he finished filling the tank. He adjusted a tarp over the bales of hay, which, strangely, were wrapped in thin plastic.

"Wonder why they wrap them," Harry said.

"This is the rainy season. Maybe they want to protect them from moisture if they're going far. Seems like the tarp would do that though. And I sure don't see any thunderstorms on the horizon. Let's just see where they're going."

The truck had been facing north, but made a u-turn as it pulled out of the station. Not strange in itself. Both men knew their jurisdiction extended into Arizona in cases like this, but, of course, they'd let local SCABS authorities know if they spotted something suspicious.

Harry replaced the gas nozzle, tightened the gas cap, and jumped in without going back to the clerk for his change. He stayed a few cars back and kept the hay truck in view. He moved at a normal rate of speed, and when they came to a junction, an intersection really, with a sign reading 95 South, he took that route.

"I didn't think you could go south from Yuma," Harry said.

"But I took a look at my map before we left the break room. Arizona stretches a ways below us---probably about thirty-five on this highway. You go south and a little west and then you end up in San Luis on the border, and just below it, San Luis Rio Colorado. In Sonora, not Baja. I think we better let our local guys know about this, and alert the Border Patrol at San Luis. It's probably a load of pot." Jake was already texting. Harry kept an eye on the truck, staying in the right lane and going exactly 65.

"Bring up the map, okay, Jake? Any towns between here and San Luis?"

"Yeah," Jake had the answer almost instantly. "There's Somerton— we're almost there--and halfway between it and the border with Sonora, there's Gadsten. Glad I don't live in this desolate state."

"Don't knock Arizona, there's towns like that in California."

The truck kept moving right through Somerton, which probably had a couple thousand people in it. The hay truck slowed to the speed limit. So did the SCABS vehicle.

"They've got to know we're tailing them now," said Jake a few miles down, when they were traveling almost due west.

"Don't see how they couldn't. No need to approach," Harry decided.

"We'll pull up on the side when we get to the line and wait to hear from the Border Patrol. We better get a thank you. Wait—what the hell? The highway turns south here, but they sped up and went straight. It's barely a road. I'm goin' in, after them. Hang on."

Less than a mile after leaving the highway, they could see the river, but the ground beneath them was dry. They were on an embankment higher than the water that had cut its way through in many seasons of flooding. Not exactly the Grand Canyon, but a high enough embankment that it would be perilous to drive off it. The truck did just that, as Harry and Jake stared in disbelief. It came to rest with just the top of its cab showing, bales of contraband floating off the back, where a tailgate had either broken off on impact, or, more likely, been lowered from a button in the cab. All four men were half-crawling, half-swimming out of the windows, which must have been fully lowered before splashdown.

Harry brought their vehicle to a halt just short of the small cliff, sending up a huge cloud of dust and gravel. He and Jake jumped out and saw that the four men were not running or swimming to the other side of the river, which was the state of Baja California, not Sonora. Instead, they had donned life jackets and were moving around in the water rounding up the floating bales.

Harry drew his gun and was about to point it at the men when he heard a voice in the sky. The sound was followed quickly by the clacking and whirring of helicopter rotors, which made it hard to make out the words. Harry lowered the gun and listened. When he strained, he could hear the words "DO NOT PERSUE!"

He put the gun back in its holster and waited for further instructions from what he realized was the Arizona Border Patrol helo. "GO TO CHANNEL 19" were the next words. Jake already had the radio out of his vest and had put it on speaker. The rotor noise diminished as the chopper withdrew a ways.

Harry moved close to Jake and listened. The four men from the truck continued their work unperturbed, pushing the bales toward the far side of the Rio Colorado. It almost looked like they were smiling or whistling while they worked.

"We realize this is not in your manual," said the helicopter pilot over the radio. The chopper itself was drifting slowly out of sight. "There is no river border with Mexico in your state, and this is the only one in ours. It's common in Texas, so we've been brought on board, and they alerted us two weeks ago that there was enough water in the river they might try it. First time it's happened here that I know of. But it won't be the last. The river is the boundary--here it's between us and the Mexican state of Baja California--but there's no halfway mark. The minute they touch water, or even wet mud, we have to back off. It would be an international incident if we went after them. Sure a good thing you didn't fire your gun," said the pilot.

"I wouldn't have." Harry said. "I don't think. I'm freakin' glad we notified you, though, and glad you got here when you did."

Jake, who had been cursing at the helicopter, and chomping at the bit to chase the perps with or without permission, sighed heavily. "Guess we can't do shit. That sucks bilge water."

Harry ended their call with the Arizona pilot, but not before asking him how he knew about the splashdown.

"Guy at San Luis called me right after you texted him, just in time for me to get here from the airport. It's just east of the wide bend between Yuma and Somerton. Said he had a hunch."

"Come on," said Harry.

"If we leave now, we can be back by dark."

Loose Ends

As dusk descended and the SCABS truck neared San Diego, Jake turned to his partner. "Is there anything we could have done to get them?"

"Not much, really."

"Who would ever think."

"We will next time. I guess they could put up a barricade at the point they jumped, but they'd just take an angle and do the same thing," Harry conjectured. "It sure feels weird to have to just sit there and watch them swim with their bales of pot. But the law's the law, and this one is big time."

"Yeah," Jake agreed. "They must of known at the gas station and went with plan B. Didn't even look like that truck was four-wheel-drive. You think they'll just leave it?"

"I doubt it. People in Mexico don't waste anything and labor's cheap. My guess is, as soon as the bales were corralled, they got on their phone or radio and called their bosses. More likely there was already somebody on the way; the bosses were probably tuned in to the conversation we had with the border guys at San Luis."

Harry continued, "What they'll do, most likely, is send a couple of guys in a good four-wheel drive with the bed full of old fence boards, roped together. They'll lay it out as a road and drive the old pick-up right out of the river. Then they'll dry it out and clean it up a bit, do some minor repair if necessary. Those guys are all mechanics, and the rescue vehicle will have spare parts. They'll transfer the load to a different truck or a van and use the wet one for other jobs till this dies down, then put different plates on it. Don't ever underestimate the organizational skills of the cartels, if that's what this is. They're not just cruel, they're smart. And some might say they're not even cruel, compared to the opium wars in China last century."

"I see the lights of the El Cajon Valley," Jake said, abruptly changing the subject. Whad'ya say we stop at the Big Steer Steakhouse for a nice, juicy rib-eye. If I have to eat another fast-food taco, I think I'll be sick."

"I'll go along with that."

There was plenty of parking at the steakhouse when they arrived, because it shared a big lot with a Home-Handy store, set further back— both were across a busy frontage road from a mall, and there was easy freeway access. When they had satiated their appetites for high quality beef, they exited through the back door, at a much more leisurely pace than they had used to enter. There was a small group of men hanging out across the way, in a tree-shaded square within the parking lot.

"If you ever come by here at 6:30 am, you'll see dozens of them," said Harry, "waitin' to be picked up for a day's work. Of course, we can't do anything about them. They could have valid green cards. Our job is at the border--people we know just crossed illegally."

"So why do you s'pose they're there now?"

"Just hangin' out, probably. Maybe some of them spend the nights, there in those shrubs. Shopping carts are easy to come by," Harry answered.

Jake was suddenly alert. "Hey, doesn't that guy look familiar?"

Harry looked, and immediately recognized the man but preferred

not to let Jake know that right away. "Naw, those guys all look alike," he said with an uneasy laugh.

"I swear I've seen that one before."

The agents returned to their car, and Harry was still in the driver's seat, when the man they were talking about strode purposefully toward them, with a long, easy gait. Harry thought about rolling up his window, which he had lowered, and peeling out before the tall Mexican got to the truck, but was afraid that would look even more suspicious. So he sat still.

The Mexican man smiled and said hello to Harry, but kept his Texas-style hat low so Jake couldn't see his face. He pulled a folded envelope out of the pocket of his shirt, and tossed it through the open window, onto the dash. "Didn't expect to see you here," he said, still smiling. "Guess this is as good a time as any to get this to you."

"Uh, thanks. We gotta get goin'. See ya," Harry said, visibly agitated. Jake was staring at him, so he said the first thing he could think of, by way of explanation.

"I didn't recognize him at first. Almost forgot I 'd asked him to give me an estimate on a little deck I want built at my house."

"He sure was familiar. Can't place where from right now, but I'll think of it. How do you know him?"

"Uh, the judge gave me his name. My landlord." Harry had rolled his window up and started toward Fletcher Parkway, the six-lane arterial that brought shoppers to the mall. He didn't touch the envelope. Willing it to just disappear, he looked straight ahead. Distracted and nervous, he gave the truck too much gas as he pulled out to turn left when the light changed. The envelope went zooming across the dashboard and slid off it, coming to rest in Jake's lap. Both men noticed at the same moment that it was partially opened, and several hundred dollar bills were visible. Harry's face blanched as he tried to maintain his composure. Jake said nothing.

Harry pulled over to the side, and Jake handed him the envelope, again without words. Harry put the bills in his wallet, all but one, mumbling "special charity fund," and that was the only part that wasn't a lie. He gave the other bill to Jake, smiled and said, "Buy Trish something."

Back at the complex, Jake appeared to act normally. He mentioned what a shame it was that Harry had to drive all the way back out to Santee, when he had been so close to his house. Harry agreed, and as he walked toward his car, called out, "See you tomorrow."

"No," answered Jake. I got tomorrow off. Trish's birthday."

The next morning Harry arrived at the Otay Mesa buildings earlier than usual, and got in the truck for a solo patrol of The Edge. He drove to a spot not too far from the last place they had used the OTIS, thinking he might take a look with the binocs. He found it hard to concentrate on tracking. His thoughts were scattered. He had no idea it was Trish's birthday. Had Jake told him and he just wasn't paying attention? And did the remark about buying her something ring false or was it a convenient ruse? He puzzled over the coyote showing up there and thinking it was all right to approach Harry in his truck when his partner was there. Didn't he remember that Jake was there that time he was driving the flower van, the time it really was an accident that he got away?

The silence of the high desert at mid-day was oppressive. The vest Harry wore over a white t- shirt and under a short-sleeve, lightweight blue denim shirt felt thicker, hotter, heavier than it ever had. Truly, it was Harry's heart that was heavy. He wondered why had he started this crazy game. It could ruin everything. "Everything I've worked so hard for," he started to tell himself, then corrected it—"more like everything that was handed to me." Why had it been so easy to pick up where he had left off?

To just waltz into this job after an eight-year lapse in his life, as if he were still in Dover before that night his world fell apart. Whatever the reason, he had a job and he liked what he was doing. He liked to think that it was helping society, and strangely, the part he was doing wrong, that would get him fired in a minute, probably jailed for years, that part felt even more like it was right, in the most basic, moral, human way.

Harry took off his vest and service revolver and locked them in the toolbox in the truck's bed, just behind the cab. Wearing only the t-shirt, his jeans, boots, and a baseball cap, and carrying a bottle of water, he took off walking, heading for a high, craggy rock. Some of the sparse local population claimed it looked like an angel with folded wings, but natives saw it as an eagle that represented their first chief, centuries ago. The view at the top would be spectacular, and it was thought by many to be a spiritual place. It would take about an hour to walk to the top and another hour to walk back, if he decided to return.

"That's crazy," he told himself. "Nothing will come of it." Yet, he knew Jake too well to believe he had been fooled. Jake knew payoff money when he saw it. Harry wasn't afraid of going to jail, and he didn't care much about the money. It wasn't for him anyway. What he feared most was not having this job. It was his second chance, and at his age, there wouldn't be a third.

At the top, he had four magnificent views. To the south, where his vision settled first, he saw The Edge and the border itself, looking pretty much like it always did in their surveillance, only smaller. The westerly overlook included that layer of liquid-silver iridescence that he knew to be the Pacific; and the faint outlines of tall buildings just in front of it, shades of lavender gray and soft blue-green--downtown San Diego. To the north, on the right in the far distance, were the Chocolate Mountains, which did indeed look as if they could have been gigantic Hershey kisses. To his left, close to the horizon, was a big patch of dark blue under the bigger patch of matching blue sky. The once great Salton Sea, not so great anymore.

Melli had told him how it was inadvertently formed when a levee broke and the water flowed to a natural basin. What had immediately become a Palm Springs-type resort destination started to dry up as weather patterns changed and the levee was repaired. Fresh water with nowhere to go. What didn't evaporate was heated by an unrelenting sun. Runoff from fertilizers and pesticides created a stagnant sea. Birds once attracted by the rising water levels began to die off by the thousands and fish could hardly survive. Efforts to fix it had so far met with failure. Later, the stench became unbearable and the people stopped coming, except for a few hardy or stubborn desert rats.

Yet from up here, it looked unspoiled and lovely. To the east, far in the distance, were the sand hills they'd driven through—could it have been just yesterday? Yesterday, when everything in Harry's life was okay. The sand, when viewed from afar, was just as glorious as the water, the trees, the ocean. Nearer, in fact immediately if front of him, was another edge, a sheer drop-off, at least two hundred feet down. He wondered how many people had let themselves fly or step off at this exact point, and what their reasons might have been. He speculated about whether anyone would miss him. Would they find his body? Probably. He'd left enough clues. If he just stepped off, it could look like it was an accident—there would be no way to prove otherwise. His life insurance would pay off. Harry's body tensed. If he checked out now, his life insurance would go to his ex-wife, because he'd never bothered to take her name off the beneficiary papers. That meant John Saunders, who used to be his best friend and who then became his wife's best friend, would make out big time.

The thought swiftly transported Harry back to reality. He turned and started walking briskly down the grade to the truck, determined to explain to Jake how he got caught up in this sticky web. Only halfway down did he think of his mother and whisper "sorry" for his moment of weakness. The trail, if you could call it that, widened about halfway down and curved around the side of a foothill, revealing his truck, and parked next to it, one he knew to be Jake's personal vehicle. Too convenient. Before he had finished his descent, Jake was in front of him on the trail. He stared a second or two, then shouted sternly, "Agent! You're out of uniform." But as he said it, he cracked a big grin and offered Harry an un-opened can of ice- cold beer. Suddenly Harry knew what had been bothering him more than anything else. It wasn't losing the job so much as it was losing Jake's respect and friendship.

They found a thick incense cedar close to the trucks and sat together in the shade. The first thing Jake did after they settled was to hand the hundred dollar bill back to Harry.

"I can't take this." He said simply. Harry tried to read his eyes, to see if this could be some kind of trap.

"Is this the hottest damn day of the year do ya' think?" Harry asked.

Jake fielded his question in the usual way, Harry noticed. Ask him the time, he tells you how to make a watch: "Sometimes, in fact quite often, the hottest day is next month. There was one October we recorded the hottest and the coldest day of the year

both. But, yeah, it's a scorcher." "Hey, I have an idea." "Oh yeah, what's that?" Harry watched his partner closely.

"There's this creek with running water year round. Cold water.

You can drive almost up to it.

Whad'ya say we go take a swim?"

"Bathing suits."

"Harry, loosen up. You're still way too East Coast. We're fifty miles from civilization, and we're almost cops. Who's going to arrest us?"

The creek was exactly as Jake had promised. Cold, refreshing, private. Of course, they kept their weapons within reach.

After a bracing swim, both put on undershirts, jockeys, jeans and socks, and both restored their "back-up" guns to their regular hiding places in the socks. Their vests and shirts remained nearby, Harry having retrieved his from the tool box.

They checked the sun's angle instead of reaching for their phones to determine the time.

"It's about three," said Harry. He felt much more free to talk, knowing there was not even a remote chance that Jake was wearing a wire. He didn't want Jake to know he'd even thought it. Then he wondered if that might be the reason Jake had suggested the swim. All at once, Harry wanted to talk. "Jake, I got some questions, and I bet you do, too. How do you feel about wasting the rest of the afternoon?"

"Nothin' I'd rather do. It's my day off, remember. I already fulfilled my duty—took Trish to brunch at the Hotel Del. Tonight she's going out on the town with her best girlfriend, Maria, and a couple other women, I think. I don't like it much. Nothing wrong with Maria, just, well, good-lookin' women out on the town, temptations, you know? But the more I complain, the more determined she is to go, to prove a point, I guess. So I told her to have a good time. She'll call me when she gets home, maybe before. So, ask away."

The first question is obvious. How the hell did you find me out by the spiritual high point? I didn't know you knew about it. I didn't even know I was coming here. I found it by myself last year and asked Melli about it."

"The answer's just as obvious as the question. GPS." "You put a GPS on my truck?"

"Our truck, and no, I didn't put it there—the Force did. It's on every vehicle in the fleet. You gotta know that. There's never a minute of the day they don't know exactly where we are, or have a way to look it up if they want to know."

"Yeah, I guess I knew that. But you had to ask the SCABS higher-ups for my location, didn't you? I'm surprised they gave it to you. Isn't that just for or the director's use?"

"I didn't have to ask."

"You hacked in and got it yourself?"

"Well, hacked isn't exactly the word I'd use."

"You sure have liberal access to the company computers, my friend."

"That's because I know them better than they do. Better than any of the supervisors or the director himself. Don't tell Abe I said that. That's not to say their skills are lacking."

"No, you're just some kind of wonder-boy magician when it comes to electronics."

"I grew up at the right time. A computer in every classroom. I never met one I didn't love. It took up a lot of my time. You'd be amazed at some of the things that can be done."

"I am amazed. I'm wondering how many of those things have been done to me."

"Harry, what do you remember about the day you hired on?" "Every detail. You want me to go over it?"

"What the hell—go ahead. I saw you that day but wasn't there for all of it. And since I'm the one always doin' the talking, I'd like to see it through your eyes."

Hiring On

"I woke that morning to a light tapping sound that I couldn't quite place. I knew it wasn't a car in the street—those sounds don't carry all the way back. Something like the click of the meter through the pipes when Melita takes a shower, but not quite. It was a different sound, one that took me back somewhere in memory, to Spring in New England, when I was a kid." Harry looked over at Jake who was trying to conceal his phone, which he was replying to a text message. "A light, misty rain--that doesn't happen here, especially not in the summer. You know, 'It never rains in Southern California—the clouds'll only warn ya.' Soft delicate rains--not exactly SO-Cal style. He rolled out and the minute he twisted the control stick on the blinds, I was transported to a different time and place."

Harry cleared his throat as a subtle way to let Jake know he wanted his attention. "It was mesmerizing, and it really was rain. But I wondered at first if it was a bad omen, you know, coming on the day of my interview. I knew Phil-the-mill Bradshaw was a cousin to my former friend John, but I had no idea how close, I mean, bein' on opposite edges of the country. I was up way earlier than I needed to be—maybe the drizzle sounds. The old guy I rented the house from would have called it 'channel fever.' Bill Nelson, the retired judge, he'd spent some time in the Navy. Most guys around here have done the same. Most old guys anyway. You know what the expression means, don't you?" Harry paused and looked at Jake.

Jake had just placed his phone back into his jacket pocket.

"Yeah, when the ship's been out on WestPac for six or eight months, the guys get pretty anxious for some good home-port nookie."

"When they pull into that channel, there between Pt. Loma and North Island, all those sailors, with their crisp white uniforms coverin' up their hard-ons, they line the rail lookin' for girlfriends or wives and kids in the mosh-pit of people and news cameras."

"I was never a sailor," Harry went on, "but I could imagine what they felt, and I had that stomach-churning sensation about a meeting that would dictate the direction of my future. I went out and stood in the yard till I was soaked. There I was in my plaid boxers in the middle of an impressionist painting where the artist ran out of every color but green. I didn't take it as a bad sign. Besides, I'd just talked to my mother and she didn't just think--she knew--that I would be hired. I felt so good out there in my very private yard, I took a piss right where I was. Must have looked like one of those Greek cherub statues."

"Okay, I got the picture. That may be more information than I need." Jake being Jake gave Harry a big ole grin.

Harry continued on. "So off I go into the cold cruel world, armed with the map Phil drew for me when I met up with him earlier, and my trusty Thomas Brothers. Still have that map. I can still smell the oiled wood of Phil's lobby area, combined with my breath mint and that woman's—the secretary's--perfume. I noticed there were lots of windows, all frosted— no looking out to daydream."

"And no one looking in, either."

"I was sitting there waiting in one of those leather chairs with the brass nail-heads all over them, staring at the round table with magazines arranged in a neat circle and memorizing the leaf design of the carpet. As I recall, it was neutral and soothing, but I wasn't feeling soothed. Was it like that when you interviewed?" Harry asked Jake.

"No, not quite. Some day I'll tell you why."

"Phillip Bradshaw came through the door like a racehorse when the gate opens. I noticed his silver hair first, of course—no thinning or receding.

He looked too young and in shape to have hair that color. I stood to shake his hand, but it was awkward. He just said, 'No, sit,' like he was talking to a dog. He gave me this thick folder, about SCABS. He said he wasn't quite ready but I was glad—it gave me a chance to cram for the test."

"You were on that thing like stink on shit the minute he left." "No shit—you were watchin' me?"

"Me and my p......Phil, yeah, we had the camera on--that was the plan. Phil saw it as a gamble—he hoped John really knew what he was talking about when he said how great you were, and that it wasn't just his guilty conscience talking."

"What the f--? You both know about my friend John, bein' with Lara? I'm not even s'posed to know about that."

"I didn't know you did. Guilty conscience could have been about anything. I'm sure there are a lot of details I don't know."

"I wasn't a dirty cop, not then anyway, and I didn't cheat on Lara, not technically. Someday maybe we'll talk about that too. So, now some things are starting to make sense. I remember you were in Phil's office when he called me in. He introduced us, said we might be partners if it worked out. Then you left. Things working out wasn't up to him, he said. Abe, the director, made that call. Something went on with Abe. Something crazy. But first Phil told me that guys usually work in pairs or have back-up nearby, that our pay is hourly, that there were no women agents on the force."

"None then. Only two now," Jake clarified. "Not because we discourage them, just none that want to work for us, I guess. None that are qualified. We have to borrow them occasionally from other departments."

"He said if I got hired, not to ever piss Abe off or get on his bad side. Then he looked around like he was in a spy movie and handed me the forms,"

Harry turned his head. "He said to pay attention to the yellow sticky notes. I was sweating like the quarry in a greased-pig-catching contest."

"Do pigs sweat?"

"This one did. I started to feel foolish for even trying, what with an eight-year gap and a few other deficiencies. How could I hope they wouldn't check with Dover, or that the record there would conveniently not mention my last week of work. You knew about that, didn't you?"

Jake remained silent.

"The first sticky was under 'special skills,' specifically languages. I had plenty of skills, but I didn't even speak English right, according to everybody in California."

"Phil doesn't either."

"Phil's kept his accent. Cultivated it, even, I think. He can get away with it—people see it as cute. I decided to lose mine. Back then, the only words of Spanish I knew were si and no, adios, amigo and senorita. The note said to put 'English, some Spanish. Currently studying to improve foreign-language skills' on that line, and I did. Close to the truth, I guess. Under 'reason for leaving my most recent job,' another note said to put 'Cultural—desire to learn more about the world by moving to a new environment while still young enough to benefit from the experience.' It was better than anything I could have come up with, so I used it verbatim.

I rubbed the notes with a moistened finger and crumpled them into my sock. Phil said he'd add his comments, and next thing I know I was in Abe's plush office."

"How'd that go?"

"I suspect you already know. First he told me to relax, said he noted that my father and grandfather were both cops. I told him 'yes, sir' and he said, 'call me Abe, Harold.' Guess what I answered?"

"Yes, sir, Abe?"

"You got it. He said I sounded like I was at boot camp, then he said there was no problem with my credentials at Dover, that I was their golden boy. You coulda' knocked me over with a feather. Then the real shocker, he said, 'We do have this inconvenient time gap. Phillip Bradshaw says you were assisting your sister in Texas during a long illness".

"Where did that shit come from, I wondered?" "Yeah, I lived in Texas. Yeah, I got a sister, but we're not that close. And she lives in Florida. I went along with it, needless to say, but I wasn't very happy with Phil for throwing that one in with no warning."

"It was the best we could come up with. Got you hired, didn't it?"

Harry nodded, but had barely heard the question. "Tell me about this 'we'."

Jake chuckled. "I went into Phil's office again right after he walked you over to meet Abe. I pulled out a little machine the size of a cell phone and Phil turned white. He said, 'Oh, Jesus, Jake, please tell me that's not what I think it is—you haven't bugged Abe's office, have you? You're going to get both of us fired."

"Did you bug it?" "Hell, no. I told Phil I might have accidentally given you the wrong 'good-luck' pen. The one I still had in my pocket wasn't the one with a miniature recorder-transmitter."

"My God, Jake, what if Abe checked out that pen?" Phil had asked.

"I doubt if he'da been able to tell. And it was programmed to self-delete. But, shoot, I was young then. Brash and impulsive, that's what Phil called it. Guess I could add arrogant."

"That sounds pretty personal, what Phil said."

"That's not the half of it. Harry, I shouldn't be telling you this—it's my neck in a noose if you ever let on--but you've saved my butt a few times. I grew up without a dad. My mom divorced him when I was four 'cause he was a binge drinker. He'd get violent with her sometimes. She was pretty devout in her religion, and divorce was a big sin, but she said it would be worse for me to grow up with that as my example of how to treat women. As a side benefit, she stopped getting hit. But she couldn't re-marry or she'd be ex-communicated."

"Did you ever see him?"

"A few times, till I was about eight. Then he just kinda drifted away."

"Must have sucked to not have a father. Do you know where he is now?"

"I heard he got sober. His new wife got him into rehab. I hope he's happy." "So your mom raised you by herself?"

"No, she met Phil, and she left the church."

"My God. Are you saying Phil is your step-dad?"

Jake laughed again, a self-conscious chuckle. "Called him Pop once, right in his own office. It was after he interviewed you. I said it

was too bad about the stuff on your record. The stuff I had to clear up. I said hacking wasn't as easy as it used to be, that I had taken care of it, but that it was a hassle, and then I said, 'You owe me big, Pop.'"

"Wow." Harry took a few seconds to absorb this news. "How did he react?"

"He gave me one of his lectures: 'Jacob, you're being careless and dangerous. I know this is a secure room, but you start calling me that here, you might slip up and say it sometime in front of someone. It might not be taken well if people knew. There's no reason anyone should know unless one of us screws up.' I was offended—told him I wasn't a screw-up. I must've sounded like a ten-year-old kid, but he softened. I still remember the words, "No, you're not. I'm just sayin,' better to be extra careful in this matter, especially with the way you stuck your neck out for me on this one. And, yes, I do owe you.' I think he took a risk helping you get hired because he thought your maturity would help me. Remember when he introduced us?"

"Yeah, he called you over. Called you Jacob, and introduced me as the candidate you 'took a special interest in.' Now I know what he meant. He called me Harold S. Dugan, and I said no one ever called me Harold S. except my mom, and then only when she was pretty pissed."

Both men laughed again, as they had six years earlier.

The agents stretched, put on their vests and shirts and headed toward their trucks. On the way, Jake said, "That part about your sister. Abe needed an explanation— something that would fly. Of course, we couldn't tell you ahead of time; we didn't know you at all. But there was another reason—I guess you'd call it a test. Phil wanted to know how good you were at thinking on your feet, manufacturing solutions on

the spot. He was pretty thrilled when Abe said, 'Well, kid, give me the details,' and you came up with a gem."

"You mean, 'You know, Abe, I wish I could but my sister is--was a very private person. When she--just before--you know, she made me promise not to talk to anyone about her situation. Not made me, but asked me to.'"

"You said you never did find out why it was so important to her, but that you gave her your word and your word was more important than anything, even the job."

"You laid it on thick."

"I had nothing to lose. I had a mentor once, who said the best way to conduct yourself in life is never to lie. But if you ever have to, make sure the reason is valid, and make damn sure you do it well. I was fine with it. Just before I got up to leave, when I said I'd been a good cop and could be again, that if he hired me he wouldn't be sorry, I was looking him straight in the eye, leaning toward him. God, I hope that was the truth."

Jake smiled. "It was."

They started to go separate directions, but Harry turned around and moved close. "One more thing, Jake."

"Shoot, partner. We're in a safe place."

"There is no deck. You knew that, no doubt. The guy who gave me the money isn't a contractor, he's a coyote—the one who got away when we stopped the flower-delivery van."

Jake jumped. "I knew it. I knew I'd seen him, even though he tried pretty hard to keep his face hidden from me. So, are you sayin' him getting' away was no accident?"

"No, I'm not sayin' that. I wasn't cutting him loose, not consciously anyway. But there was something in that look he gave me, something that froze me in my tracks for a split second. And then all hell broke loose."

"So how did you hook up with him?"

"He found me. I still don't know how, but I doubt if it was accidental.

I was in Hookey's, the local watering hole, winding down the evening with a shot of Scotch, and he slid onto the stool beside me. Took some guts on his part, I'd say. I was still in my work uniform. He asked if I remembered him. He was familiar, but while I was trying to figure it out he told me. He said he had looked into my eyes when he got out of the van and saw compassion there. I never would have used that word for me, but I guess he knew me better than I knew myself."

Harry thought about the word compassion.

"It wasn't that way at first," he went on. "When I came to this job, I was gung ho, 100%. Catch all them dirty wetbacks, lock 'em up and throw away the key. Or at least throw them back into Mexico. Then two things happened—two ordinary things. First, there was this guy who painted the house I'm renting, the exterior. I watched him and his small crew, and I knew how much the judge paid him, which amounted to about minimum wage for him and a little less for the others, when you broke it down. They did a good job. The guy was Mexican. He came back a couple months later and asked for Mr. Nelson, so I called him. The judge drove right out, and the guy, Juan, asked if he could borrow some money. He said he needed it to pay the guide to get his cousin across the border. Said he'd saved twenty-five hundred dollars and needed seven hundred more, that he would pay it back in two weeks. Damned if the judge didn't just reach in his pocket, without a single question and hand the guy seven hundred dollars. And what's really crazy--he got it back on time." Jake listened patiently and nodded his head.

"The other thing happened about a year ago, Harry went on. Melli had accepted, with my approval, some white chickens from a neighbor. Silly-looking things with soft feathers and furry feet. Silkies. They're very docile and the neighbor's other chickens were picking on them until one got injured. We already had some nice pens not being used, and I got to enjoy the clucking sound and the idea of fresh eggs. But one turned out to be a rooster, and they love to brood, so we ended up with chicks that grew up. Then one day this guy was working in the canyon, on the neighbor's side of the fence. Late June, about 98 degrees, and he was cuttin' tall dry weeds with a scythe in the middle of the day. Almost certainly undocumented. Melli was feeding the chickens and this worker came to the fence and called to her—she didn't know I was listening. She went to the fence. With some hand gestures and a few English words, he asked if he could buy a couple chickens for three dollars each. She didn't flinch, just asked if he wanted hens or roosters. When he said it didn't matter, it seemed like it must be for food, but that was as much as he'd pay in a store for a plucked one, so maybe not. She put one of each in a box and threw in some food and met him by the street. She said he could have 'em, but he wouldn't accept that—he made her take the six dollars."

Harry drew circles in the dust with the toe of his boot. Jake remained silent but didn't move away, so Harry kept talking: "Maybe along the way, I have developed compassion. El Coyote paid for our drinks and asked me to come to his car with him. In the yellowish gleam of the street-lamp, I saw two people, a middle-aged guy in back and an old woman in front. El Coyote said something in Spanish and the guy got out. He was about thirty, name was Rigoberto. We shook hands. El Coyote

told me how Rigoberto had saved for almost a year, when he first found out his mother had cancer, so he could come here and get her. She got a green- card back when they were more generous, worked here many years, the "guide" told me. He spoke excellent English and looked right at me. 'She sent money back to her parents who were caring for her kids while the dad worked in a mequiladora near the Arizona border. Enough money, between both parents for them to eat and go to school. Kids grew up but couldn't get work visas. When Mama got too sick to work, the family she cleaned for took her to a hospital here and got her signed up, some way. She was there several months. Now she's ready to die and Rigoberto has taken her from the hospital. She can't travel alone, of course. We'll go back in my car, to the town in Sonora where the family is, so she can be with them for her last days.' Then he put the first envelope in my hand and said, 'I know you're a good person— maybe if you see someone out there who looks like me, you'll know he's also a good person, too, and let him do his work.'"

"I just gave him a touch on the shoulder and walked away so he wouldn't see my face. That first envelope had two hundred dollars in it. I started a fund, which I use only to help people who need it more than I do. That's what I gave to Elena."

"Have you seen the Coyote since? Out on The Edge, I mean?" "Couple times."

There was another period of silence, then "Harry?" "Yeah."

"I came out here not just to give your C-note back, but to tell you that I was thinking about asking for another partner."

"Understandable. What happened? Change your mind?"

"I saw something in your eyes when you came down off that hill. Same thing you saw in Rigoberto's, maybe. Or El Coyote's. I guess I got compassion, too."

"Shit, man," said Harry with a half-smile, "what's happening to us?

"I dunno. I guess we're just regular people, after all."

Lady's Choice

Harry pulled his car into his usual parking spot, on the left half of the driveway, his body still vibrating with that other-worldly feeling that sometimes accompanies tense situations. His day had started here, then taken him to the SCABS compound, then to the inner drama of his thoughts. There had been the cool of the swimming hole and the warmth of true friendship radiating through a heavy conversation. What felt like a week's worth of ups and downs had taken place in less time than a normal day's work. He should have been past the point of exhaustion, considering all the emotional strain, but he didn't feel tired. He was running on nervous energy.

It was comforting to see Melli's car parked in its spot, next to his, and it was an even more pleasant feeling when he heard her familiar knock at his front door twenty minutes later.

"Thought you might like to celebrate with me, she said, holding a towel in one hand, and in the other a bottle of inexpensive champagne.

"I'm always up for a toast," he responded, feeling grateful to have such a nice young woman for a neighbor and a friend. "What's the special occasion?"

"Well, you might have noticed that I've been on the missing persons' list," she began. "I've been hiding out in my cave with my nose in the laptop."

"I thought I'd seen a little less of you," Harry answered, choosing his words carefully, for he seldom paid much attention to Melli's exact whereabouts.

"I was showing up at work, of course, but I didn't want to do any field trips or personal stuff until I had finished writing and submitted my grant request. Got it in on time, just barely. That was two weeks ago. Just got notified today that they've agreed to fund it. I'm a happy camper. Since my work on the campus is part time, I need to get paid for my research in order to live the lifestyle to which I've accustomed myself. This will keep me going for two years at least."

Harry nodded, not fully understanding the complicated world of academics, but glad he didn't have to renew his contract every year or two. And glad nobody graded his written reports.

He got two glasses from the cupboard and put them on a small tray. "Back in a minute," he said, and went to dig out his bathing trunks and a towel. A few minutes later, 103-degree water swirled, glasses clinked, and Harry, with very little embarrassment, told Melli about his skinny-dipping experience in the rugged high desert. "Earlier today, butt naked in a pristine pool, and now sipping champagne in a hot tub with a beautiful woman much too young for me--I guess today my life is about as decadent as you can get."

"No, not quite," Melli said.

"What do you mean?"

"This is as decadent as you can get," she said, as she placed both hands at the center of her chest and loosened her bikini top. Shrugging first one shoulder and then the other, and without taking her eyes off him, she exposed the two most beautiful breasts Harry had ever seen. It could have been the light from the newly-risen moon on her wet skin, or the vibrating excitement of the day he was still carrying, almost like an electrical charge from the psychological roller coaster of events. But secretly he knew it was neither. Beauty may indeed be in the eye of the beholder, and context may have played a part, but the sight Harry beheld was the loveliest he could recall in his entire life. Perhaps just a bit smaller than average, and perfectly natural, Melli's delicate breasts, now presented for his visual enjoyment, were a gift from the gods. No breasts, unless they were sculpted on a statue of Venus, could be more perfectly formed, more gloriously exquisite.

Harry sat motionless, stunned, like a wild animal in the sudden glare of headlights. While he wondered what, if anything, he should do, she leaned forward, allowing her smiling lips to brush his. She glanced away, then back toward him.

"If you're not interested, that's okay," she said. "I won't be offended. No questions. We'll just pretend this never happened." Her right hand moved under water, searching, and she brought her bathing suit top to the surface in front of her.

"No, no, don't do that." He reached gently for the soggy piece of cloth in her hand, placed it on the tray next to his glass, and wrapped his arms around her, lifting her gleaming form out of the water and onto the smooth cedar slatted deck that wrapped itself around two sides of the square tub. He was appreciative of the delightful, and delighted, woman who was sharing herself with him, and thankful for the solid wall of the house behind them to muffle their sounds of pleasure. The day that he had thought, for a fleeting moment, might have been his last became the longest and most memorable of his life.

All the next week, Harry was so unbearably cheerful that Jake was finally able to figure out what was going on.

"It's not 'going on,'" Harry insisted. "It happened. Once. It may never happen again. It was just some kind of confluence of our moods or some--"

"Harmonic convergence?" Jake asked with a wry smile.

"Happy coincidence is more like it. Just a nice moment. Maybe it will happen again. I hope it does."

"Whether it does or doesn't makes no difference to me," Jake said, "but it seems you are much in demand by the fairer sex these days."

"What do you mean?"

"This morning Trish asked if I would arrange for her to have a private audience with you."

"With me? Do you know why?"

"I have no idea. She won't say. But I'm fairly certain she doesn't have the same thing in mind that Melli did. She's strictly business."

"That's a relief. I mean, well, Trish is an attractive woman, but she's your attractive woman. How do you feel about us having this talk?"

"Sure. I trust her." Harry thought Jake answered too firmly, too quickly. But he knew that he wasn't Trish's type, and visa versa.

"Well, if it's important to her and you have no objections--." "Good. Tomorrow's Saturday. Can you be at the Golden Pheasant

Coffee Shop on El Cajon Boulevard at 10:00 am?" "Yeah, I guess so." "Good, that's settled. Now, let's get to work."

The next morning Harry was a few minutes early, as was his habit. At precisely twelve minutes after ten, Trish came in, looking just a bit less than crisp—a wisp of hair out of place, the buttons on her blouse not quite centered. Harry had only met her a few times in passing, but heard her name almost every day and felt like he knew her pretty well.

Certainly he had no trouble recognizing her. She was vibrant and bubbly, chatting before he pulled a chair out for her, sort of a mild apology, more like an explanation for her tardiness. Something about rearranging her schedule and having to look for a parking place on the street.

"I'm glad you picked a booth in the back," she started as soon as she was seated. "This is something I've been wanting to--something that has been bothering me for quite a while. I just, you know, I feel so bad for her."

"Who?"

"Maria, my best girlfriend. We've known each other for years, since I was barely out of my teens and we were both waitressing at the Charter Club. I was her maid of honor at her wedding. I doubt if I'll ever be able to return that favor." A hint of bitterness chilled her voice, then it went right back to cheerful. Harry couldn't help thinking Trish looked and sounded as if she were now just out of her teens.

"See, she's a really nice person, got a heart of gold and works hard, and she's a wonderful mother, probably better than I could be."

"But?"

"But, she's got this problem." She looked around with narrowed eyes, fidgeted a little. "I prob'ly shouldn't be telling anybody, especially someone like you." Harry wondered what that remark meant. "But it's killing her. Well, not killing, you know what I mean, like it's driving her crazy. She can't ever relax—never knows if this could be the day her world crashes around her. I'm her best friend, I gotta help, right?"

"Help her with what, Trish?"

"It's not her fault, really. All she wanted was a better life—she was the third oldest and her parents were having a hard time just to make ends meet and feed the little ones. The bigger kids found their own way out, one way or another. They lived in a colonia east of Tijuana. The man, the guide, he said he could promise her a job, and she would have a permit and there would be good pay to send home and plenty of food to eat."

"So she came into the country illegally? When was that?"

"In 1998—she was sixteen. But she thought it was legal—that's what she was told. The man took advantage of her. Now, she should be able to get her citizenship. She has an American husband. Even the family she works for will help. But no, she still can't get her documents."

"Because she came in without papers?"

"No.""She doesn't have enough money for the fees? Maybe I--."

"It's not that. They're not wealthy, of course, but they could come up with it. And they would. Honestly, Harry, I don't think she'd take any money from you."

"You're holding back something. What is it, Trish? I can't do anything unless I know."

"Something bad that happened to her. It's not her fault, but she got in trouble. I think she should be the one to tell you. Will you talk to her?"

"Well, I don't know how I could help."

"And you have to promise not to turn her in. Cross your heart and swear to me." "I don't know, Trish; these things get complicated."

"That's just the point. She's worked so hard, does so much for others, and she can't live her life in peace. At any minute they could jump on her like vultures and take her away from her two children. They're not even teenagers yet. Please, Mr. Dugan, you have to help. I can bring her to you now."

"Bring her? Is she here?"

"She's in a stall in the ladies' bathroom. Please, will you talk to her? And promise not to get her in trouble, even if you do nothing to help?"

Reluctantly, Harry agreed. Trish brought the woman, who looked younger than her age. She was 31, if he heard right. Then Trish said to her friend. "He promised. I'll wait outside."

Their waitress appeared and hovered a minute, to see if the new diner wished to order. Harry saw Maria's face about to crumple and waved the server away. Maria started speaking in awkward bursts. Her English was passable but not smooth. Most likely she had learned from her kids.

"All I want is to live in peace, here, with my family. I did nothing bad, Mr. Harry, but they say I am bad woman. They will put me in jail or send me away—away from Carmen and Jose--and mi espousa, my Victor, my love. Please, senor, I am not a whore. I had no choice. I was sixteen years, barely a woman.

"Not yet a woman, according to our law."

"He found me a job as a maid in a dirty hotel. But he made me do things--woman things--with him, and with his friends. The man who said he would help, would get me a new life, a good life. That is why I don't believe anyone who says he will help. This man came to our house in Mexico; he made promises. Good things for me and my family. I had some money my parents didn't know about. I could not tell them because it was from begging. From taking my brothers---one was a baby. I went to touristos and said our parents were killed on a bus. Yes, I lied. I was a child then, and I wanted to help, to buy food and clothes for the little boys. Instead, I gave the money to that awful man, Pedro, and he made me do things, and when I ran away he found me, and he beat me."

She had started slowly but now her sentences rushed at him like a runaway train. "When my bruises healed, he gave me a green card and took me to a place, a place of whores, and the police came. They did not send me back, because the card in my purse, they thought it was real. Maybe it was. They let me keep it, and they said I had to promise not to be a whore. I tried to tell them, but Pedro and his friend, they say I was whore, that they owned the building where police came, that they saw me take money. The judge said I could get out of jail. I was there four days. He said if I do anything bad again, he will make me stay in jail long time."

"You were sixteen?"

"Si, but papers say eighteen."

"Trish says you are legally married?"

"Si. To Victor, we met when I worked at the club. It was restaurant, but name is club. I used a card Pedro gave me and I got job—I could not go back to that awful place with Pedro. Thank God, he left me alone after that."

"How'd you get the waitress job?"

"I was in front of courthouse, sitting on bench, too sad to cry. That's when a lady came and sat with me. Nancy Webber. She had parking tickets, she said. She asked why I sad, I say no job. I say I need work and I show her my papers. She say she is manager of a place, Charter Club, a nice place, I learn. Too nice for me. I don't know how to be waitress, but Miss Webber, she is kind. And Trish, she is there and she take time after her shift to help, to teach. I am very lucky. Work five years, even though the card I had, the date is passed. No one ever asks. Never see Pedro again. But I meet Victor. He is from Espain, but citizen in U.S. He treats me nice and takes me to meet his parents, then we get married.

Trish, she help me, many ways. Always my friend. She is Godmother to Carmen and Jose."

"Have you ever tried to get your citizenship?"

"Si. Trish ask Jake and he saw my record, says I have conviction, I am criminal, so I no can get papers. But this man who works downtown, he is like a lawyer, very good, they say, but I keep giving him more money. We are not rich, and it costs so much—I want to give him more, but by now, should be enough. I work again, because my ninos are in eschool. For a family in Rancho Bernardo, I work, cleaning. I take the bus. But we do not have as much as El Gato wants. Victor, he is a driver for take people to doctor, his job good but not much pay. I wish someone could make El Gato Grande give me what he promises. Trish says maybe you help."

Harry tried not to appear startled when he heard the familiar name. "Maybe, just maybe, I can, but you have to help, too, and be brave. I have friends. I have ways to clear your record, but you have to do something for me, for you, and for other people like you." Harry was already feeling pangs of regret for what he was about to propose, or more accurately, for doing it without consulting his superiors, who most likely would be able to be convinced. But there was something about the timing, the momentum, and his imperative need to get El Gato into jail. Not that it would make Elena any safer, but it sure would make him feel a vindictive sense of satisfaction to nail the bastard.

"What you want me to do? If I help, the judge he will know I no have documents; he'll send me back, won't he?"

"I think I can prevent that."

"Can you promise?"

"I promise I'll do everything I can, and I have a strong feeling it can work. What I will promise is that El Gato will not get your papers, ever. He is a sly fox and a liar."

"You know El Gato!"

"Yes, I know what he does, and I've met him. He's a bad man but he's a coward, too, so you can help us catch him and put him in jail."

"Will I be in danger?"

"Not much. Leonardo Delgato is so arrogant, so sure of himself, he chooses only people who are vulnerable. You know what that means?"

"I think so. We have much to lose, we want to believe, so we make it easier for him to lie."

"Maria, you are one of the smartest women I've known." "So what would I have to do?"

"You would visit El Gato again and give him some money." He handed her one hundred dollars. Tell him that's all you have now but you will get more. Ask him to tell you again what he will do for you, and how much more you must pay. He'll probably answer you because it's just more lies. You would carry, in your brassier, a small recorder. You know El Gato. Do you think he would ever reach under your shirt to look for a recorder?"

Maria's eyes dropped, looking into her lap where she twisted a cloth napkin in both hands. The lids fluttered, then she spoke. "It would never cross that man's mind to think I might do such a thing. I agree with you. I would be safe. But anyway, I want Victor to know."

"That's all right. Tell Victor, but no one else. You must give me your word on this. If you do this for me, I'll do all I can to help you and I think your chances are very good. As a bonus, we will keep many people from being hurt by this devious, greedy pig. Can you meet me here Monday at nine am?"

Maria nodded, "Si. I don't work Monday." Then she continued in a whisper. "Pedro raped me, and the others raped me. If I didn't want to do it, it was rape, wasn't it?" Her eyes pleaded for an answer.

"As surely as if he had a gun to your head," Harry said.

Maria took his hand in both of hers--he was afraid she was going to kneel--and spoke mostly in Spanish with "bless you" and "God be with us" coming through every few words.

Harry stood, "Do you need a ride home?"

"No, I can walk from here. That is why we chose this place. I must go now and pray."

Outside, Harry wasn't sure whether he would see Trish, but there she was, about twenty feet away, leaning against a white sedan. He walked over.

"So, do you see what I mean?" she asked.

"Yes, and I learned something important today, about an old friend." He said the word with a sneer but added "enemy, actually" just in case. "Trish,

I must confess, when you asked to meet me, I thought it would be about something else."

"Jake's drinking?"

"So, you feel there's a problem?" Harry asked.

"I don't know what to do about it." Her lip trembled, almost imperceptibly. "I know sometimes he drinks too much, but not always. I don't think he's an alcoholic. I went to one of those meetings once. Al-Anon. Don't tell Jake that, whatever you do. I mean, he never hits me, and well, I really believe in us—our relationship. I just wish there was someone I could talk to about it. I don't want to get him I trouble. Like, his job is everything to him, and he's so good at it."

"Trish, you have my word anything you said or say will be held in strict confidence. There are probably people, professionals, that you could talk to anonymously, but honestly, that doesn't always mean things will improve."

"I guess I've sort of made peace with it. The situation could be worse."

Harry hesitated, not sure whether it was a good idea, but offered: "If you need or want someone to talk to that knows him, I'm a decent listener. Not good at much else, but--."

"Thanks. I know your intentions are honorable, but I'm just not sure how Jake would feel, and I respect his feelings more than I need relief."

Harry wanted to add that it might be time for someone to help, to intervene, but wasn't sure himself if it was to that point, and he sensed he should leave things just as they were. He gave Trish a stiff hug, then, holding onto her shoulders as if she were the daughter he'd never had, he said, "I learned something else today, Trish. You're a very grounded, caring person and the most loyal of friends. You can be proud of that."

Disappearing Angel

Harry and Jake had just got their marching orders from Phil, and as Harry had been hoping, there was some leeway at the beginning of their shift.

"Cup of coffee?" Harry asked.

"Sure, I wanted to see how it went yesterday with Trish." As soon as they were seated in the air-conditioned break room, steaming cups of brew between cupped hands, Jake said, "So."

"So, I found out it's about her girlfriend."

"That would be Maria. She has a record and can't get her papers, but I don't think it's Trish's duty to help her."

"Apparently Trish wants to help her. And, crazy as it sounds, I want to help her. But there's another angle, and maybe that's the only reason for my generosity. We got a chance, a real good one, to put away El Gato."

"No shit? Tell me."

"I talked to Maria, too. She's been victimized repeatedly—paid money she was saving for her family's needs to come across the border, thinking it was for a legal job, then was raped and forced into prostitution. Got away from it early, thank God. The arrest and conviction might have been a frame-up by her coyote-pimp, retribution for her running away. She was sixteen, for God's sake."

"Wow. Trish never told me all that."

"Maybe she thought you didn't want to know." "I guess that's possible."

"She cares a lot about you, Jake. You're lucky to have her. She wouldn't do anything to jeopardize your work."

"But you might?"

"No way, partner. Maria's going to do it for us--help us set up the fat cat. After that, seems like they'd be willing to offer her a get-out-of-jail-free card. It's the least they could do."

"Maybe so, but no guarantees."

"Yeah, tell me about it. Sometimes I think the courthouse downtown should be called the 'Hall of Injustice.'"

"You gonna bring this up to the big shots, get it official?"

"I don't think there's time for that. We gotta strike while the iron's hot."

"You're kinda goin out on a limb, aren't you?" "Maybe just a little."

"That's an understatement. But it's your party. There's one thing I can do, now that you paint me a better picture, Harry. And I think I should--make it go away, her conviction. Wouldn't be the first time, you know. You're pretty sure she's telling the truth?"

"Not a doubt in my mind. And that woman of yours would have figured it out if Maria was putting on a show. She's pretty astute."

"Yeah, the bimbo thing is a bit of an act—for me I think." "Speaking of acting, I've got a favor to ask of you."

"Seems like you've got a whole pocketful of them. What now?"

"Well, this El Gato thing has got me thinking—about another of his victims."

"Elena, right? I don't think you ever stopped thinking about her." "It's been over a month now since I've seen her, or heard anything,

and it's driving me crazy."

"If The Shrimp did anything to harm her, you'd have known about her. I'm pretty sure he's moved on. You need to let it go."

"It will be easier to let go if I just get a sense that she's all right. I borrowed Melli's car today; I thought maybe we could just do a drive-by look. Not even slow down. We'd have to make sure he didn't know it was me."

"And just how do you plan to go about that?"

"Well, I thought if we approached from the north, and you were driving. I'd be on the other side, slumped down a little, with a different hat on, you know, in case they have a camera pointed at the street."

"And they wouldn't be looking for me."

"Well, probably not. It seemed to be me they were focusing on, so I don't think you showed up on the earlier film. But just in case, I brought a little something."

"I don't know."

A few minutes later they approached Melli's car, a hybrid, and Harry pulled a bag off the passenger seat before he sat in it. Jake settled in and asked, "Okay, so what's in the bag?"

Harry pulled out a well-used Texas-style cowboy hat, one neither he nor Jake would be caught dead in under normal circumstances.

"Jesus Harry!" Jake hissed through his teeth---what do you think this is, Halloween?"

"Not yet." Harry pulled one other item out of the bag and said, "Now it is." He held out a fairly good quality fake mustache.

Jake chuckled and took the disguise, holding it as if it were a tarantula and muttered something about what some people will do for their friends. "How do you put one of these things on?"

The light-hearted mood subsided the minute they approached the grocery on their right. Things were different, barrels on the front porch entry area had been moved, signs were not where they had been before.

A new poster was taped to the inside of the window, on a diagonal slant, near the entrance: "Under New Management." Jake's gaze went immediately, and discreetly, to the places he knew the cameras had been set up. Thank goodness, they were still in place, wide-angle lenses focused in both directions, on two poles at the street, giving a pretty good overall view of the front of the store, as well as recording any traffic, vehicular or pedestrian.

Jake saw his partner's body go slack, like one of those old-time string puppet figures that dropped into a pile of parts when you pressed a button underneath it, then had the miraculous ability to stand up again with another touch. Harry hunched down in the seat, wearing a cloth roll-up type fisherman's hat with an old Padres team logo, and what you could see of his face showed only fear.

"Harry, it's probably a good sign," Jake managed. "You know the brother-in-law got citizenship, and he was pretty well set financially. Maybe he bought them a new store in a better area."

"Yeah, or maybe--" He couldn't bring himself to say out loud the horrible thing he visualized.

"We better get back to the compound asap." "Why, do you think El Cameron has made us?"

"Not a chance. I'm worried some of our own guys might see us and have us both committed over at Mesa Vista."

Harry had to smile despite his concern. Neither said anything further on the twenty-minute trip back to the parking lot at the compound. They sat in the car a minute after it was turned off, feeling the oppressive heat start to creep in.

Before he opened the door, Jake found a switch to roll both front windows down part way. "Hey, new guy, I got something I gotta tell you. Two things. About the day I went over and babysat Elena."

"Okay, go ahead."

"Well, you know there was a crew there pretending to fix the plumbing--actually fixing the plumbing. But that's not all they were doing."

"I know, they were protecting her and watching El Camaron's parking lot." "And one more thing."

"What else?"

"They were setting up cameras, good ones but tiny. They're still there, I checked." "You could see them when we drove by?"

"Only because I knew what to look for. They're wide-angle and well-camouflaged; they'd probably show everything that went on near the front of the store the past month."

Harry perked up. "Jake, is there any way you could look at those tapes?"

"There may be."

"Now? Let's go. What's the second thing?"

"Uh, yeah. That day, before I left, right after Elena tried to give me the money back, I-- well, I guess I wanted Elena to be safe as much as you did. Now, I want you to swear, you never heard this from me.

Harry was intrigued. "Okay, you got it."

"I had a piece on me, a drop gun. I picked it up when I grabbed those two drug runners in El Cameron's van. I wasn't gonna tell anybody.

But, you know, it can come in handy sometimes, to have one that can't be traced to you."

"What happened? You lose it? Did you have to use it? Oh, God, I think I know."

"No and no. What I did, you probably guessed, was to give it to Elena. I made sure she knew how to use it and told her to keep it on her all the time. It could buy her safety or at least a few minutes, if things got really gnarly."

"Um, well I guess that's a good thing. Thanks." "Thanks?" "Thanks for caring about her and thanks for telling me."

"Yeah, now let's get outta here—it's hot as hell. I'm gonna see if I can get some resolution to this thing that's drivin' you bananas, so maybe you can get your mind on your work, or at least on some other woman."

"What are you planning?"

"You're gonna' get a computer skills update—provided Papa Phil doesn't ask too many questions."

"How is that gonna help?"

"Let me amend that," said Jake. "Provided Phil and you don't ask too many questions. Wait in the lobby while I check."

A few minutes later, Jake appeared at a doorway and motioned to Harry to join him. They went halfway down a hall and took an elevator that Harry didn't even know was there. It wasn't marked as an elevator entrance. The second floor was a maze of wires, neatly arranged in rows on metal grill-work that looked like see-through walls. It was cooler there than the offices, and much cleaner. No carpeting, not a speck of dust anywhere. There was the constant hum of motors running and a slight movement of the air. Harry had never seen so many wires and switches in one place. There were no windows, but good artificial light. The room was probably two thousand square feet. At one end, where Jake led Harry, was a room composed of a half-circle of screens, monitors bigger than most people's television sets, and consoles on a desk of the same shape. It looked like a movie set, the cockpit of the Starship Enterprise or something like that. It was closed off by thick glass panels, one of which was a door. Jake walked up to a sensor at the door and leaned his face near a pad that must have had a reader for his eye. Harry heard a click but the door didn't open. Then Jake took a small item, a flashcard, from the coin pocket on his pants and inserted it just below the pad. Voila, the door moved— not out like most doors, or sliding along the wall like a pocket door, but straight up. It was only then Harry realized how high the ceilings were and saw more bundles of wires.

"Fiber-optics," Jake said simply, when he saw Harry looking. "One the size of a human hair can carry as much info as a thousand copper wires."

"Whew—that's a lot of data."

"Now, turn your head the other way, so you don't figure out what I'm doing and try to hack in here."

Harry laughed, but followed the directions. "It would take years for me to begin to figure this stuff out."

"I guess you're not much of a threat. Now let's sit down and see what happened on Hollister."

"Harry was amazed, and a little relieved, by what he saw on the screens. The pictures were clear, not a trace of fuzziness. The big screens made it easy to spot faces, and a few of them were familiar. Jake slowed the action when appropriate, and he could zoom in to show a close-up of a

button, or anything he chose. The date, camera number, and location were on a bar at the top.

"Well, there's your lady-friend," Jake said, "and she doesn't seem to be under any duress. Her whole family's around in this one; they've all been appearing from time to time. Looks like they're getting things ready to turn the store over and move their personal belongings out of the house. Lucky for us everything has to come out to the street by that dirt driveway. I'd say it's a normal move."

"You don't think they're doing this because he threatened them?" "Look at their body language, Harry, and their faces. These are not

tense people. Yeah, they're working hard, but it's with a sense of accomplishment or anticipation."

"You think they might be going to Mexico?"

"Doubt it. The brother-in- law, Arturo, he just got his official citizenship. Remember, SCABS helped set up the application? Phil says Abe put him on the fast track. That's his truck right there." Jake used a blue laser to point it out on the screen. "A nice new one, local plates."

"Can you read those? Maybe we can track him through the DMV."

"I can read all the letters except the last one. Maybe we could find a clearer view. I don't know anyone at the DMV, and SCABS doesn't

have formal access to its records. You'd probably be best to do it officially, clear it with Phil and maybe Abe. Honestly, if you want my opinion, I think you ought to give it a rest. If he was gonna do anything to hurt her, he'd a' already done it, and we would have heard about it, you can bet on that. No, the shrimp's out in his ocean looking for other fish to fry, if you'll excuse the mixed metaphor."

Just the same, Harry memorized the six digits he saw. His next statement came out like a child's whine:

"But I don't have a way to get in touch with her."

"It's too soon, Harry. She'll reach out to you, I'm sure of it. Just give it some time. She has your card, doesn't she?"

At just that moment in the video Elena appeared. Jake zoomed in as she reached up above the front door, on the inside, and pulled two items down from what must have been a 2 x 4 header. One was a velour bag like some brands of whiskey might be sold in, about the right size for the gun, probably wrapped in cloth of some kind to hide its shape. The other was a wallet-size card, but they saw only the blank backside of it. She slid both items into her handbag without any fuss and left the store, for what turned out to be the last time. That night, at home in his bed, just before he turned out the light, Harry reached over and patted Melli's shoulder. She lay next to him in a slightly curled position, facing him. "I'm so glad to have you here with me for the night," Harry said.

"Me too. I know you're the adventurous type, Harry Dugan, but I don't think we'd have been able to relax very well doing what we just did on my platform."

Harry was in a serious mood, but couldn't help chuckling a little. Melli seemed to have that effect on him. He wasn't quite tired enough for sleep, but didn't want to leave the bed either.

"Mel," he said hesitantly, "how would you feel about talking a little bit?"

Melli rolled onto her back, stretched her arms and wiggled her toes, then rose up against the headboard, tucking a pillow behind her.

She reassured him. "Let a female give you a little lesson in bachelorhood. You pretty much can't ever go wrong with a woman wanting to talk after sex. One of our main complaints is that men don't want to talk. Grunting a few words and rolling over to sleep is about the best we can hope for."

"So, how's the research going?" It was a lame start, but Melli seemed not to notice and started chatting merrily about how ravens had colonized almost everywhere humans lived, but only in the last few decades had found ways to live in true deserts. And then only when humans came every weekend by the droves, and thoughtlessly left garbage for them to feast on. Or for the rats to come after, giving the ravens even more protein. Harry was trying his best to pay attention but his mind kept drifting.

"…..And now the tortoises are endangered. I'm worried."

"What was that about the tortoises, something about dune buggies running over them?" "Yeah, and a more serious threat, the ravens have learned to pick up the young ones." "Don't the shells protect them?

"They used to, till the crow relatives realized they could carry them high in the air and drop them on flat boulders."

"Smart birds."

"They're related to mynah birds, too, you know. Harry?" "Yeah, what?"

"I can tell you've got worries on your mind. Is it something you want to share with me?"

"You're a mind-reader. But what's bothering me isn't something you want me to be sharing with you, trust me."

"Ah, worried about someone of the fairer sex, huh?

Another bachelor hint: talking after sex, good. Talking about another

woman after sex, big no-no."

"That's what I thought."

"But that's most women, Harry. I'm not planting any rose-filled garden and white picket fence here. I'll be your lover and your friend for a while—a long while maybe. If the lover part ends, I'll still be your friend-- unless you marry a jealous woman."

"Like that's ever going to happen."

"I'd like to think we can talk comfortably about any subject, even this. Is the woman you're concerned about in trouble?"

"I don't know. I don't think so, but--." Harry did not finish.

"Is she someone you've been intimate with, if you don't mind

telling me."

"No."

"Only in your fantasies?"

"You know me already, Melli. Or you're really psychic." "Sometimes I wonder. I think we all are, to some extent, if we just

let ourselves go with it. I will at least plead guilty to being pretty intuitive."

"You're tuned in to nature, and to human nature. She is someone I met on one of our jobs, but I can't say too much about that part. She was sort of threatened by one of the bad guys. Now she's moved, and every indication is that it was by choice. I still keep wondering, though."

"Do you think she was forced to move? You're a cop. Can you investigate?"

"I can't go there--or I won't. It could put her in danger. But I have checked out the scene, in a way."

"Are you wondering if she's safe, or are you wondering if she wants to see you?"

"That's a good question. Probably more of the latter, now that you put it that way. Melli hadn't asked the woman's name."

"Harry, I care for you a lot. If I could help you, I would. But I will say that my gut feeling, my psychic feeling, if you want to call it that, is that she's okay and that she will get back to you. Maybe it will take a couple of months. She's probably more worried for you than you are for her, but I believe she's thinking of you. Now it's time to let it go."

"That's what Jake said."

"There's no point in your tearing yourself up about something you can't do anything about. Just stay busy, be positive, and let things happen the way they're meant to. Now, I have one more question for you."

"Go ahead."

"Have you ever made love twice in one night?" "When I was young." "You're still young." She moved closer.

"Melli, are you suggesting--." She answered by parting the hair on his chest with her chin.

A Bad One on the 125

There wasn't anything going on at 5:40 pm on the 125 that demanded Harry's attention. The darkness of an early winter evening had descended on San Diego. There was a fair amount of traffic, but less than normal for the commuter hour, because many people had the day off or left work early. Some were headed to the mall for last-minute shopping— many stores were open until 10:00 pm or even later. Harry and Jake had volunteered to be part of the Christmas Eve skeleton crew for SCABS, because neither of them had families (although Trish might have disagreed). Their shift was set to be from 11 to 11 starting with two hours at the compound, some patrol time, check-in at 6 for another two hours at the desks, then back on the road until quitting time. They would be paid for two full days, but that wasn't the reason they did it.

Almost three months had passed, and Harry had pretty much stopped thinking of Elena, or if he thought about her, he didn't mention it to his partner. The darkness had fallen, but the winter chill in San Diego was a far cry from the three-foot-deep snow Harry used to shovel just to get out of his driveway a lifetime ago. Southern California was a different world from the one Harry had inhabited in his childhood. Christmas was pretty traditional. He thought he really should get in touch with his sister directly, even though his mother kept him posted. It had been a long time since Harry had thought about his family or the rose-covered cottage.

He thought it odd how a certain date could trigger such memories.

"So I guess this is different than New Hampshire on Christmas Eve, huh?" Jake said, by way of breaking the silence.

Apparently he was on the same wavelength.

"Other than thirty degrees colder and three feet of snow to shovel or drive through, Dover isn't much different than here." Harry paused, but when Jake made no answer, he continued, feeling a pang of nostalgia.

"When I was a kid, it was like living in a holiday card, a Currier and Ives scene in real life, back when my dad was still alive and my sister was living at home. Even later in the rose-covered cottage. Of course the roses weren't blooming in the winter—just a bunch of dead-looking canes all over the front of the house, and there was usually lots of snow to wade through and ice on the roads, but it was heaven." His voice trailed off and he focused on the road ahead to keep the sadness from taking hold.

Harry spotted the trouble ahead before any of the drivers around him. It was always his policy to "drive forward," as he called it. He kept his eyes moving, checking as far up the road as possible every few seconds, as well as keeping an eye on the rear-view and side mirrors.

He'd paid attention in all the required driver safety courses and learned his lessons well. He always knew where other cars were, and he made it a personal policy never to be behind a truck or high-profile vehicle. All this, combined with the height of their seats in the big pick-up gave both him and Jake an advantage on the road. They were southbound on the 125, coming up to an area with a wide curve and a slight uphill incline. Most people probably didn't notice it, but there was always a slight fluctuation at this point, an almost imperceptible slowing in the flow of the great freeway snake.

The speed might change only by a few miles per hour, and there was never any apparent reason for it, but Harry knew the simple fact was that some drivers drove for distances with no change in the amount of pressure they put on the accelerator. Maybe they learned to drive in Florida or Nebraska, or somewhere else absolutely flat and devoid of changes in the natural topography, but they tended to go up steep hills at 40 mph and down them at 80. Whatever the reason, it was a freeway fact, and other drivers adjusted for them, usually without noticing or thinking about it. But today, one driver must have been going too fast for the situation, or another too slow, for it was obvious by the way brake lights started to strobe and cars screech and swerve that two of them had come together. The lane cars were jumping out of was the number two, second from the left, so Harry positioned himself in it, turned on his emergency flashers, and slowed to stop a good fifty feet behind the accident scene.

Jake didn't have to ask what was up. He had already grabbed the flasher, positioned it on the roof, and hit the ground running before the truck came to a full stop. Harry launched himself out of the vehicle, lit half a dozen flares and threw a few as far as he could to the rear, on both sides of the affected lane.

Turning his attention forward, even in the jerky light of moving tail lights and distant street lighting, Harry could see that a silver SUV had plowed deep into the back seat of a mini -van. He saw figures moving, including Jake bounding toward the passenger side of the mini-van. Harry could see that one passenger was a man, strong and athletic, probably in his late twenties, pulling the driver out of the minivan and throwing him over one shoulder, then heading directly toward him.

Flames were coming from the place where the vehicles met. About ten feet from him, the exhausted man, probably the driver of the vehicle in back, stooped and laid his burden on the pavement. With first-aid kit in hand, Harry ran the short distance, got the attention of the bigger man, the rescuer, and pointed to a place on the shoulder in front of a road sign. He knew that would be safer.

Harry mouthed the words "over there" and "safer" to the rescuer, as it was impossible to be heard over the din of traffic, screeching brakes and people screaming. Harry also heard a siren in the distance, which gave him some comfort. He grabbed the shoulders, the other man found strength somehow to pick up the legs, and they got the limp form onto the shoulder. The victim was a young Asian male in his late teens. He was unconscious, with blood spurting from a wound on the upper arm, blood that did not appear to be arterial.

They both leaned over the injured person, Harry pressing a clean gauze bandage on the wound. An ambulance pulled up in the northbound lane. "Apply pressure," Harry said, grabbing the man's hand and pulling it toward the bandage. At that time he noticed a strong odor of bourbon whiskey, not from the victim. Over the three-foot-high corrugated metal divider, he got the attention of one of the paramedics, pointing to the victim, then to the cars; immediately after that he sprinted toward the flames. When he got to the passenger door, Jake was banging on the door and window, yelling hoarsely at the jammed car door, "Open, damn it!"

An elderly man sat belted in place, bruised and unconscious but looking peaceful. He wasn't quite dead. Harry saw his chest rise and fall ever so slightly.

Harry also saw flames, too high and too close, and knew they had run out of time.

Instinctively, he was expecting the gas tank to blow sky high any second.

"Come on, buddy, we gotta get out of here." He took Jake's elbow gently but he felt pressure pulling back.

"Can't leave without him." Both Jake's hands were on the door handle. He was straining with all his might, but it wouldn't budge. When he tried to remove his hand to make one last lunge at the window, it

wouldn't release the handle. Suddenly everything went black. Jake had the sensation of floating or flying, like lying on a tire tube out in the middle of the Colorado River in a big current. No, more like moving across mud or gravel, sliding down a slope that wasn't steep or slippery. Then noise and heat and something big hitting him, and Jake's world went black again.

Harry had no clear memory of getting to his truck, but he was tailing the ambulance, on its bumper, making every illegal turn and swerve, going through all the same traffic lights. When the emergency vehicle entered the ambulance bay at Paradise County Hospital, Harry parked haphazardly in a loading zone and dashed through the nearest door, then turned and ran down the hall in the direction of the ambulance entry.

No one seemed to notice him at first, but when he got to the double-wide steel doors of the emergency room, a nurse who must have been an MMA "cage" fighter in her spare time, challenged him. With her arms folded firmly across her chest, under bosoms in a straight-jacket of a bra, she snapped: "Sorry, sir, only medical personnel beyond this point.'

"I'm his partner. He needs me. I need to be with him. Please." "Sorry, there are reasons for our rules. If you make a scene, it will

only make it harder for us to treat him." It sounded as if she'd repeated the same words, in the same monotone, hundreds of times.

Harry reached for his badge as he responded, "I'm next of kin, for Chrissake!"

"I don't see your name on the I.C.E. info. There's a number for his mother, and his boss at work, apparently--doesn't say where he works, and--."

Harry flipped open his wallet to reveal a shield, which only he knew did not represent police or fire, but was official in its own capacity.

"He works with me! Homeland Security. And I'm his brother; now open that door." He pulled himself up tall, puffed out his chest and walked toward her with the badge held out. She relented and pushed a button.

Harry stood at the head of the hospital cot, with one hand touching the sheet near Jake's head, as emergency room workers bustled about on both sides. Sometimes moving quickly and jerkily, sometimes standing still, they were talking to each other in soft voices and words that were more like a secret code than the language Harry knew. But they seemed to accept his need to be close and pretty much ignored his presence.

When Jake was wheeled off to a room in intensive care and no other patient needed immediate attention, the crew drew a simultaneous breath and their body language changed.

"Is he going to be all right?" Harry asked, to no one in particular. The doctor had left, but the nurse in charge took a moment to answer Harry.

"He's suffered smoke inhalation, a concussion, and somehow a broken jaw. That's serious. We'll have to wire it, and he won't be eating anything solid for eight weeks, at least. But it's the burns on his hands we're worried about. They're pretty deep. Any idea how that happened?"

"Oh yeah, there was a man in the car—injured but might have lived if we'd'a got him out. This guy—he pointed the direction where the gurney had rounded the corner-- wouldn't give up—wouldn't let go of the door handle.

The nurse, a man about thirty-five, put a hand on Harry's shoulder and a wedding ring was plainly visible. "I know how you feel," he said, "if it was my wife Charline, I'd be going crazy. It's pretty sure he'll make it."

"We're partners, but not that kind. We work together. So what about his hands? They'll heal, won't they? He'll be able to use them normally?"

There was a hesitation, a deep drawing of breath. "We'll do our

best."

"I need more info than that."

"Burns are unpredictable. They'll probably heal eventually, if they don't get infected. He needs to take care of them, and someone needs to take care of him. He's not gonna be able to wipe his own ass, to put it bluntly."

"If Trish won't, I will." Harry knew the nurse didn't know what he meant by that. "When can I see him?"

"We've given him a pretty strong sedative--not an induced coma, but almost. His heart rhythm is fine, so he should be awake by late tomorrow. He'll be drugged, though. You'll have to check with the main desk to see when he comes out of ICU and whether he can have visitors."

Harry knew there was nothing more the man could tell him, He put out his hand to express appreciation, but realized the nurse was still wearing latex gloves. He nodded instead and said, "Thanks man."

Catching Up

Harry poured a cup of hot coffee from the white plastic automated machine on his white counter and walked toward the sliding patio door that led to his backyard. Halfway there, he stopped suddenly, and on a whim, changed direction. He took the steaming cup across the living room, careful not to splash its contents on the light beige carpet.

He thought about sitting in the chair closest to the window to maybe catch a glimpse of Melli, or at least enjoy the birds at the feeder, but something compelled him to keep going, through the door and onto the path of blue beach pebbles that circled the front yard.

Melli had been visiting his house a couple of nights a week since their interlude on the spa deck. She occasionally fixed a special meal and invited him to spend the evening in her room, but essentially they led separate lives, and that's how they both liked it.

Today, however, Harry just wanted to be as close to her as possible, and wished he could tell her the fantastic news he'd received.

Before stepping outside, he picked up the muffled sound of voices, but they were accompanied by music—recorded music. Definitely not loud, and not the classical he was used to hearing emanating from Melli's part of the house or yard. This was from a folk album by Judy Collins, lamenting that "he loves that damned old rodeo more than he loves me."

It was Harry who had bought the record player, as a Christmas gift for Melli a year ago. It could handle cd's as well as old-fashioned vinyl LP's, and had a radio, too. She'd been ecstatic. Even though she didn't have room for it, Melli made a place. She stored a small collection of vinyl under the sink in her bathroom and had bought at least two more since the holidays, both at garage sales. Unable to resist and still holding the coffee cup in his hands, Harry followed the music. He stepped into his yard, walking first toward his little truck, then circling back, hoping his neighbor/tenant/occasional lover would see him from her open doorway. Instead he saw her, sitting on her patio. "Lovely day for January, isn't it?" he asked, feeling trite and a little foolish.

"Just another day in paradise," she repeated a well-worn phrase. "Can't beat Southern California living. Care to join me?"

"Yep, we're lucky. He entered thorough the half-width lattice door, and she patted a place next to her on the love-seat sized bench. Harry quickly accepted. She turned slightly to her side, balancing her slender body effortlessly on the edge of the bench so she could face him directly. That was one of Melli's traits that Harry found attractive: she always looked him right in the eye when they talked.

"You're a bit late going in. Do you have the day off?"

"Not quite. I'm going in late because I might have to testify in a court case." His voice trailed off.

Melli guessed that he didn't want---or couldn't--- talk about the case, so she changed the subject, asking something she'd been meaning to for a while.

"So, how's your partner doing?"

"Okay, I guess. The doctor says he's got a good chance of healing completely and may be able to come back to work, with some limitations, in four to six more weeks."

"That's a long healing time. I know burns are serious, but on such a small part of the body, I--well, I guess there's a lot I don't know. But he had some other injuries, too, didn't he?"

"Yeah, a concussion and a broken jaw."

"That seems odd."

"It is odd," Harry answered. "The jaw takes a long time healing, but the burns will need constant supervision for months, you know, keeping them clean and all."

"Will everything be normal, you know, being able to bend fingers and use them like he did before, and feel things?"

"Doc thinks so. I talked to her the other day. She said Jake's hands came free from the metal just in time."

"Amazing—seems like a miracle. And the jaw—what's the deal with that?"

Harry chose not to tell her what he knew about how Jake's jaw became broken. "They had to wire it together. It will heal completely, too. Luckily our bodies have almost infinite capacity to repair themselves. But it means close to eight weeks without solid food, only what he can get through a straw. And he better not vomit. If that happens, they have to cut the wires to keep him from choking to death, so they watch him pretty carefully. He will lose weight; good thing he's not skinny.

"He's certainly not fat."

"No, but he did have enough meat on his bones to get through this without excessive physical trauma."

"His attitude okay?"

""Yeah." Harry did not elaborate.

"I have another question for you."

"Shoot."

"What's got you in such a happy mood?"

"Oh, nothin' special. Just feeling good about Jake," he lied.

"Come on, friend, I know better than that."

"What makes you think so?"

"Well, today, you were singing along to 'Someday Soon.' You were singing the words. You weren't doing that yesterday, or the day before. I don't know if I've ever heard you sing. Did you hear from the lovely angel in white?"

"My God, woman, can I not have a thought without you being in my head? It's scary."

"I'm not psychic, Harry, just intuitive, as most women are. You don't have to say anything about her if you don't want, but I'm happy that you're happy."

"Well, it's not like we're dating or anything like that. I just got a call from her yesterday--mostly about her court appearance. That's where I'm headed later today. Elena is going to testify against the Fat Cat. She's not worried, and I don't think she needs to be. He's not the type. I'm surprised he didn't take a plea. He still could. Mainly I was just relieved to hear she's all right, and actually things have been going good for her family, just like Jake thought. Oh, and she asked about him, of course."

"Harry, you're such a decent person. I hope things go well in court." She hesitated, then added "and otherwise. Will you be seeing Jake, too?"

"I'll go there first."

"You see him every day, don't you?"

"Yeah, one day I was late and he was sleeping, so I didn't wake him, just sat there." "He knew you were there."

"That's what he said."

Two hours later, after circling a crowded parking garage until he came upon someone who was actually leaving, and making the long trek and elevator ride to the burn unit, Harry stood in the doorway of Jake's

room. Harry lifted a thin laptop computer off of a box in his arms and put it on the table opposite the bed. He then set the bright red, white and blue cardboard box on the rolling tray that stuck across Jake's bed, even though it reached a bit beyond the tray on both sides. He smiled at his bedridden partner.

"I told you I could get a meat-lover's pizza in here without getting caught," he announced proudly. Jake managed a one-sided smile.

"I can't eat pizza. All my food comes through a straw. All I can do is smell it. Don't get me wrong--the aroma is to die for."

"I'm not through." From his pocket, Harry extracted a curious item, like a drinking glass with a thick bottom. Also inside was a one-serving can of tomato juice."

"What the fu--?"

"This, my friend, is a miraculous gadget and a magic potion in a can. Watch me as I extract it and miraculously open it without tools."

"Yeah, so it has a tab on it—big deal."

Harry just smiled and went about his plan, which was to take a slice of the pizza and, tearing it into smaller pieces, put in the strange contraption, which turned out to be a battery-operated single-serving blender, probably made for a portable bar. He then added half the can of tomato juice, replaced the lid and whirred away.

He produced two coffee mugs and two large red plastic straws, the largest size that would fit in the space between the wires holding Jake's teeth together.

A nurse who had been passing and apparently heard the blender sound stuck her head in the door. "Everything all right in here?" she asked.

Harry flashed his most charming smile and said, "Sure thing, we're just having lunch." When he heard her footsteps far enough down the hall, he poured the unattractive but wonderful-smelling mess from the blender into the mugs, gave one to Jake and cupped his hands around the other. Here's to protein!" he said, tapping Jake's cup and starting to slurp.

After downing his drink, he said, "Good, huh?" "You lying sack of shit," Jake said. "I didn't say it was the best meal I ever had."

Before Harry had to dig too far for more polite untruths, Jake rescued him saying, "Funny thing, but it really does taste like pizza."

"It is pizza. I'll make us a second slice."

The nurse reappeared as he poured the next batch, and this time she exhibited more interest.

"Did you say lunch? You do know he can't eat solids, don't you?" She eyed the blender.

"Of course. We're just having some liquid pizza," Harry answered, grabbing a plastic cup and pouring a bit of slush into it. "Here, join us."

"Well, I'll be," said the good-natured nurse, declining the offer with a shake of her head. "Who would've guessed?"

Harry opened and closed his phone to check the time, even though there was a clock in the room.

"Well, buddy," he said, I need to get goin'—I have a trial to attend. Don't say I never did anything for you." Jake chuckled, or made the sound that Harry had come to recognize as a muffled laugh, the best his friend could do under the circumstances.

"Thanks, man. You gonna leave the pizza?"

"Yeah, if you don't want thirds, maybe the staff will like it. See ya."

"Harry?"

"Yeah?"

"You gonna be here tomorrow?"

"Yeah, probably at my usual time, around nine. That okay?" "That's good."

Harry met Trish at the door as he turned to leave, and gave her a solid hug. Not the awkward, stilted kind they used to exchange, but a spontaneous, sincere hug.

"Today's the day," he said with a smile he hoped didn't look falsely confident. "We're going to put away Mr. Leonardo Delgato, once and for all."

"Go get em', Tiger," she smiled back and gave him a quick kiss on the cheek.

An Intervention of One

By the first of February, Harry knew the corridors and elevator buttons at Paradise County so well he could have negotiated his way to Jake's room with a blindfold on. Usually he brought something interesting for Jake to drink, since alcohol was out of the question. Yesterday, it had been a whole coconut, and, amazingly in such a security-conscious world, he had also carried in a knife that looked like a machete and was sharp and strong enough to whack open the hard fruit in one swift blow. Jake might not approve of everything Harry did on his behalf (and certainly hospital authorities frowned on it, though they stopped short of evicting him) but one thing could be said for Harry's daily visits. They were not boring.

Today, he brought with him what looked like a bottle of champagne, but was actually a high-end brand of sparkling apple-cranberry juice.

"Today, my friend," he announced as he proffered the bottle and two crystal flutes, we are celebrating."

"And what is it, might I ask," Jake said, lifting his glass in a vain attempt to raise a half-bandaged pinkie finger, "that requires a formal celebration?"

"The fat cat is in the cat cage and the wicked witch is dead,"

Harry sing-songed the words and did a little shuffle in front of Jake's bed. "They convicted Delgato?"

"Yep. Jury came in about an hour ago—guilty on all counts but one. Should keep him in the cat- box for a long time. We were afraid he might have pulled some strings, but this judge and jury couldn't be bought.

He'll appeal, of course, but not much chance he'll be walking the streets and preying on unwary immigrants. Not for a long time, anyway. I think they're raising glasses and toasting this decision on both sides of the border."

"Cheers," Jake said as he put straw to flute and bent it to fit the angle to his mouth.

"It couldn't have happened without both of our star witnesses. One of them alone might have been a 'he- said/she said,' even though the recording made it pretty clear. Still, it could have gone either way. But with two very credible women—well, the jerk didn't have much of a chance. He won't be stealing the last dollar from any more desperate people. I'm so glad Trish's friend came through for us. And Elena--wow-- she was absolutely perfect, and looking gorgeous. Her whole family was there in the room."

"You get a chance to talk to her?"

"Naw, it just didn't present itself, and I felt a little awkward seeking her out when the verdict came in, but I saw them all still there, hugging and high-fiving. I smiled as I went by and asked her to call me when she had a chance. She smiled back—so radiant--and said she would. Hope she meant it."

"I hope so, too, man. You got it bad for that lady."

Harry didn't respond, realizing that Jake was right, even though he'd done his best to put her out of his mind.

After finishing his glass, Jake put it on his tray, and Harry was happy to see he seemed to have almost full use of his hands, although the bandages, much thinner and lighter than the earlier ones, still made it cumbersome. His tone changed, he looked Harry in the eye with a serious expression, and said, "Harry, I had a visitor today."

"You mean besides Trish and your folks?" "I do." "Phil—I bet it was Phil the Mill!"

"Wrong, although to be fair I should mention that he did come by once about a week ago."

"Was it someone else from work?"

"No.

"Then I guess I'm out of guesses."

"You'd'a' never got it anyway. It was the kid driving the SUV— the silver one in the accident."

"The accident on the 125?" Harry asked trying to wrap his mind around the situation.

"The very same. I thought it was really weird because we were just talking about him yesterday."

"Do-do, do-do." Harry hummed the theme from the old "Twilight Zone" T.V. show. "That is a pretty ironic coincidence."

"Yeah, remember how I said I thought of him as a hero, and you said there was another way of looking at things."

"I said I saw him as saving one life but taking another."

"And I couldn't figure out what you meant because I didn't know he'd been drunk."

"Well, not falling down drunk, maybe. But, under the influence enough to cause an accident."

"Odd how he can go from hero to murderer in an instant, with just the change of one little fact."

"That's how some people would see it for sure—somewhere between the second and fourth drink, he became the perpetrator of a crime. All the good deeds in the world won't bring back that man who died."

"Too bad. It was Christmas Eve, and he was coming home from a party at work— probably thought he was good to go. I was wondering, though, Harry--."

"Yeah, go on."

"Well, I didn't have anything to drink that day---I don't think, anyway." "No, you didn't."

"But do you think if I had—like just one or two--would I have been more relaxed, maybe a little looser. Would that have made it possible for me to, you know, get the old guy outta there?"

"No, Jake, you couldn't save him, but you sure coulda died tryin', like you almost did anyway, you stubborn son of a bitch. So, what did the kid want?"

"I guess kid is the right word. He didn't look over twenty- five. Poor guy--his life is ruined now. What he wanted was to meet me in person so he could thank me--for trying so hard, for getting hurt in the process. He may have just been curious about how bad my injuries were. I think he's having a hard time with the guilt. Says if I'da died too, he didn't think he'd be able to live with himself.

"Do you think he's suicidal?"

"No, not any more. I think he's accepted responsibility and hoping the court or jury will go easy on him. He's never been in any trouble before, and he's got a wife and kid."

"What a shame."

"I assured him I'm fine and about to be released any day now." "Good snow job."

"Well it shouldn't be too much longer. Harry, I hope you don't mind me getting all nostalgic, but I got something I wanna' talk about, but first I gotta ask you a question. You got a bit of extra time today?"

"'For you, buddy, always."

"There you go—bein' too good."

"So what's up?"

"Well, somehow I ended up with a bump on the back of my head that caused me a pretty noticeable headache, and a broken jaw, which seems could only have happened from the front, and I lost some time, but I know I didn't black out from drinking. I'm just trying to wrap my head around what went down at that scene on the 125, and since you were there and I know you won't lie to me, I gotta ask."

Harry sighed deeply, then drew a verbal picture for his friend. "You were hanging on to that door handle with both hands like

they were glued to it, and I think at the end, they might have been. The heat was so intense I can't describe it, but I couldn't get you to give up. I could see the flames, growing like a huge wall, edging closer to the gas tank. I knew the whole place was about to blow. There was nothing more we could do but save ourselves. The man was out already. He wasn't going to suffer. But I couldn't get your obstinate ass to move. I had to do something, I knew but I didn't have choices. Only one, and I couldn't wait. I got myself angled so when I hit you, it would knock you back and away from the vehicle, and I let you have it in the jaw with all my might."

Jake smiled, as much as the wires would let him. "And your might is pretty mighty, I might add."

"Cute. Maybe when they fire you from SCABS, you can be a late-night comedy writer."

"Then I tried to pick you up and carry you off the road, but it was more like half carry, half drag. I had you by the armpits and when I felt the

air suck in, that tenth of a second when I knew it was exploding, I threw myself across your body and hung onto your thighs. I guess my instinct told me it would protect both our faces, and make us heavier, not to get thrown by the force. As it was, we tumbled or twisted or rolled some and ended up on the bank. The medics were on us like flies on stink, but I convinced them I was all right and made for my truck."

"Were you--"

"Was I what?"

"Were you okay?"

"A few scrapes and bruises and minor burns. My ears didn't quit ringing for over a week. But nothing Melli couldn't take care of. She's a gem—a dear friend."

"Wow, that's a lot to take in. Guess I better thank you for saving my life."

"Just wish you could have saved his. Oh, by the way, don't know if I told you or not, but the other guy, the driver, was the man's grandson. Nineteen-year-old college student. He's going to recover fully—out of the hospital already."

"This is just all so surreal. But I know you—you would've been holding onto that door handle, too."

"Prob'ly."

"So you said you had something to tell me."

"Yeah, I do. Remember that time we were talking, just before Thanksgiving, I think it was, about both of us being able to work the bad shifts 'cause we're single with no major family ties?"

"Yeah, I remember."

"I was wondering why you hadn't ever asked Trish to marry you, though of course it's none of my business."

"In a way, it is. You're as close as the rest of my family." "Well, it does seem like that's what Trish wants."

"It's what she thinks she wants."

"But not what you want?"

"I'm not sure I know what I want, bro. Trish makes me happy, no doubt about that, but I'm scared. I don't know if I can make her happy. I sure don't want to disappoint her, or lose her. It's okay with us now, kinda like if it ain't broke, don't fix it, you know?"

"But I sense you feel like you're missing something."

"I am, of course. I want a family, and she's made it clear she does, too. Yeah, but she's too ethical to let that happen until we're committed by the "m" word, and anyway there's also some doubt."

"On your part?"

"On her part. She thinks she wants a ring, but does she really want me. I come with a lot of baggage. What if I hurt her. She thinks she can change me.

"She's wrong on that count. There's only one person that can ever change you." Jake gave a look like he understood, but hurriedly moved on.

"We fight sometimes—you know that. She says we only fight when I've been drinking."

"You ever hit her?"

"No, never have. I pray that I never do" "Sorry, Jake. Had to ask."

"But I got to thinking about when we fight, and I know she's right. I don't get stupid or mean drunk, not in quite a few years; at least that's how I see it. But when I go back in my mind, and think about the disagreements and fights, the ones that hurt always came after a few

drinks. I got to wondering if I should change my drinking habits. I'm not an alcoholic, but--hey, what's with the eye-roll?"

"Sorry, didn't realize I did that. I don't think you're an alcoholic, Jake, but it's just that every alcoholic I've ever met says those words."

"If you're going to change, don't do it for Trish. Do it for yourself. That's my advice."

"And I respect your opinion. That's why I brought it up now, even though I can't talk to her about it. When that kid came in today, he looked me in the eye and said this about himself: 'Yes, I saved a life, but I also took one. There's no way to get away from that—no way of denying that responsibility. It's done. All I can do now is go on from here and make the rest of my life a living memorial to him. I want so bad to be like you, to be of service to others in whatever way I can, and to dedicate it all to Mr. Chan.' When he said those words, something inside of me changed, fell apart, opened up. Harry, for God's sake, it could have just as easily been me. I've got behind the wheel with a good buzz on too many times."

Jake pulled out a notepad with good bond paper in the clip and a pen. "So, here's the deal, Harry, I know myself, and if I try to give up

alcohol totally, chances are I'll fail."

"Most people do."

"But I can't just do nothing. Not when I know I've got a problem and I know it affects other people. Loved ones and strangers alike. I know the experts say this won't work, but what have I got to lose? This is my proposal. I'm doing a contract with myself, and with you and Trish and my parents, and I'm making a promise in writing. Two promises. One, I'll limit myself to two drinks at any one event, absolutely never more than three, if it's a long day or special occasion, and they'll be an hour apart.

And two, I'll never get behind a steering wheel if I've had any alcohol at all. Period. I'll arrange for a designated driver or get acquainted with a lot of cab drivers. You think this will work?"

"I think it's got potential. Only time will tell." "Write it down for me please, just like I said it."

Harry took the pen. He looked at it for a moment and confirmed in his mind that his trust in Jake had not been misplaced.

Husband-To-Be

Harry couldn't believe he was spending Valentine's Day afternoon back at the hospital. Jake had been released the week before and was doing quite well at Trish's house. His jaw was still wired and he still needed some help with personal things, like food preparation and using the bathroom. For some strange reason, he had asked Harry to join him at the hospital for a late lunch in the main floor cafeteria. Harry switched around his schedule.

The room was crowded, brightly lighted, and filled with the normal sounds that seemed somehow reassuring to patients' families and loved ones. It didn't take Harry long to spot him, or them, he should say, because Trish was with Jake at a table against the right wall, near the center of the cafeteria. Jake smiled broadly, revealing the absence of metal wires.

Harry noticed immediately and raised two thumbs up as he walked toward the seated couple.

"Wow—congrats!" he said cheerfully. "They let you take the braces off early." "It's been seven and a half weeks," Jake answered, "but who's counting?"

Seeing his friend smile again was such a treat to Harry that nothing else mattered at the moment. Harry also noticed that Jake was wearing a lifeguard-type whistle on a string around his neck, but decided not to ask about it yet.

"So, I have to ask. Why here? You finally get to eat real food, anything you want, and you choose a hospital cafeteria. Doesn't make any sense."

"Oh yes it does. These people gave me my life back, after you saved it.

Trish made me realize my life's worthwhile. Besides, their food is pretty good—you might be surprised." Jake stood. "Let's go get in line."

When Jake took a tray and set it on the stainless steel bars that served as a non-moving conveyor, Harry noticed that his hands were still bandaged at the palms, with flesh-colored pads and matching tape. Something that looked like tiny, thin finger-cozies covered each of his digits, but he could bend them easily. Jake caught him looking and held up his hands. "Have to change the finger socks pretty often," he said with a smile, "but I can do almost everything for myself now."

After finishing their meal, the three friends sat without speaking, watching the room, not really paying attention, in that comfortable silence that isn't possible with strangers or the barely acquainted. Finally, Harry offered a comment on the meal. "You know, that wasn't half bad for hospital food."

"Not half bad? Come on, you can do better than that. Out with it." "Okay," Harry laughed. "You got me. I didn't expect it to be so

good. It's one of the best meals I've had in months." "Me, too." Trish announced.

"See, I'm not crazy after all." Jake said, with an intriguing, shy half-smile that hinted at more. "The food here is great. I expected it after so many weeks of only being able to smell it. Lunch isn't the only reason I asked you two to join me here." With that, Jake got up and walked to an

open space nearer the center of the room. As he put the police whistle to his lips, Trish's face flushed. She nudged Harry and whispered loudly to him, "Oh, God, what's he up to now?"

"Damned if I know," Harry said, just as the constant low-level jangle of background sounds and voices was interrupted by Jake's shrill, warbling whistle.

"May I have your attention, please?" Jake said it as a polite but firm request. Almost everyone in the room quieted down and looked at him. "I am here with the two best friends in my life."

Trish was still looking at Harry and smiling.

Jake continued. "One of them is a woman named Patricia Meadows." Harry had never heard her full name. "She has shown me, especially in the very difficult last two months, the true meaning of life, and I want to spend the rest of mine with her." Harry noticed that Trish had gone pale and her eyes filled with tears, staring directly at Jake as if in a trance.

As Jake spoke, he moved toward Trish, and the color returned to her face. "I want you to all be my witnesses, if you can stay a minute or two." The diners made encouraging sounds. As he approached her, he reached into his shirt pocket and leaned forward, with one leg stretching out behind him.

"Oh dear, not the knee," Trish said, and she forgot to whisper. Then her hands covered her lower face and the two precariously balanced teardrops rolled down her cheeks. On one knee, with diamond solitaire— traditional but not ostentatious--in his hand, Jake wrapped up his plea. When Trish didn't answer immediately, he went on: "I know you didn't get to pick it out, but the jeweler said we can come back together if you want, and trade up."

"Of course he did," Harry thought to himself, somewhat cynically. Jake sounded nervous. "If you don't like them, that is."

Trish regained her composure to a degree, stammering, "Oh, Jake, not like them? You picked them out."

"Well?" asked someone in the impromptu audience.

"What's your answer?" joined another.

Trish, now fully in charge, responded to the questioners without taking her eyes off Jake's.

"My answer is that if my husband-to-be chose these rings, I will be proud to wear them the rest of my life."

Jake pulled her toward him, lifted her into his arms, and made a sweeping circle of the room before depositing her back in her seat and sitting down in his. The motley assortment of spectators roared their approval and broke into applause, then slowly began to disperse.

A New Face in Town

Harry was enjoying a leisurely Saturday morning, knowing he had the whole day off. The paper spread out in front of him proclaimed in dark headline, "Mountain Lion Spotted Directly Across from West Hills High"; and "Border Patrolman arrested in Death of Mexican National, says victim threw rocks; victim's friend says it was because the man was taking video by cell phone of him being beaten." Harry thought about the street that fronted West Hills, and how many times he'd driven the busy four-lane arterial. 'Mountain lion, wow'—but it was pretty rural to the north, and to the west was a popular and large hiking park, Mission Trails, maintained jointly by Santee and San Diego. About the other news flash, he would reserve judgment until he could learn more facts.

The bigger news in the headlines had more relevance to Harry and the new life that he was now living. The larger than life title read: "U.S. Angry Over Release of Drug Lord After 28 Years in Prison for Killing of U.S. Agent." This meant trouble was brewing somewhere in the Mexican underworld and revenge planned for whoever it was that put this drug lord behind bars. All Harry knew was that he needed to alert the rest of the SCABS team that Rafe was out of jail and to place a notice in every member's inbox back at the office.

His reverie was interrupted by a knock on the front door. A bit early for a Saturday, he thought, but wasn't in the least disappointed. He checked his clock for he had not yet put on his watch. Almost nine. That's not bad. He threw on a white T-shirt to go with his plaid pajama pants, went to the door and swung it wide open.

"Hi, Melli, you're early--you're not Melli." In front of him stood a young man, a boy really—good-looking, a little shy, but quick on the draw.

"No, I'm not Melli, and I'm also not selling anything, not even salvation. My name is Randolph Elton Saunders the second. My dad's cousin Phil gave me your address. He would have let me borrow a car for the week, too, but my Dad already set up a rental at the airport."

"Well, come in and sit down." Harry offered, trying to buy time to figure things out. Whoever he is, he must be sixteen if he's got a driver's license. Harry felt like he was swimming in murky water, trying to discern light at the surface. Who is this kid? He seems to think I should know him.

"I just flew in this morning from Dover. Man, I hope it's not too early," he said as an afterthought, noticing the pajamas. "I've been up for half a day." Seeing Harry's blank stare, he tried again. "My dad is John Saunders. You know him well, or did, I should say. He was your partner on the Dover police force."

"Yes."

"And," he hesitated, as if unsure whether or not to say more. "I have information, through a third party, about someone else you know—a woman named Lara."

The name Lara stopped his heart mid-beat. Did he hear right? Slowly it came to him. If he was John's son, he must be Lara's son, because John didn't have any kids before that. The kid didn't know how to break the news to Harry that Lara and John had hooked up. Of course, Harry thought, that was it--this was their kid. Their son. Makes sense they'd have a kid—maybe a passel of them. But here he was, in the flesh, in Harry's house. Seemed nice enough, polite, and Harry had invited him in. Maybe he was going to tell Harry the big secret, or maybe he was going to just try to tell him something about Lara while pretending she wasn't his mom. Sounded complicated.

Harry caught his breath and hoped he didn't exhibit symptoms of shock. Then Harry came to his senses. Wait a minute. Randolph Elton was a teenager—that couldn't be. Geez, she must have jumped in the sack with his best friend the minute Harry's Datsun passed the city limits sign.

"So, what brings you out this way to begin with?" Harry asked the poised young man sitting to his left on the sofa.

Well, we're on spring break, and I thought it would be a perfect chance to check out Cal Poly in Pasadena, where I hope to get accepted."

"You're not a senior are you?" Harry asked incredulously.

"No. I'm a junior this August, but it's not too early. Some kids have been trying to get set up since the beginning of their sophomore year. It isn't as easy as it used to be, you know."

"And it costs a lot more, I hear. I wouldn't know for sure—I just went two years to a community college, and then got into the police academy. I don't think college was even required back then to be a cop, but the academy was pretty heavy duty. After that, they offered in-service educational opportunities. But enough about me. Tell me why you want to go to Cal-Poly." Harry found it surprisingly easy to talk to this kid.

"Oh, it seemed like a good fit for me, with the curriculum I'm taking and the majors I'm interested in. Then there's the part about it being in an exotic, far-away locale. California holds kind of a fascination for a lot of people in New Hampshire. Myself included."

"Your first trip here?"

"Yeah, we were going to come out as a family one time, a few years back, when my younger brother was eight. You know, do the

Disneyland thing, go to Universal studios, and visit San Diego too. It fell through for some reason—never did find out why."

"Well, I can see why you'd be interested in California, and why you might want to visit with Phil, or why your dad might want you to, but--sorry if this seems rude--I still don't have the foggiest notion why you looked me up. It's not as if you had to drive by on your way to Phil's."

"Good point. I've heard you mentioned and learned a fair amount about you over the years. I guess I developed a curiosity. I have some questions I want to ask you, and some important details I want you to know."

Wow, thought Harry, this was starting to sound like a scene in a novel of mystery and intrigue. He didn't say it was his dad that mentioned him— maybe it was she. Maybe the kid just likes drama. "I'd be happy to have you spend some time here---I don't have much to offer in the way of food—I mostly microwave frozen meals when I'm home. A lot of times on the job I eat in restaurants. You don't drink coffee, I suppose?"

"No. But I would have a cup of tea, with milk and sugar. If you have it, that is." Harry remembered that Lara drank tea a lot, and that's how she took hers.

"Tea I can do. That's within my area of expertise." He smiled and was relieved to see Randolph smiling. He brought a cup of tea for each of them and threw some round crackers and a sliced apple on a plate. He wondered whether to make more small talk or just get right to the point. "So the questions—you couldn't get the answers from your dad or his cousin?"

"No, I haven't even talked to Phil yet, other than to let him know I'd be there sometime today. I did promise Dad I'd check in and make that

my home base before I go up to Pasadena. They want me to take the bus up there instead of driving. But the stuff in my head, and on here"—he produced a flash drive —"are directly related to you."

"Whoa, wait a minute. Slow down. First, about driving up there, I agree with them. L.A. traffic is a nightmare, even when it's good. How long have you been driving?"

"About two years now."

"Two years—that doesn't seem possible."

"Yeah, well, I just got my license two weeks ago when I turned sixteen." "And you're allowed to drive by yourself?"

" Daytime only. And with no one under twenty-one in the car. I think I can handle L.A. I know how to use a G.P.S."

"We can get back to that, but my other question is, why me? I just don't see why I should have any importance in your life." As Harry spoke, his eyes were fixed on the little black device between Randolph's thumb and index finger, as if looking at it could somehow help him decipher its contents. This was like a game of chess and it was the kid's move.

"I know you were my dad's best friend, and I guess you're not anymore, and I think I pick up a sense of loss from him. And you were very important to my m-- to my friend's mom Lara. There are some things I thought you should know, and maybe some things for you to tell them, or Dad anyway."

"You have a lot of respect for John, don't you?" "He's always been good to me, just like a father." "Like a father? He is your father, isn't he?" "Of course. I meant like a father should be."

"Okay. Well. I'm glad you two get along. A lot of kids and their dads don't at your age. So, how is it you know this Lara woman again?"

"She's, um, my friend's mom."

"And what's your friend's name?"

" Um, Butch"

"Randolph, is that what everyone calls you?"

"No, my friends and family call me Randy. You can call me that, too, if you want to."

"I think I will. Randy, I believe you are doing this with the best of intentions, because you really care about your dad, and the loss of his bond with me, so I'm going to make this a little easier on you. I know about your Dad and my ex-wife. I know they're a couple. I've known that since 1997 and had it confirmed several times. I didn't know they had any children, but I guess I'm not surprised. So relax, it's all right to refer to her as your mother."

Now it was Randy's turn to be in shock. "But how—they were very careful, I know. Dad didn't even let on to Phil, although he called him quite often, just to hear about you, I think. Whew, I need a minute to think about this. You've always known? But how did you find out?"

"Two things I heard over the phone, on two calls to your dad. The dog and the music box."

'Rusty? You recognized Rusty's bark?" "Wouldn't you?" "I guess I would. What about a music box?"

Lara loved music. So did I. All kinds, except rap, but I don't personally believe that fits the category. Movie music and old rock and classical—I was probably the only guy in New Hampshire who had season tickets to both the Dover Symphony and the New England Patriots. Your

mom even more than me. She was always humming tunes if there wasn't an actual song playing."

"Still does."

"So the music box was a gift from me to her because it played her song. Lara's Theme —from an old movie you've probably never heard of. When I heard that very music box playing at John's house, it was clear to me. I think I stopped listening to music on that day, or liking it anyway."

"Well, I guess that explains some things. You know the big secret, always have. But you don't know all the secrets."

"So, clue me in."

All in good time. First, I want to hear something about you. I know it's really personal, but I have a special interest, which I'll explain later. I want to know about your situation with the police department—how it was you came to resign. It's the one thing Dad won't talk about, though I suspect he knows quite a bit. I want to hear your take on how you and La —my Mom came to split up."

"Wow, you don't want much, do you?"

"If I'm ever going to be a cop, follow in the family footsteps, I need to know how things work. Something bad happened to your career, and I don't think it was your fault."

"That about sums it up. I was set up—I don't know who and I don't know why, and I've long since stopped caring. I also set myself up. Did something stupid that caused me to lose Lara, but I did it with the best of intentions, sort of like a no-good-deed-goes-unpunished situation. It all happened the same night."

"So, what happened exactly?"

"I was told to pick up information from a snitch, and I met a guy in a car just as they said, and he gave me an envelope. I've still got it. Turned out they were taking pictures and planned to accuse me of taking a bribe."

"Was there money in the envelope?"

"Don't know—probably not."

"What do you mean you don't know?"

"Never opened it—it represented everything evil in my life---it was picking up that envelope that put me in a place to meet Carrie-Jo. And that killed everything I had with Lara. Not that it was her fault; she was just a poor abused woman who needed help."

"Was she hurt when you met her?"

"Yeah, roughed up pretty bad, sitting on a curb at eleven pm I just wanted to get her away from the jerk that hurt her and into a shelter. She was so frightened that she just wanted someone to stay with her and hold her, like a kid would, to keep the monsters away."

"So you stayed the night with her?"

"Yeah, I held her and we both slept. And nothing else."

"Man, I can't believe being in bed with a chick and not, you know, doing it—it would be almost impossible."

"For you, because you're sixteen, I was thirty-one and I loved Lara. I never had any desire for another woman, even if she was beautiful."

"Was Carrie-Jo beautiful?"

"Could have been. That night all I could feel for her was sympathy."

"Wow, that's a lot to think about. You didn't have to tell my Mom, did you?"

"Yes, I did. She knew—women usually do. She would have found out anyway, because they took pictures of that, too. The cops or whoever was doing their dirty deeds. They got a real bonus that night. She would have found out and it would have been worse. She used to say that she probably couldn't forgive an affair, even though I said I probably could, when we played this "Truth Serum game."

"I know about Truth Serum."

"You know about that game?"

" Boy, your mom certainly shared some personal stuff." "Yes, she did. Uh--"

"Why do I sense there's more to this than you're letting on?"

"Well, the part about that game--that little bit she didn't exactly come out with on her own."

"What do you mean?"

"Well, I sort of came across it in her journal."

"Her journal? You read her journal? That's supposed to be a big no-no. I didn't know she kept a journal."

"I didn't either, till she asked for some help on her computer. It was running real slow, driving her crazy, but she wasn't sure if she had used up all the memory and needed a new hard drive, or if there was something else wrong that could be corrected. "

"And of course, it was you she turned to for help."

"Well, I do seem to have a knack for tech stuff. Grew up at the right time, I guess."

"You're sounding pretty humble about that. You're prob'ly a freakin' genius, like my partner Jake. But I can't believe you went looking for your mother's journal just 'cause she gave you her password."

"It's more like her journal came looking for me. I was adding up all the programs to see how much of the memory was used up, and something just didn't compute, pardon the expression. There was a big chunk that didn't show up on any of the lists, didn't have a name, but certainly affected on the computer. I was just doing what she asked me to do when I ran across it. I sure didn't expect it to be anything dramatic— just stuff about her job, like which clients wanted what color curtains, crap like that. You know she's doing interiors on her own now, and getting a bit of a reputation as a designer locally?"

"Didn't know that, but not surprised. Go on."

"Well, that's exactly what it was, for the past fifteen years, but to know how to best set up her electronics, I had to see how much there was and start at the beginning. I saw one phrase that caught my attention. It didn't seem possible and I had to check and make sure there wasn't a different item caught up in there, something she copied accidentally or otherwise, like from a magazine or a novel. You'll see what I mean."

He again held out the flash drive.

"Let's put this in your computer—I'll show you."

"Randolph, I don't think I should be looking at your mother's most personal writings."

"Yes, you should be; in fact, you have to. There is something in here that affects you, and you need to know. It's better to hear it from her than from me."

Reluctantly, Harry led the boy to his office, the room that housed his PC, a small dresser, and a TV. His single bed usually served as a perch for the princess. He pulled the spare chair over to the desk and they both sat down.

A screen came up with dates on the left and writing next to each one. The first set of numbers had already etched a hole in Harry's heart and it startled him to see them in black and white. July 7, 1997. 7-7-97— the day he drove out of Dover for the last time. Seven certainly wasn't his lucky number. The words were poignant, right from the beginning, and Harry could not help himself. He let the tears well up in his eyes as he read:

July 7—Today the only man I ever loved left. I don't know if I'll even see him again. And it's me that sent him away. What hell have I wrought? Am I a fool? I didn't know he'd go so far. Maybe if he stayed in Dover, I could somehow get over--but no, I don't think so. How could I ever lie in his bed, how could I touch him, knowing that he had touched her, held her close all night long? I don't blame her. I can't imagine what it might be like to be trapped with a guy who hits and hurts you. I always used to wonder why those women didn't just walk away, but I've met some women through work who helped explain. Sometimes it's fear of losing children, sometimes worry that he'll come after them or people they love. Jerks like that threaten them. One I know of put bullets on the mantle, held her arms behind her as he showed her each one. He said this for you, this for our daughter, this for your mom, this for your dad. She was a brave woman. She left anyway, with the daughter, worked her way across the country as a live-in maid. He never followed through, but some of them do. Carrie-Jo, I hope you made it. I know it's not your fault. And Harry, it's not your fault either. It's just me.

July 8----I went to the doctor today. The feeling was just too strong and I was a week late. Could have been the stress, but I've always been so regular. I just didn't want to trust one of those drug-store tests. This is too important. I got a call this afternoon, and my intuition has proved to be correct again. I am carrying Harry's child. Now what do I do? Well, there's one thing I will not do, that I know. I should tell him, but I don't even know how to get a hold of him this minute. I'll just have to wait till he calls. But I don't want him to turn around, because nothing else has changed. Maybe it's best to wait a while.

July 9--Got a call from John Saunders this morning. He wants to bring the dog over this evening. He started working a day shift, and he doesn't want Rusty to be alone in the house all day. I told Harry I'd be the one to keep Rusty, and I'm glad I can at least do that—I've been missing him. Rusty, I mean. Of course, not as much as I miss Harry. John also decided to buy Harry's truck, and has put the money in our--my account. I told Harry he didn't owe me anything. I'm fully capable of taking care of myself, and anyway it was my idea, and him without even a job. If he did try to give me something, I wouldn't accept it. Work is going well.

July 10--I am so, so very sorry, dear God. I never thought. I always had control of my emotions, and I wasn't even drinking, like that would be an excuse. I won't be doing any drinking at least until April, so no drowning my sorrows in alcohol today. I have to look at myself in the mirror and deal with it. Am I a whore? No. Am I a very foolish woman who gave in to her overwhelming sadness, loneliness and fear, finding solace in the arms of a long-time friend? Yes, especially a foolish woman. Is there any excuse for what I did, for what I allowed to happen? No. There was no forcing, no pressure, no seduction—I just fell--fell from grace, fell from common sense, fell into—what--I can't even call it passion--maybe consolation? I've heard when a mother loses a child, her libido suddenly increases—a physiological thing, sort of nature's way of trying to make up for a loss. But my loss was different. Still, I was feeling loss—loss of the man I loved and planned to spend my entire life with. Why was I so sensitive about what he did, which was really a decent thing to do? Why was I so mindless? I wish things could be back like they were —only a week ago?

July 20---It's been a while since I've noted my thoughts here, but it's like sometimes I just have to talk to someone and there's no one I can share this with. I called Harry's mom today. I needed to get Harry's cell phone number. He probably gave it to me, but in all the confusion, I couldn't remember if I got it or where I put it. Anne Dugan is such a nice woman. I know she feels bad for Harry, but it's like she feels bad for me, too. I couldn't bring myself to tell her I'm pregnant, but I will have to before long. I don't know how much Harry told her, but the news was all over town about his "indiscretion" as well as the suspicions about him being a bad cop, which he definitely wasn't. It must be just as hard for her as it is for me—losing Harry. And not too long ago, losing her own husband, becoming a widow. I can't imagine. She's a strong woman. I hope I can be more like her.

August 1--I guess it's no surprise that I've been seeing John. Once a bond like that is formed, it's most likely to strengthen over time; and we do feel happy when we are together—not just the sex part, either. Sometimes I catch myself humming and thinking I've gone back in time to all the good years. But there's no going back, and going forward will have some major hurdles. I don't even know how John feels about the future, though we both agree the present feels pretty good. And right now no one but me knows about the new life inside me. I've got to call Harry soon.

August 10----Well, I told John today. I couldn't believe his reaction. The thought about the timing, that this life could possibly have started before "us," never came close to crossing his mind. He was so sure, and so supremely, genuinely happy. I just couldn't have imagined a more positive reaction if I had tried to write it myself. He's already making plans—wants us to get married immediately, but of course that's impossible because of a little detail regarding me. I'm still married to Harry. 'Oh, yeah, that,' John said. 'Well, we'll have to get to work on the paperwork asap.' Then he went on with plans for me to move into his house and rent this one out if it doesn't sell right away, and which room we'd make into a nursery, and what toys we'd buy for him or her. I don't think I've ever seen a man so exuberant, anytime. Now, what do I do? Who was it that said "O what a tangled web we weave, when first we practice to deceive?" I swear I never had any thought of tricking John, but I don't want to break his heart, either.

September 30--Today the papers came back, postmarked Fort Stockton, Texas. I've spoken to him a few times, including today to let him know how much I appreciate his cooperative attitude with the divorce, and how strongly I wish him happiness in his new life. He says he's met someone in that godforsaken town and plans to stay awhile. I never thought I could find contentment with anyone else, but now I find myself hoping Harry can be as happy as I am. I've decided not to say anything to him about the baby, and the people here, including Anne Dugan, will be told it's John's child. Let them think what they will of me.

October 8—Good news, the house sold today. We had a week of unusually fair weather—Indian Summer, they call it--and I think that helped. Winter in New England is not the best time to sell a house. We went in for the ultra-sound today, and the doctor couldn't pinpoint the exact age. (Thank God.) We set the due date at 266 days from our first week together. April 2nd. If he arrives early, I don't think it will be a problem. And I do mean he—they were able to tell us we're having a boy.

John would like to name him after his two grandfathers—Randolph and Elton. That's fine with me. I'm just so glad he's healthy and has such a loving father.

Randolph sat very still but signaled Harry that he was ready to talk. "Well, that's the main part, that I wanted you to see, anyway. I think you realize you needed to know. Or at least, had a right to know."

Randy's voice came as if from another dimension, and it took Harry a few seconds to register what he said. The taste of salt still on his lips, he responded to the boy, the boy he now knew was his own flesh and blood."

"Well, whether or not I needed to know is moot. I do know now."
"Are you sorry I told you?"

After two seconds hesitation, Harry said, "No, not at all—you did the right thing. It's just a lot for me to process right now, as I imagine it was for you. The big question is where do we go from here."

"Where do you want to go?"

"It should be what you want, Randy. You are an intelligent young man, strong and kind with a good moral compass. I don't know if I can take credit for any of that with my genes, but I want you to know I'm proud to have you as a son."

Randy enveloped Harry with a bear hug, the strength of which he couldn't imagine coming from such a young kid. Tears flowed with no embarrassment, then tissues, then more words.

"So," said Randy hesitantly, "I guess you're leaving it up to me how to handle this. Is that right?"

"Yes, I am."

"Then I say some secrets are best left undisturbed. We both know we are father and son, and we're both better off for it, in my opinion. But I don't see where it would make anything better for anyone else to know.

And it might make things a lot worse. Do you think this can be a private matter, just between us? We'll become close, I hope, like an uncle and nephew might be, but we'll have a pact to never divulge this one fact, no matter how tempted. What do you think?"

"I think you're a young man wise beyond his years. I accept your pact." Harry held out his hand and his son took it and shook it with a firm grip.

"Is there a place around here to get a good burger?" Randy asked. An hour later, back at Harry's house, Randy made a comment

about getting on his way to his cousin's.

"But you're not supposed to drive after dark, are you?" "Well, I guess not, but--."

"Let me give Phil a call. I think he'll be all right with you staying here, and you're probably feeling some jet lag coming on. That's a comfortable bed in the office."

"And Melli? "

"She's a tenant—lives in the front bedroom and yard space. Pretty much comes and goes on her own. She's also a close friend."

"A friend with benefits?"

"You might say that."

"All right. Go ahead and give Phil a call."

Harry awoke to the smell of coffee. He noted on his clock that it was 5:45 am, but he felt rested. He found Randy in the kitchen.

"D--. I almost said Dad. I need to be careful about that. Harry, I'm glad you got up early, 'cause there are a couple more questions, if you don't mind."

Randy put two saucers on the table, each with a piece of peanut buttered toast and a half banana, sliced. "First, well that lady in the motel, the one that got beat up. You were with her all night—in the same bed---

and you didn't, well, you know, do anything. That must have taken a lot of, like, control. How did you do it?"

"It wasn't like I had to even think about control. Under different circumstances, maybe. We had a few drinks. She was an attractive woman, or would have been.. But at the time, she seemed more like a wounded animal. The poor woman led a life of misery and would probably go back to it. I like to think maybe my influence, and the shelter I took her to in the morning, got her off to a start on a better road. As far as feeling horny, well it just didn't happen. I guess the empathy factor over-ruled it."

"Oh, so you were drinking. That might have clouded your judgment. Now the other. You mentioned an envelope you got when they set you up. What did you say was in it?"

"I don't know. I've never looked at it." "But you still have it?" "Yes, it's taped to the back of my favorite picture.

" I can't believe you never opened it. I'da been dying of curiosity." ""It signified the end of everything I held dear. I just couldn't

bring myself to look at it."

"Can you now? It must have been important to someone."

"Or just a blank piece of paper to set me up—or some cash, which I wouldn't feel right about spending."

"I don't see how you can just leave it sealed. It's driving me crazy and I'm not even involved."

"Okay, why not. Wait here a minute."

It took Harry only a brief moment to retrieve the photo, as it was something he kept where he could bring it out every now and then, just to stare at and think. He showed his son the photo of Lara with, basically, his two fathers, returning from a pleasant day of sailing. She was smiling, without a care in the world. Randy asked for a copy and Harry agreed to make one, feeling it could do no harm. Then he carefully slid the envelope out and opened it with a table-knife.

"As Harry read, silently, his face grew pale and his body stiffened. When finished, he folded it and started to return it to the envelope."

"Wait a minute," said Randy. "What did it say? Come on, what's up—you gotta tell me. We don't have any secrets from each other."

"It's not that, it's just--this is pretty heavy duty stuff. And you're young."

"In less than two years, I'll be an adult. I'm not exactly naive. Besides, we have a bond. No secrets from each other, one from the rest of the world, right?"

"I'll start reading—you tell me to stop any time you want to." Harry began. "I am a man of twenty-one. Five years ago, as a scout

working on my Eagle badge, I had what was supposed to be the honor of a ride-along with a police officer. E.B. Nelson. It turned out the opposite. I should have told someone years ago, but forgive me, I was scared. I feel so bad for the others after me. I chose you to get this, Officer Dugan, because when I checked, I found you to be the most honest detective on the force, the one who might go against the "code of blue."

Nelson took me to a park—part of our job was to check the restrooms, make sure there was no illegal activity going on, he told me. He sent me to check the stalls, starting at the back. Then he put yellow tape on

the door, locked it from inside with one of those hotel security devices you can order from the "techie" catalogs. He faced me and said, 'Son, we can do this the easy way or not,' as he patted his gun with his hand. Then he turned me around, leaned me over a urinal and raped me.

My mom's a single mother, works hard. Nelson knew her name and address and where she worked. He said if I didn't want anything to happen to her, I'd keep quiet. But I can't do that any longer. This letter has passed through several hands to get to you; hopefully it wasn't opened and re-sealed. You're my best hope. I know how hard it is to get a conviction, but I'm willing to testify. Call me."

Randy was uncharacteristically silent. When he did speak, it was in hushed tones. "I see what you mean, Harry. But there's something else. I've heard my Dad mention that guy Nelson. Seems like it was a long time ago, and even then, in the past tense, but I think he knows something about it, and maybe about how and why you were set up. When's the last time you talked to him? "

"A few years ago. I called him when I got the job, and once or twice after that—never talked very long."

"You ever Skype?'

"No."

"You know what it is, don't you?"

"Yes, I'm not that far back in the dark ages."

"I think you ought to Skype with my Dad. There's something here left unfinished. It may be too late to do anything about this Nelson guy, but I think my dad should know. He's Chief of Police now."

"I didn't know. I'm happy for him, really. But I don't know about this Skyping."

"It would be good to clear the air—you and him have more in common than you do separating you. It would do you both good, and, who knows, you might find other occasions in the future to Skype."

"I don't even know how to go about it. "

"I'll set it up. Then you e-mail my dad. Say you ran into me at Phil's and got his e-mail and you want to ask him something. It's 10 am back there; on a Sunday—he's probably home."

"What if Lara sees the e-mail?"

"They have separate computers—he doesn't do much except family photos and e-mail, but he checks it often. While we wait, you can show me the garden."

Ten minutes later, John responded. Randy set things up and went outside to read. Harry saw his old friend's face looking, of course, like a completely different person, as he was sure he did. He hoped his nervousness didn't show through. After a few pleasantries, Harry got to the point, about the envelope. Instead of reading the young scout's letter, he paraphrased it. He told John how he was feeling guiltier by the minute for not checking it out years ago.

"I can imagine, but you don't have to worry about that part. I saw that letter. I wasn't ever going to tell you this, but you deserve to know. There was a guy, not Nelson, but someone who wanted you out of the way. He knew you were likely to be appointed next Deputy Chief and he was eying the job himself. I don't think I need to mention his name."

"Not if I mention it first. Warren Roth?" "The same." "How far did he go?"

"He made deputy, then stagnated. He wasn't qualified, finally realized it and took early retirement. I think he's selling cars."

"Suits him."

"He found out about the letter to you and decided he could use it against you, with the help of two other detectives. I hate to say it but I was one of them. I went along, not because it meant saving my job, but because I knew what he was up to and thought my best chance of saving you was to be on the inside. Sorry it didn't work out, man."

"You were one of the investigators, taking the pictures?" "I was there." Harry blew out his breath but said nothing.

"I swear I had good intentions. And I managed to see the letter you just told me about. Roth called me over and handed it to me. Said to go to the coffee maker and steam it open, then meet him in the men's room. After he saw it, he told me to shred the letter, put a $20 in the envelope, reseal it and get it back to him. I said I would as soon as I took care of my morning business and headed for a stall. 'You don't need to come with me?' I asked, only half joking, because I knew he had doubts about my loyalty to him. Sucker said 'no, I'll wait here' and leaned on the sink. Well, that blew my chance of making a phone call to you with the info, but I had one other option. I'd just got this new camera—you know I'm into photography—one about the size of a graham cracker, and I always kept it in my pocket. I coughed while I snapped the picture, then flushed. I came out and handed him the letter, keeping the envelope. 'On second thought, I think it should be you shredding this,' I said. I'll take care of the money and get the envelope back to you." As you know, what I put in the envelope was a copy of the letter from my camera. We mighta had a chance if that woman hadn't gotten in the way."

"Was Roth protecting Nelson?"

"No, just cared about his own ass. Nelson was a wild card."

"Yeah, a freakin' pervert wild card who kept hurting kids because I didn't open a stupid envelope."

"Wait a minute, friend. You're forgetting that I saw the letter—had a picture of it." "So, wha'd you do about it?"

"I waited a couple months, then I called Nelson—used the old hanky over the phone trick, and told him I was acquainted with you. I said when you left town, you went to the state capitol and were working with the D.A, and you had the letter-writer—I mentioned him by name---and three other former scouts who were all about to testify —that he was going to be arrested any day, and just thought he might like to know."

"Did that accomplish anything?"

"You might say so—the next day the bastard ate his gun." "My God."

"So, I hope that makes you feel better. I guess you met my son. He's out there on a wild hair about a California college. I figured it wouldn't hurt him to meet his cousin. And Phil can watch out for him— he's barely sixteen."

"Yeah, we met, briefly."

"Just hope he doesn't develop an interest in the border patrol and want to move out there for good."

"It's like the border patrol but a separate agency. I don't think you have to worry about that—seems like an East Coast kind of kid. You ought to have him check out M.I.T."

"Good idea."

"John, I'm glad I called. You definitely have made me feel better. I hope I can return the favor."

"What do you mean?"

"It's time you knew. I don't have any hard feelings. I've known about you and Lara since a month after I left. No hard feelings, I swear."

"How'd you find out?"

"Rusty told me. Give Lara my love, and my best to both of you. Seriously. And, John, I really appreciate what you did for me, and what you tried to do. 'Til next time, friend."

'Til then."

The Truck is Back

After the Skype call, father and son showered and dressed. Harry tilted his head a little to the right in gesture of satisfaction.

"Guess it's time to take you to your cousin's." "Take me? I can drive, you know."

"I know, but there's no use paying for a rental when all of us have vehicles. I thought maybe, if you're okay with it, I could go with you up to Pasadena, maybe tomorrow. You can be the driver. I'll navigate."

"Yeah, that sounds good. You want to follow me to the airport now and turn in my car?"

"That will work," Harry said.

"One thing we need to do before we get in the car." Randy held up the flash drive one last time.

"Yeah, that's right. How shall we do it?" "I say, get me your biggest hammer." "You would."

Harry let the boy have the honor of smashing the hard drive into small pieces, but as an added precaution, on Randy's suggestion, they also made a tiny fire in the backyard fire-pit. "Did you delete the one on your Mom's computer?" Harry asked.

"Actually, no. I was afraid if I did, she might notice it missing and know I knew. I'd rather take my chances the other way. The odds of anyone else ever finding that in there are very slim."

Harry pulled up in Phil's driveway, and immediately was waved in by the friendly figure at the front door.

"Had breakfast yet?" Asked Phil-the-Mill, and they answered in the negative, because neither one felt their p.b. and b. snack constituted a meal.

After a nice meal prepared by Phil's wife, Harry headed to SCABS with Randy in his truck, since Phil thought it would be nice for his young cousin to get a look at the workplace. Halfway there, the phone buzzed with a sound Harry knew to be an alert signal; he hit the speaker button. "This is important. All units proceed to south end of Hollister Avenue. Contact S.D. Police upon arrival."

Harry knew Jake was back at work and on duty today, but probably at or near the compound, waiting to hook up with him. He hit the button on his phone that rang the radio in the SCABS truck they usually shared and was relieved to hear Jake's voice. "What up, bud?" Harry asked.

"It's the Shrimp's operation in that parking lot on Hollister. How far are you?"

"I'm pretty close—5 miles, maybe, but I've got a ride-along, Phil's sixteen-year-old nephew. Not sure what I should do. Do you know anything more?"

"The truck's back and something is going down, according to dispatch. The cops are trying to decide whether to go in."

"Can somebody tell them to hold off 'til we talk to them? And find out what to do about the kid—I can't get Phil on his phone."

"I'll see if Phil answers the radio. I think he's on his way to the site. Hold on." After a minute, Jake's voice came across the radio again.

"Phil says take him with you but park a safe distance away and instruct the kid under no circumstances does he leave the truck or unlock it for anyone but you."

Harry turned to Randy. "You heard that, didn't you." This isn't game-playing, it's life and death. You need to do what he says."

Harry had increased his speed and was passing under the 5, just a minute or two away from the scene. He reached into the console and pulled out a pocket- size spiral tablet with yellow pages, the color of a legal pad, and a pen clipped on. He threw it to Randy and said, "Maybe you can be a witness from where you are. Use this to take notes." As he screeched to a stop on Hollister, safely off the road, Harry could see the SCABS truck, his and Jake's, parked almost a block down, halfway into the parking lot. He jumped out and ran, telling Randy as he left to lock all the doors.

Jake was talking to a cop who had a radio unit in his hand. He was trying to get something across to the cop and was turning red in the face.

"What's happening?" Harry yelled.

Jake looked up at Harry as he was running towards them.

"Cops want to go in, but I'm trying to tell them it looks like a trap." "What do you mean?" Harry asked.

"I think El Cameron has set them up. They think the truck is empty, but I bet there's a dozen or more of El Cam's soldiers with guns in the truck— an ambush.

The cop turned to Harry. "He's crazy, man. Can't be anybody in the truck."

"You know that for sure?" Harry asked, hoping to stall the cop, who was apparently the one who would give the go- ahead order. He could see at least ten cops in modified riot gear raring to go, like rodeo bulls leaning on their gates.

"Yes, we checked with an infrared heat detector—your buddy here showed us how. There aren't any humans in the truck, just a lot of contraband, we think."

Jake interjected, "There's some kind of ramp under the truck angled on the ground and it could serve as a shield for the bastard to bring in men and set up an ambush."

"Bring in from where?" the cop asked, his patience wearing thin. "We've been watching ever since we did the OTIS check. Nobody has entered the truck, I can tell you that."

"From underground!" Jake was screaming now, and it only served to make the cop in charge think he was crazy.

"You're talking nonsense!" the cop said, and picked up the hand mic to give an order. Harry snatched it from his hand in such a way the cord snapped where it was attached to the main unit.

"What the hell?--I should arrest you right now."

"The man knows what he's talking about—there's a tunnel, and that ramp looks suspicious."

"You're both crazy."

"Want to stake the lives of ten cops on that theory. Or want to give us a minute to prove ours?" Harry asked and noticed Jake looking at him like he'd gone off the deep end.

"Let me slip up to the truck and see if I can open the door and release the parking brake. Even if you're right and no one's in it, it rolls down the parking lot to where you are, and you take it from there. But first, you get the OTIS back here and check, so no one walks into an ambush."

"I'm on my way," Jake said, and before Harry realized what was happening, his partner was halfway to the truck. Keeping his head low,

Jake swung the door open, moved the gearshift handle to neutral, and released the foot lever. He jumped out and gave a big heave against the doorframe with his shoulder and chest. The truck rolled forward and came to a stop against a police car near Harry. As it did, it revealed a two-foot by two-foot square hole and a slab of asphalt the same size in front of the hole. Both had been under the truck's bed. The aluminum ramp had been mysteriously pulled up into the truck body. The sound of gunshots was heard, coming from the hole in the ground, and also from the truck itself, but no shooter could be seen and no bullet hit any person. The riot squad had sprung into action, with cops coming from everywhere, encircling the truck with guns drawn and pulling a battering-ram-equipped vehicle into place near the truck's sliding back door. The OTIS had been brought back and was being set up again, and a loudspeaker blared the Spanish words for "Come out with your hands up. You have no choice. It is the only way to save your life."

"My God," said the cop who had called Jake crazy. "You guys were right. How did you know? You saved us from walking straight into an ambush. A tunnel—never would have though it possible. Right here, under the noses of Homeland Security. That's their fence, and all their construction equipment right behind it down there in that field."

He pointed south.

As the main cop spoke, a technician operating the OTIS announced, "There's a bunch of them—fifteen—sixteen, no seventeen. Looks like seventeen."

"Are they armed?"

"Trying to tell, it looks like a couple of 'em might be holding guns."

Again the loudspeaker blared in Spanish: "Put down your weapons, push them to the door and open it a crack. Push all the weapons through it, so they fall to the ground, or we will explode the entire truck."

"Can we do that?" Jake was asking.

"You mean legally or practically?"

"Both."

"No and probably," Harry answered.

Just then the truck's aluminum, rolling door started to vibrate and jerked slightly up from the bottom, about three inches. A hesitation, then another creaking noise, and few inches more. Then guns started falling and hitting the asphalt, as armed police stood by. Automatic weapons and small revolvers—more than a dozen. Harry was hoping none of the Mexican, or more probably Indian, cartel employees would try to be a hotshot and take out a few cops before he went down.

"Let's get another look at the infrared," said the cop in charge. He checked it himself and, satisfied with what he saw, gave the order in English, to be translated. "Lie down on your bellies and come out feet first, then turn around and put your hands high in the air."

Seventeen small, brown, unarmed men complied, were handcuffed roughly and led to police cars, three or four in each.

"Well, that went better than I thought it would," Jake said to Harry. "Maybe one of these guys will lead us to the Shrimp if they don't find him in the tunnel."

"Yeah, I think we can wrap up this chapter. Come on with me—there's a neat kid I want you to meet, Phil's cousin."

Together they walked to Harry's personal truck. When they got there, they found a window cracked open, as if by a gun, and no sign of the boy.

"No!" said Harry. "It's the Shrimp, and he's got Randy. God help us get him back alive. "

Jake looked at Harry with concern, " Did you say that Rafe was let out of prison?"

It appeared that Harry and Jake were thinking of the same thing at the same time. Both spoke the same word.

"Phil."

Harry and Jake both ran towards their pick up truck. As Jake threw the shifter into drive, Harry reached over to assure him that it would be all right.

" Hey, Jake, just keep us on the road. We will catch up with these s.o.b.'s soon enough, and Randy will be okay." Harry tried to keep the look of reassurance on his face, but deep inside he knew what these drug lords were capable of doing. Jake had stepped down on the gas pedal so hard that both of the truck's rear tires were spraying dirt and dust everywhere.

"Yeah, but, I think Phil was on the arrest team that brought down Rafe."

Just then the units radio in the truck reported that a man, fitting the description of Rafe, was seen driving a stolen vehicle onto the Viejas Casino property.

The dispatcher sounded confused as she stated, "With him was a boy and a clown." Her voice inflection questioned what she was reporting. Jake impulsively mimicked her report before making eye contact with Harry, who was squinting his eyes and scratching his head, mouthing the word "clown." Then, he recalled the Tribune's headlines that read, "Convicted drug trafficker Rafael Felix was shot to death Friday in the Baja beach resort of Los Cabos by a gunman wearing a clown costume."

Goodbyes

Jake drove their truck towards Tocayo Avenue, which skirted the northern boundaries of San Ysidro and, where they could merge onto the 905 freeway towards the 805 north and eventually onto the 8 east towards the Viejas Casino. Jake pressed his foot on the gas pedal so hard that Harry, who had barely gotten his seat-belt fastened, was now curious about just how the Kumeyaay tribal police and the Viejas Casino security would be handling this situation.

The tribal police were not as equipped with the latest technology as the local, state and federal law enforcement agencies were. They were barely a police department to say the least. But with recent federal funding from the Bureau of Indian Affairs, the Kumeyaay tribal police department had a few new computers along with radio dispatch that allowed them to communicate with the other agencies, as well as sometimes providing support when necessary.

Jake looked over at Harry quizzically.

"We are gonna call this in, right?"

Jake paused and watched Harry ponder. "Right. Harry?"

Harry was hearing Jake's voice, but not listening. As Jake reached for the trucks radio, Harry motioned for him to stop.

"Please keep your eyes on the road, will ya?", "And no I don't want to call this in just yet."

Harry and Jake sat in silence for the next four or five minutes.

Jake was now focused on getting to the Viejas Casino, which was located in Alpine, CA, on the Kumeyaay Indian Reservation.

The casino was owned and operated by the Viejas Band of Kumeyaay Indians, which caught a lucky break when then Governor Arnold Schwarzenegger signed a modified compact granting them unlimited slot machines in return for higher payments to the state.

There were many residence in San Diego county who opposed this casino because statistically they attract crime. As time passed though, the very same individuals who fought against the casino, could be found gambling their retirement checks away, shopping at the casino's mall, or using the casino's inviting amenities. Although generous as well as entertaining to the many who frequent the casino on a daily basis, the Indians are still struggling.

Jake was now driving at high speeds, passing every car on the road. Harry opted not to interfere with this process as he was all consumed with what was going on inside of his own head. As their truck reached the Harbison Canyon area, located in a canyon between Crest and Alpine, it was Jake who broke the silence.

"So we're heading to the casino?"

Harry turned and looked at Jake in a very serious manner, "Yes and there will be tribal cops there too.

Jake, still needing to respond only as Jake would, even in this situation, "We're going to have our hands full".

Jake turned onto the Willows Road exit, and drove a short distance when Harry spotted several different vehicles ahead of them as they approached the Viejas Recreation Center. Harry motioned to Jake to slow down and pull over to the side of the road.

"We will not be welcome here", Harry said as to caution Jake.

Responding in kind, Jake's reply had been much more serious than Harry had anticipated. "We are always welcome here at Viejas, but I do understand that this time is different". While Jake was completing his sentence both were looking at one of the tribal officers walking towards their truck. Jake had recognized him.

He turned to Harry as he was opening the driver side door. "I know this guy Harry, we've spoken a few times in the past".

Before Harry could respond Jake had already departed the truck and headed towards the two men. Harry had wondered to himself if he should have called this one in. As Harry sat in the truck, watching from a distance, he thought of Randy. Harry was not an impatient man, but he wanted to do something, anything to keep his son safe. He was about to get out of the truck and signal to Jake that it was time to go. Just then the radio dispatch announced that there was a robbery in progress at the Viejas Casino. The tribal cops were already in motion, waving bye to Jake as they walked hurriedly towards their own official police vehicle.

As Jake jumped up into the SCABS truck, the tribal cops had turned their car in such an angle, stretched across Willows Road so as to not let anyone in or out. Harry opened his window and started yelling at the tribal officers.

"We need to get in there and help".

One of the tribal officers got out of his car and addressed Harry.

"You are not permitted to be a part of this, as you are not belonging to the tribe, and that you are now interfering with a tribal police matter" the officer said. Harry, already halfway out of the passenger side window, was so upset, he continued all of the way out of the window, so he could approach the tribal officer and explain to him about Randy.

While Harry was climbing out of the window, his service revolver had slipped out of it's holster. Harry was so preoccupied with trying to get to Randy, he hadn't noticed.

As the two men were now in a heated discussion as to who's authority governed the casino property in this situation, sound of gunshots could be heard. Harry again made a motion towards the casino, as the tribal police were now telling Harry he would be arrested if he were to continue his efforts. While Harry was engaged in a debate about why he needed to get into the casino to help Randy, Jake had managed to make it past the two tribal cops unnoticed. Suddenly, a cloud of dust coming from the Viejas Grade Road, which was part of the fork that merged with Willows Road, where the tribal police and the SCABS truck were parked.

The tribal police were not expecting any vehicles to exit from Viejas Grade Road, because it was a road used mostly by the Indians living on the reservation. As the dust cloud was getting closer, Jake was in clear view of the car as it approached.

It was the same stolen car identified by dispatch earlier, which had brought them to their current location on the Viejas Indian Casino property. As the car got closer, Jake was now staring at the driver, who was dressed in a clown costume. He knew Randy must be either in the car with his head down or possibly back in the casino. Without over thinking what his options were at that moment, and because the driver was pointing a gun in his direction, Jake drew his service revolver and fired several shots. By this time, there were four additional local police vehicles with armed officers ready to assist pulling onto Willows Road.

Harry heard the shots coming from where Jake had ran to, but the dust was so thick, he could not see very well. He yelled as he ran towards Jake. Harry was not the only one yelling. By now there were several casino security officers as well as an additional tribal police vehicle and two more tribal cops, all armed and adrenaline was at an all time high.

The car being driven by the man wearing the clown costume headed towards the local police vehicles, who had positioned themselves in a barricade across Willows Road. The car stopped suddenly, and the clown opened the passengers side door and, got out, using the vehicle as a shield. There was a long pause as the dust was still so thick, not allowing anyone to see what was happening. All at once, the clown reached up and placed the car in drive. As the car rolled forward, the clown started shooting. Harry was caught in a crossfire, still trying to get to Jake, who had apparently been struck by one or more of the clown's bullets. The sound of gunfire and bullets whizzing by Harry's head, along with the heavy dust from the dry dirt filled Viejas Grade Road, made things feel as if they were going in slow motion.

Harry reached for his service revolver while stepping back into a place where he could take cover. He did not realize that it had been missing all of the time he was standing in the middle of the road pleading with the tribal police to let him in. Now he was concerned for his own ability to defend himself. He could hear the tribal police talking about one of their own who had been badly wounded, but what else he had heard was something totally unexpected. The tribal police officer who Harry had been arguing with when the dust filled the air and the shooting began, was lying on the ground just feet away from Harry as he remained crouched low behind some nearby boulders and shrubbery.

Harry overheard the tribal cops ordering a search for Harry as the main suspect for this shooting. Harry had to think fast. The dust was still thick enough that he had a good chance of getting to the SCABS truck without being noticed. Once he got into the truck, he located the spare key, started the engine and made a quick u-turn towards the local police vehicles that were still unaware of the tribal cop being shot, or their belief that Harry was a suspect. Harry drove past the local cops and gave the usual wave as he passed by and drove to the freeway exit.

Harry knew that he would soon be on every police scanner.

He decided to make a turn towards Arizona instead of heading back to San Diego. Harry was now in a difficult situation. He had worry and concern for both Randy and Jake, but he also needed to clear his name. As Harry drove east he knew he would only be able to stop once for gas before his name and picture would be scattered all over the news. Harry pulled his truck off onto Pine Valley Road, where he filled the tank and bought a case of water and a few sandwiches from the deli cooler inside of the Pine Valley Store. On his way out of the store, Harry looked around to make sure he was not already being followed.

He was quick to get back on the road and make it to someplace safe where he might come up with a realistic game plan. He figured if he could make it to the Arizona border before dark, he might be able to ditch his truck, which was very noticeable and, then find a place to stay out of sight.

*** Fast Forward ***

It was a cool crisp February morning. There was a slight breeze blowing from the southwest. Staring out at the beautiful Mingus Mountain range, also known to the Yavapai Indians as the Black Hills, which is located within the Prescott National Forest, traversed by State Route 89A, approximately midway between Cottonwood and Prescott, Arizona.

A man in his 50's, who at first glimpse could have passed as homeless, reached over and picked up the transistor radio from the mid century looking table that was beside the chair he was sitting in. The sounds from the radio grew louder, and the man was intrigued by hearing his own name spoken. As the news reporter continued, the man sitting in the chair, running his hands through his unkempt hair and unshaven face, appeared to become more concerned. The news reporter gave information regarding incidents that occurred relating to a manhunt for a killer of an Indian at the Viejas Casino in San Diego County CA. Not just any Indian, one of their tribal police officers. The man reached over and turned the radio off . He stood up from the chair he was sitting in and moved towards a workbench, staring out the window at a black pickup truck, which was covered with an old tarp and some tree branches. The man staring out the window was Harry Dugan. A man who had fought for the life of a child. A child that Laura, Harry's ex-wife, with whom he thought she had with another man, was kidnapped by the man wearing a clown costume.

The same Harry Dugan who had guarded and protected our nation's border at three international border checkpoints along the United States and Mexico's international border in San Diego, CA.,is now wanted for murder. As Harry stood there looking out at the truck he bowed his head with worry about Randy and Jake. He also felt a tinge of reality and thought about his life as a cop in New Hampshire.

Then Harry's mind wandered back to a more recent time, to a moment where he almost went to a sand castle festival. In his mind he listened to the radio call from dispatch regarding suspicious activity, landscapers loading boxes into a truck. Harry was remembering the events played out as they did that fateful evening. It was almost too much for him to process. The images of Jake and himself arriving on Viejas casino, then the radio call indicating that there was a robbery in progress. Harry could recall the heated discussion with the tribal cops regarding the whereabouts of the driver and Randy. Harry walked back over to the chair and sat down. A barrage of thoughts were now running throughout Harry's mind. The shooting during the casino robbery. Randy and the clown. Jake. Overhearing a conversation about the tribal police shooting and Harry, himself being a suspect. Harry remembers the panic when he could not find his gun. The recollection was surreal, as the shots rang out, everyone was yelling and all of the confusion that ensued. Harry took a deep breath and let out an even bigger sigh as he recalls Jake calling out to him during the commotion back in San Diego.

Harry wondered to himself if Jake was still alive.

As Harry's mind was being occupied by these thoughts, he was alerted by the sounds of a vehicle approaching from the only access road to where he had managed to find as a place to lay low for a while. As he watched out the window at the large white van with bright blue and green lettering on the side, Harry wondered to himself, will today be the day they bring me to jail?

Harry sat back and watched the delivery driver drop a package at the front side of the building. There was nothing unusual for anyone to see, including the delivery driver. Harry had hidden the truck and managed to find himself a safe place in a storage area of the back building of this small compound up in the hillside. As he watched the driver get back into the vehicle and slowly roll down the long dirt road, he wondered who was living here and just how long he would be able to remain unnoticed. Harry managed to observe the van as it reached the end of what was considered the driveway. He caught a glimpse of a sign on a post that read USDA Forest Service.

"Great!" Harry blurted out sarcastically. "A government facility."

Now Harry was more concerned about his location, and just how long he had before the GSA employees and contractors would be returning to their workplace. Harry had also noticed that the license plate on the van was an Arizona license plate, giving him a sense of just where he was as it related to the California-Arizona border. Harry was thinking when he had made it through the border patrol checkpoint into Arizona. Harry and Jake often drove out to Yuma for one reason or another, in their official SCABS truck, so there was nothing out of the ordinary when Harry passed through that checkpoint, but this time was different.

"It must have been shortly after I went through" Harry thought to himself, "That the All Points Bulletin went out".

Harry completing his thought, "I must have driven a few hours more".

Harry was guessing where he was in relation to the Viejas casino. He did not recall any signs as he made his way into the north central countryside, but he did remember seeing a sign indicating the town of Mayer. He could only guess where he actually was, and it would only be a matter of time before he would be found. He needed to figure things out quickly.

Back in San Diego, at the SCABS compound, Philip Bradshaw and Abraham Fox were addressing the SCABS team with details regarding what happened at the Viejas Casino. Philip spoke directly to the tribal police departments handling of the shooting and how to approach Harry, if they should encounter him. "I am not about to take their word for it" Philip said.

Continuing on Abraham Fox added, "We will still need to proceed with common sense and caution".

The updates included additional details on what had happened to Jake as well. The room went quiet when the SCABS team members heard that one of their own had been shot. Some were almost ready to let their emotions get the better of them. Just then

Abraham Fox spoke directly to the heart of the matter. "I assure you all that Harry is a good SCABS member and that he will be contending any of the accusations regarding the shooting".

"Also", Abraham continued, "Harry and Jake are close like brothers, and I am sure that both of them feel the same towards each and everyone of you too". A young woman interrupted the meeting, addressing Abraham Fox. The young woman and Abraham Fox left the meeting in a hurry. As the room filled with a low rumbling of chatter among the SCABS team members, Philip Bradshaw spoke.

"We are still gathering evidence from all of the local cops that were at the scene", he paused, then pounded his fist on the desk as if to demand silence.

"All I am asking is that you use your better judgment".

Bradshaw dismissed the room full of ancy young men, who were not all that patient when it came to long winded briefings. He then walked into the office where the young woman and Abraham Fox had gone into just a few minutes earlier. As Harry was exploring his options on where he would go to next, he decided to have a look around the storage facility. While looking through several boxes, he ran across some Forest Service uniforms. Harry managed to find a shirt and pants that fit. He already had work boots that matched. He also found other articles of men's clothing. During his time looking around the facility, he found a can of black spray paint and used it to cover up the lettering on his truck.

Nobody had picked up the package left at the front door of the facility yet, so Harry felt as though it was safe enough to get a closer look at the outside of the building. Just to the left of the door that he had opened, was two older vehicles. From the looks of it, neither of the two were operational. Harry noticed that each of the vehicles had license plates still attached. It only took him a matter of minutes before he had switched the license plates and painted over the SCABS lettering. Harry was aware of his predicament as he tossed a box that had a Forest Service uniform and some additional supplies in it. He moved fast and with a purpose as he tossed the branches off from the truck and jumped in.

Shortly after the SCABS team members were released from the updates regarding the Viejas Casino incident, Philip Bradshaw was seen leaving from the back parking lot of the SCABS compound. He drove in an almost reckless manner, but did not appear to lose control at any point.

Philip Bradshaw arrived at the Paradise County Hospital just a few moments later, where he was escorted to the intensive care unit.

He was not allowed to go into the room, but was looking through a window. Behind the glass was Philips golden boy, Jake McGinnis. A tear filled Philip Bradshaw turned to thank the doctors and nurses for their jobs. As he started to leave the ICU, Philip turned as if to say goodbye to what appeared to be an incoherent, almost lifeless body, just lying there, Jake opened one eye. Whether it was possible or not, Philip thought he saw a smile on Jake's face. Before he could confirm any of it was real. Jake's eye was closed.

Just then Philips radio had a dispatch announcement indicating that the man in the clown costume had been shot and killed during an armed robbery at a nearby ATM. As the dispatcher continued her announcement, she also spoke of a young man resembling Randy had been found in the back seat of the stolen vehicle. Philip raced over to the scene to see if it was really Randy.

"I hope he is going to be ok", Philip wondered out loud, adding, "And I sure do hope Harry is going to get out of this one alive".

Just as Harry was trying to find a place to get some shade and do some planning, he took his eyes off of the road for a split second to grab a water bottle from the box on the front seat, missing the reduced speed ahead sign. Within seconds of Harry passing an Arizona Highway Patrol, he was getting pulled over. The officer who pulled Harry wasted no time figuring out who he was, and that the license plates on his truck were stolen. The officer also was not into small talk either. Harry knew the drill, as he faced the truck and placed his hands behind his back. Although unusual, the officer did not put handcuffs on Harry, but just opened the back door of the cruiser and sat Harry inside.

Upon arriving to the Arizona Highway Patrol holding station, Harry was placed into a small, uncomfortable, but air conditioned room.

"Strange," Harry thought to himself. The room had a bed, small sink and a toilet. "Yup, this is jail".

Harry noticed as they were arriving, that the building he was in could not have been more than one thousand square feet. He also noticed that it was all office accept the one cell he was occupying.

"This is going to be a long night", he thought to himself.

Suddenly he was alerted to the sound of an incoming helicopter. Then moments later he could hear a door open and footsteps. Harry could only feel a lump in his throat and his heart started racing.

"This is it", Harry thought. "I am going to spend the rest of my life

in jail." Before he could finish his thoughts, Philip Bradshaw was calling out Harry's name. "Dugan, Dugan" Bradshaw called out.

Harry was now in disbelief.

As Philip Bradshaw stood in front of the jail cell door, Harry was already tearing up. Harry was ready to go to jail for killing a tribal police officer in San Diego. Harry felt that Philip Bradshaw would be the right man to take him back to California to stand trial. Bradshaw handed Harry a form. Harry's demeanor had changed once he read the top of the form that indicated he was a free man.

"I could just kiss you", Harry blurted out to Bradshaw.

Philip Bradshaw was not a very emotional person, or did not tolerate horse play, but in this moment, he was glad to see Harry still alive and well.

"You do and I will file sexual harassment charges".

Philip smiled and continued, "Let's get going, it's going to be busy once the reporters find out you are here".

On the helicopter ride back to San Diego, Bradshaw explains how Rafe was shot and killed after Randy had already gotten free from the stolen car. Harry was also given some mandatory time off from SCABS. Now that he knows that Randy is ok and safely back with his mother, he can relax. As

Harry walks up into his home, there standing in the driveway is another familiar face, Melli, who in one hand is holding a stack of mail that had been piling up while he was away and in the other, a bottle of scotch.

"Just in case", Melli said as if to reassure Harry that meant welcome home. As Harry and Melli went over all of the details of the Viejas Casino incident and off of what ensued afterwards, he was dividing his attention as he sorted through the pile of mail, which looked even bigger because of all of the advertisements.

"Oh shit", Harry said under his breath, looking up a Melli, he continued, "I got to go back to Arizona for court".

Melli looked a bit puzzled from the statement. Harry had to explain to her about the clothes and the license plates he had stolen during his stay in Yavapai County Arizona. As Melli and Harry talked and laughed through the bottle of scotch, they found their way to the hot tub, and eventually wound up in bed to sleep it off.

It took Harry a few days to finally get the courage up to call Lara to find out how Randy was doing. The conversation had gone much smoother than he expected. Harry just missed being able to speak to John, but told Lara that he would call later.

"He's right here", Lara spoke in the general direction of Randy, who was now wondering just who would call him on a landline. Harry and Randy spoke for quite a while, and before hanging up, Randy told Harry he was glad to hear that he was doing well, and also reminded Harry that he would not be following in his footsteps. Harry and Randy had a good laugh and then said their goodbyes. Harry then decided to go and visit Elena. They were very aware of the attraction that had developed between themselves. As Harry and Elena were parting ways, the hug seemed to last forever. It was not easy, but Harry felt that he needed to be alone to sort out all of what just happened in his life.

Harry's court date was finally here. He stood before the judge in Prescott, Arizona.

After a long period of silence, the judge spoke.

"I am going to set this trial date aside for now", the judge said. He continued by stating "I know your story as a cop, and as a contract employee supporting Homeland Security, and that means a lot in my book".

Harry was not sure what he just heard, but wasted no time leaving the courthouse. Harry decided to take a drive around the Prescott area. He drove along a familiar road and soon was looking at a sign at the end of a long dirt driveway. The sign read "USDA Forest Service. Harry parked his truck, got out and reached behind his seat to grab a box of items he had stolen from the facilities earlier. While reaching in, he felt a rather unusual lump.

Harry grabbed the smaller item, which looked more like a gift. As Harry gave the gift wrapped item a good once over, he slowly opened the paper. What he had found, took him by surprise. He had to take a seat for a moment to collect his thoughts.

"Closure", Harry said out loud, as he placed his service revolver into the glove box of his truck.

Harry was a little nervous as he approached the building. He walked up to the front door and placed a box of items down. He knocked on the door. An older gentleman, wearing a Forest Service uniform appeared at the door.

"Yes, how may I help you Sir?"

"I am sorry, Harry Dugan". Harry awkwardly held out the box as he explained to the man standing in the doorway what had happened.

The man in the doorway held out his hand, already knowing that there was no way for Harry to shake. The two men shared a laugh.

"Jack McGinnis, Sergeant, Forest Service.

Almost immediately Harry's thoughts were of Jake. Harry recalled the time when Jake told him about his family, and that his father remained somewhere in Arizona. Jake did also say that he had some family living out there as well.

Harry, while letting go of the box, "The Jack McGinnis?" "The very one" replied Jack.

The two men turned to walk into the facility to talk more about Harry's and Jake's work - friendship. Harry gave Jack as much information as he could about Jake. "I know your son well enough as a professional, as little as a friend, although we did go skinny dipping.

Jack holding up his hand "TMI, TMI". Harry quickly regains his wit, "I was checking Jake out for a wire."

As the two men paused for a minute to fully grasp the banter was working, there was laughter again between the both of them.

"I'm bustin your chops." Harry said as he was making the fake slow motion swing to Jack's belly, with Jack making the slow motion block.

There was a connection that was a beginning of a new friendship. Harry had to get himself back to San Diego. He would be able to go back to work soon and wanted to be in shape for that. Jack and Harry exchanged their contact information and Harry hopped back into his truck and began his drive down and out of the Black Hills towards Prescott Valley. As Harry like to take in the views of the country settings, he noticed a newly renovated racetrack, Arizona Downs.

"Nice." Harry says to himself.

Reading the sign on the way by, "And off track betting, sweet."

As Harry crosses an overpass, he noticed something out in the field, off to his right. Checking his mirrors to see if he had time to look over to see what it was. Sure enough, Harry was looking at an old trucking container in the middle of the field. Painted on the side of the container was the word FREEDOM in all caps. That was not the end of what Harry had seen. Harry decided to pull off the freeway and take the road over to where the container was.

Harry turned the corner to where his chances were better to see the entire container up close. As he came upon the container, there were two horses, right there in the field, beside the container. Harry took out his smart phone and took a few photos. He turned his truck around to get back on route 89A. Somehow he took a wrong turn. Harry was always looking at the scenery and not the directions. Instead of turning back around to go in the right direction, Harry decided to be a little adventurous.

He continued his truck down Viewpoint Drive which led him straight to a new subdivision which was actually called Viewpoint. Harry was feeling something special about this place.

He wondered to himself, "Maybe I can just stay here?" Which is exactly what Harry did.

After returning to San Diego, Harry submitted his paperwork to officially retire from SCABS. Harry was not into all of the goodbye formalities, so he managed to pack and go quietly. He also kept a low profile while saying his goodbyes to friends.

That was just Harry.

Harry had packed the last box into his truck. He turned and said his final goodbyes to Melli.

Harry waved in the rear view mirror as he took a deep breath, and then put his truck in drive.

Made in the USA
Las Vegas, NV
01 September 2025

27268949R00157